CLOCKWORK ADVENTURES

PART ONE

THE SEARCH FOR NORWALL

Written by
Alexa Rayburn

with Illustrations by
Clara Kay

Formatting and Layout Editing by
Alex Kay

Alexa Rayburn/Ingram Publishing Company
1 Ingram Boulevard
La Vergne, TN 37086
www.ingramcontent.com

Publisher's Note: This is a work of fiction. Names, characters, places, and incidents are a product of the author's imagination. Locales and public names are sometimes used for atmospheric purposes. Any resemblance to actual people, living or dead, or to businesses, companies, events, institutions, or locales is completely coincidental.

Book Layout ©2017 BookDesignTemplates.com

Ordering Information:
Quantity sales. Special discounts are available on quantity purchases by corporations, associations, and others. For details, contact the "Special Sales Department" at the address above.

Clockwork Adventures: Part One, The Search for Norwall / Alexa Rayburn. -- 2nt ed.

ISBN 978-1-7355955-5-9

Your talent, courage, and strength

through the storms

brought this story to life.

For the two best people I know.

Love always,

Mother

"Though nothing can bring back the hour

Of splendour in the grass, of glory in the flower;

we will grieve not,

rather find strength in what remains behind."

-William Wordsworth

Ode: Intimations of Immortality
from Recollections of Early Childhood

Prologue

wake up in the middle of the night drenched in sweat *again,* with my heart pounding out of my chest. I am shivering, and I sit straight up and force myself to take slow, deep breaths. The night terrors are happening less and less as time passes; I still find it hard to believe that things that happened to me when I was fourteen could still haunt me three years later.

The memories of that summer are so vivid that I can, even now, smell the spicy cinnamon smells wafting down the street from the Octagon Bakery, and hear the clacking of wooden wagon wheels on the cobblestone streets. I am running, running down one of those streets, racing against the clock, racing against many different clocks, heart pounding, clocks ticking, stinking sour-smelly-sweaty running. I know that if I don't make it in time, I will lose her forever. My heart beats wildly out of my chest; it beats so wildly that I hurt. *This* must be what it feels like to have a heart attack.

I close my eyes and flop back onto the pillows. Pulling the covers tightly up around my neck I shiver again, but it is not cold. It is summertime in Florida, and it is unbearably hot. Night washes over me and I breathe deeply, taking in slow, deep breaths as I scramble to try and make sense of it all. My mind wanders to those I am close to; the ones I love, and sadly enough, to the ones that I lost forever. It was a terrible, frightening time for me, but in the end, I began to see the incredible and horrifying events much more clearly.

I had to somehow, someway, reach down into the deepest parts of myself and try to pull out feelings and strengths I never knew existed. I am grateful I survived.

I still remember, very distinctly, the first day I saw her. Our eyes locked. She tilted her head slightly to one side and I raised my eyebrows and stared back. For me and for her, *nothing* was ever again the same.

CHAPTER 1

The Man Next Door

ONCE IN AWHILE a day begins just like every other day. But then, something unusual happens which makes this day a day you remember the rest of your life. You remember it as a turning point from which every event that follows topples down like a series of set-up dominoes toppling other dominoes, which topple more dominoes, which topple the events that happen the rest of your life. Problem is, when that day starts, you have no way of knowing that this particular day will be THE ONE. That is what happened this day, as our story begins.

Later, I would mark this day as a pivotal one, and yet, this particular morning began as every other crisp Florida morning at the Adventura Shopping Center in Central Florida. This shopping center was nothing special. The owners live in Texas, and as long as the shops are rented by hopeful entry-level business people, the owners don't care about the buildings. It's not even a mall really; just a series of storefronts linked together in two L-shaped structures. At first glance you would find it outdated and poorly maintained.

The Florida humidity makes the mildew grow exponentially mean and fast. Sidewalks, as well as the parking lot, are pitted, splotchy, black, and slimy. The Adventura Mall buildings are streaked dirty yellow, with black speckles on top of gray stains and rust-orange splotches from the iron in the sprinkler water. The parking lot markings have faded from years of brutal sunshine and you can hardly see them. The entire filthy facade, no matter where you go, smells like day-old wet socks that are lying on top of the laundry basket.

Today, a crew in tattered and mismatched uniforms climbs into a hydraulic bucket and trims palm trees in one corner of the lot. Landscaping at the base of the trees is nothing special, and palm fronds crush the dried-out plants as they fall. Mulch has been bleached out by the sun and has lost its cedar smell. The landscape crew tramples the small plants; nobody cares if weeds take over. The chief of the crew lifts a tank sprayer to his shoulder and gives a few puffs of watered-down weed killer to the hardened dirt around the base of the tree.

All the plants are wilted and sunburned from years of the Florida sun beating down, as well as the irregular watering schedule. The crew ignores the broken sprinkler system and moves on loudly to the next area, laughing, smoking, and discarding butts thoughtlessly into the landscape plants.

The Adventura is nothing like the covered malls down the interstate, which showcase spectacular waterfalls, domes of glass, fancy light fixtures, and beautifully decorated storefronts. The Adventura is the mall for business owners who have small-time budgets and narrow profit margins, not a magnet for the tourist crowd.

People streamed in and out of the Imperial Dry Cleaners on this typical Florida morning. The small, store-front shop sat on a rear corner of the shopping mall and there was nothing particularly compelling about its facade. A chipped neon sign with blue lettering had not been cleaned in years, nor had the front glass or door which advertises the business hours.

The Imperial opened its doors at seven o'clock each morning to accommodate working people, some dropping off laundry bags full of dirty clothes, others picking up crisp, clean laundry. Promptly at noon, Naji Najeem, sole employee of the Imperial for the past two weeks, took a much deserved break from working on clothes.

The short, round little man with a thick flock of silver-gray hair arched his back and stretched. His back was sore, his feet hurt, and he was tired already. He huffed a bit; he had become much more short of breath lately, and the morning rush-hour pushed him to work harder than he should have. He was, at sixty-two years old, considerably overweight with a Santa Claus belly; but Santa Claus he was not. Bending over to tie his shoes was too much of an effort and his laces were neatly tucked into the sides of his shoes. His blousey white shirt hung out over his belly and it was already stained with sweat.

Heaving a sigh, he blew air out through purple, pursed lips. He rummaged through a plastic tub under the chipped navy-colored linoleum counter for the dog leash he purchased last week from "The People's Pets Store" three doors down. He had thought that a bit of exercise might help him lose weight and ease his breathing. It hadn't worked, not yet. His futile attempts had made him *more* short of breath, but he was determined to continue his efforts.

The sticky Florida humidity did not help him one bit. The damp, exhausting heat wrapped around him like a smothering blanket as he set off on his short walk around the shopping center. He flipped the hanging sign on the front door to "CLOSED," and shut the door behind him, jingling keys in his pocket first to make certain he didn't lock himself out.

Pebby, a twelve-pound scruffy dog with a gray mop-top haircut and silver-tan long and silky ears, trotted at the end of the leash, and was anxious for her usual noon sojourn around the plaza. They first would pass the bakery and happily inhale the strong cinnamon smells. Then, they usually strolled past the bookstore cafe where the people were lining up to buy coffee and small sandwiches.

It was, however, the smell of the bakery that the little dog loved best. She tugged on the leash to hold Naji there for a few more minutes. He did not resist her pulls, but planted his feet firmly while he inhaled deeply. The smell of fresh-baked sweetberry rolls brought back memories of which they dared not speak. Memories of the home they had left so suddenly, so unexpectedly, and so unwillingly just two short weeks before.

Delivery trucks were delivering goods to the businesses and workers were picking up materials from the flooring store. There was an occasional *beep... beep... beep...* of a truck shifting into reverse, and doors slamming open and shut. The man and the tinydog stood frozen for a few seconds, as if their hearts were somewhere else.

Pebby tried to walk slowly so as not to pull Naji too fast, but she could not help herself. Walking on a leash was much harder than it looked. These past two weeks were the first time she had *ever* walked on leash and it was just unbearable! She had never before had the indignation of a human pulling her along on a string. If it was anyone but Naji Najeem, she wouldn't tolerate it at all! She huffed resolutely.

She was accustomed to flying down cobblestone streets pulling her red wagon, ears streaming straight back as she bounded through the assigned routes on a speedy run. She delivered the very best, the very freshest, and very hottest baked goods to waiting patrons. She had, through diligence and hard work, advanced to the prestigious position of Chief Delivery Dog of the Octagon Bakery, which prided itself on hand-made and home-made items, delivered fresh, delivered quickly, and delivered hot.

She looked around her now as they continued their walk. Her head was lowered, as sadness and homesickness washed over her like the sickening humidity. Her tongue hung out and she panted. The noon heat was almost too much for the little scruffy dog, who had not had a haircut in almost a month. Treena Trembly, her groomer, would be wondering where she was. She worried that her coat was getting dirty and shaggy.

Life was different here, so different! Dogs did not run free, but were leashed. She frowned as she thought about it, resenting the leash terribly. *Stupid leash, as if I am stupid enough to run away, stupid, stupid, dumb!* She shook her ears out and bore her suffering silently, so as not to burden Naji, who had his own worries.

He had left behind a fine reputation and a thriving business. Naji Najeem was highly regarded as the best tailor in the city of Norwall. His beloved wife Hannah had died in a factory explosion many years ago, and after that, he lived a quiet and simple life alone above his tailor shop. He crafted the best men's waistcoats in town, and he displayed them with pride in the front windows of his shop. People of means wandered by the windows and stopped to stare, each hand-made suit a creative masterpiece.

His shop was immaculately clean and organized; never so much as a pin or a fragment of thread littered the floor. His white tape measure hung unceremoniously around his neck each day as he unlocked his door and greeted customers. He prided himself on knowing most of them by their first names, and he acknowledged them as if they were long-lost friends. He looked at the customers that frequented his shop as family, and the tinydog who returned to his store each night his treasured companion.

As Naji and Pebby strolled around the Adventura, the sun was sparkling and there would seem to be nothing unusual about this day. But later, they would remember that this was the day when they first spotted the boy. They finished circling the shopping center and stopped on a small plot of grass behind the dry-cleaning shop.

Pebby sniffed the fresh grass and Naji took a deep breath and tried to clear his lungs before they resumed their workday. He was coughing and hacking now, and Pebby furrowed her brow with worry. He was huffing and puffing on these short morning walks, worse than she had ever seen. His thick lips, under his silver moustache, had a bluish tinge. The extra weight he carried did not help him one bit. She had no answer, and no one to ask for help. She had never felt so alone in her three years.

Out of the corner of his eye, Naji spotted someone headed toward them. He was getting older and his vision had deteriorated. The sun was gleaming in his eyes, and he raised his hand to shield them. He instinctively tightened the leash to protect his tiny charge. Pebby, too, felt someone approaching and her senses heightened.

The boy must have been about thirteen years old, with short dark hair that spiked up in front. He wore wire-rimmed glasses. His white polo shirt was neatly tucked into his black shorts and his tennis shoes were spotless. Phillip was wearing a brown canvas backpack and was carrying a rectagular black case with silver studs. He slightly leaned to one side, but the case did not appear to be heavy. He swung it back and forth easily as he walked. Pebby wondered what was inside.

There was a casual spring to his step and he hummed to himself, snapping the fingers of his right hand as an imaginary tune played in his head. He nodded his head to the music and had not a care in the world. He was deeply immersed in his private thoughts and oblivious to everything around him.

Pebby wondered again what was in the black, square, leather case. She noticed how the boy deliberately missed the puddles so as not to get his shoes dirty. Phillip looked curiously at Naji, spotted the tinydog and then, without the slightest bit of hesitation, headed in her direction. He continued to bob his head to the music. She saw him peer over the top of his glasses, and only for a moment, he slowed down and actually stopped. They locked eyes, and for an instant both were absolutely still. Pebby tilted her head to the right and blinked once or twice, brown eyes squinting in the bright morning sun.

She saw the very faint glimmer of a smile on his face, but she could not be sure. Then, he broke into the widest smile she had ever seen. His teeth were very white and perfectly straight. She saw one eyebrow arched much higher than the other, and his eyes and nose crinkled when he smiled. He tilted his head, stopped humming, and froze for a moment as they stared at each other, unblinking, as if every clock in the universe suddenly stood still.

He bobbed his head once quickly as if to silently say *hello*, snapped back to the present, and raised his hand, giving a wave goodbye to them both. He quickly hurried on and disappeared through the heavy rear door of the adjacent business. Pebby startled at the loud CRASH when the huge metal door slammed shut behind him. She looked up at Naji and he was grinning, rubbing his chin, and watching the boy with curiosity and interest.

Naji and Pebby went back to work. She was resting in her pink crate, barely listening to the people come and go as she dozed. She lifted her head and shook it slightly to make sure she wasn't dreaming. The massive fans spinning in the cleaning shop muted the noise at the front desk and the steady hum had the hypnotic effect of making her sleepy.

She dreamed she was running down the cobblestone streets she knew so well, her favorite black velvet derby perched precariously on her head. Beyond the dream, she could hear the huge paddle fans of the shop whirring at a high pitch, keeping the little place cool in the suffocating heat.

Naji tidied up the front desk, collected and filed receipts, and swept the cramped lobby which could hold only five people at one time if they were standing shoulder to shoulder. Two vinyl chairs with cracked red seats bordered a small fiberboard table on which perched faded silk flowers. A few wrinkled, outdated magazines completed the decor.

As Pebby drifted back into wakefulness she kept her eyes on the old man who was slowly sweeping. He was heaving long slow breaths which had gotten more labored in the past several weeks. *There's got to be someone who can help him get better! I can't lose him, not now. Especially not now!* She had a friend and companion in Naji, and no matter where her travels took her during the day, she would always return to Naji Najeem at night for supper and a pallet on which to rest. She had never known any other home.

Fiercely independent, she preferred it that way, or perhaps she had just accustomed herself to the loneliness; the bravado of her independence hiding the fact that she had never really belonged to anyone, least of all Naji Najeem. Truth be told, they were both fiercely independent, but found solace in a companionship which did not restrain either of them. When they closed their eyes at night, each was grateful for the company of the other. This was true no matter where they were; home, or most recently, unexpectedly, in Florida.

CHAPTER 2

The Angry Automaton

The red and black plaid blanket on which the tiny scruffy dog slept had seen better days. It had been mended many times, and by the most skilled sewing hands in the town of Norwall. Naji had seen his wife Hannah cover herself with the blanket every day as she rocked in the wooden rocker by the fire. But, that had ended two years ago when she perished in a factory explosion.

Several days after she died, Naji found himself inviting the tiny vagabond upstairs for supper, and it had become a nightly ritual for them both. Naji had fashioned Hannah's blanket into a pallet for the twelve-pound scruffy dog with silver-tan colored ears, which everyone noticed were long, and silky. It was the most comfortable bed Pebby had ever known.

Opening one eye slowly, she shivered. The fire had gone out sometime in the early morning hours. They used as little wood as possible to conserve the amount they were rationed and they hoarded it for use in cold weather. She didn't know if she woke up because of the cold, or because her inner clockwork reminded her that it was time to get ready for work. She was due at the Octagon Bakery in less than an hour.

Pebby stretched her body, raised her rump in the air, and stretched out her spine which was still sore from the long day yesterday. The life of a working pup in Norwall! She sneezed twice from the dust, and for the first time noticed the almost invisible light film that covered the cheap wooden furniture. The dust could barely be seen, but it covered every surface in the little walk-up apartment. She had been smelling the dirty, musty, stinky dust outside for a while, but now it was meandering into the small efficiency apartment above the tailor shop.

She stood and put her front paws on the seat of the recliner, where the finest tailor in town still slept fitfully. He had stopped sleeping in his bed when the breathing became too difficult; sitting half-way up in the recliner helped him rest easier. Occasionally, she heard him grunt, stop breathing for a few seconds, then take a gasp and blubber a breath. She did not need to wake him. *Let him sleep, it's only five in the morning and he doesn't open the shop till eight o'clock.* She gave him a quick licky-lick on his hand, careful not to wake him.

Slurping some water, she found a few old scraps in her food bowl. Naji had retrieved it from a discard pile at the weekly auction, where townspeople could bid on unwanted items from the Council. The white porcelain bowl had a chip out of one edge, but it had the most lovely, hand-painted lilac blossoms scattered around the periphery of the bowl. "A bowl fit for a princess," Naji had said. And sure enough, he carefully washed it each morning and fed her each evening, with whatever food he could scrounge. The ration program barely allowed him enough for himself, but Pebby would sneak out three-day-old bread from the bakery to supplement their fare whenever she could, knowing full well the penalty if she got caught. Sometimes the rolls weren't too hard, and they moistened it with soup to make a welcome feast.

Pebby nosed into her vest, which was hanging from the arm of Hannah's rocker. She carefully slid into it and pushed a small round disc embedded into the coat against the leg spindle of the rocker. As if by magic, the gears began to turn, clockwork style, and in an instant the little vest was fastened just ever so carefully around the little scruffy dog. The vest was not too loose, nor too tight. From the other arm of the chair hung a small black velvet derby, sporting a fine black net veil which partially covered the front.

The only other ornamentation on the derby was a deep violet ribbon band and a solitary deep rose-violet flower, just like the one on Hannah's favorite black hat, which still hung on a hook by the door. There remained also her oatmeal-colored fisher-man shawl, as if she was coming home any minute. Pebby nosed the hat onto her head, making sure it was at the proper angle for a lady. She took one last slurp of water, glanced at the somnolent Naji, and silently crept down the stairs to the miniature oval aperture which was her private entrance. The flap snapped closed behind her, and she stepped out into the quiet chaos of the awakening city.

The sidewalks were stained with mildew and mold, and the cobblestone streets a dusty rose-gold. They, despite the runs of street steamers every other day, were stained gray. The three suns were just starting to rise. She thought it odd that they were aligned in a perfect triangle, which she had never seen before. This was the most beautiful time of day in Norwall. The pink streaks of the sky were spectacular, radiating out from the triangular design of the three suns and lighting up the sky with streaks of beautiful rose-pink and gray. The rows and rows of three-story wood and brick buildings lining each side of the cobblestone streets were almost a luminous pink-violet shade in the morning suns. Unless one looked closely, one wouldn't notice that most of these row-houses had been hastily abandoned, their residents located in group living facilities called *Habitrons*, which attached to the factories. But, that was after the Council took control of the city. Before the Council took over two years ago, every day was beautiful in Norwall.

She inhaled a deep breath, but the air had a musty smell. She wrinkled her nose; the acid smell burned her sensitive nostrils. She wished the gray-sky had never come. The factories with their steam engines produced soot that had been increasingly dark and ominous. The Automatons patrolling the cities and factories at the behest of the Council weren't affected. But, all the plants that had once adorned the city were dehydrated and dying from the lack of rain. The humans, like Naji Najeem, were increasingly sick as their lungs became fibrotic and scarred. The buildings, so beautiful in the morning-pink sky, were darkening with soot as the years passed.

Stretching her short white legs, she trotted half of a city block. Passing her, pulling a wooden-and-metal wagon loaded with cords of firewood, was a giant copper-colored metal snail, as tall as a one-story house. A small steam engine powered the vehicle. A middle-aged, angry looking man in a black waistcoat, derby, and goggles was perched precariously on a wooden bench seat. His long, pointed nose gave him a bird-like appearance. He harbored a sour expression, and frowned as he used chubby hands to manipulate a toggle stick to stear the puffing and snorting vehicle. He did not give Pebby a glance.

On the corner of the street, tall, broad, and gleaming, sat a six-foot tin-and-brass-colored box, covered in gears of all metals and sizes. She had to squint to see the detail, but as she slowed her gait and got closer, she recognized it for what it was: an Automaton. Her activity triggered its attention and the large brass and copper gears on his back started to spin against each other, grinding softly, spinning and whirring. The mechanical man started to move in jerky, stop-gap motion. A brass colored front panel slid open to reveal a sinister face with gleaming turquoise eyes. Pointed teeth protruded from each corner of the frowning mouth and the head snapped from side to side, scanning its surroundings.

Two arms flew up in defense mode, and the machine's all-directional wheels started toward her. It aimed a cogwheel arm directly at her face, and relayed her demographics back to Council Command via its internal radio system. She was validated as a worker, with credentials permitting her to navigate the streets at such an early hour. Steam puffed from a short, stainless tube at the back of its head, three short, hot, smokey puffs.

Stinking Automats, she thought, as she picked up the pace. The robot's vicious facies came into sharp focus the closer she got. Brass gears spun wildly but silently on its back, and if a robot face could scowl, it certainly would be called a scowl. It marched a cadence down the gray, mildew-stained sidewalk bordering the cobblestone street. Menacing gear steamery-death-blasters pointed out from both arms, threatening to shoot vaporizing steam on any non-authorized living thing.

Scooting past its base, Pebby kept her head down and broke into a silent, speedy run. Her ears flew straight back, but the derby never lost its place. She knew the way and galloped joyously. *Free! I'm free!* After all, she had not attained the position of Chief Delivery Dog for nothing. It had been a long, hard climb up the ladder, with scores of fast, on-time deliveries proving her worth. Her speed was unsurpassed and she knew every nook and cranny of Norwall. There was no address she could not find, no factory where she did not know the location of secret doors where the managers could receive rations.

Gleena Glisson, the proprietress of the Octagon Bakery, had, only for Pebby, overlooked the requirement that all the delivery dogs sleep together in Habitron Quarters.

I'm the fastest and I'm the best, and I know my way around every nook in this Clockwork town, so just look the other way Gleena, as long as I show up in the mornin' ready to run, and I mean speedy run, stay out'a me business! I'm keepin' my nose down, and I don't make the

stinkin' Automats mad by trying to scoot atween their
legs, stinkin' Automats! OK, go, go, and... GO!!!

Huffing and puffing now, the tinydog galloped so fast that she was a black and silver blur. Still, the derby on her head remained perfectly angled just the way she had placed it. The clock on the tower, boasting gears of every metallic color, rang six times as the gears spun wildly but silently. The ringing of the clock was loud and deafening, so that the entire town seemed to vibrate like the lowest string on a cello, each tone lasting for only a few seconds.

In the distance, tall, shiny columns, satiny steel, as shiny as kitchen pans in the bakery, reflected the fading rose-pink of the sky. The trifecta suns gleamed, and the stainless towers sparkled, even as the gray fog rose from the factories, obliterating the crisp, fresh sky.

The bakery took up three city blocks itself, and the Habitron where the human workers lived, another two blocks. As Pebby rounded the corner, Gleena appeared like a ghostly apparition dressed in all white. A spotless Oxford-cloth apron extended to the ground from a loop that always hung around Gleena's neck. The apron was already, at this early hour, littered with flour. A tall baker's hat was perched, a little bit sideways of course, over her kinky gray hair. Her arms were out and bent akimbo, with fists resting on her hips. Knowing what was coming, Pebby steeled herself.

"Pebby! Ya 'canna' just run in here any ol'e time ye please! Orders ready to go out, hot rolls and cinnies comin offa' da line! Hurry a'fore the icin' gets runny! Why're you not sleepin' in the Habitrons? I knows ye's sneaking off to spend time with Naji Najeem, ain't cha?"

Gleena cut her eyes at the tinydog. She shook a wooden rolling pin in the air for emphasis, and Pebby galloped all the faster, ears flying straight out behind her. Ignoring the admonition, she saw a hint of a smile on Gleena's face as she brushed by her legs, slowing a bit through the bricked archway. As she made her way into the bakery proper, Pebby was nearly blinded by the reflecting shiny steel and the bright lights overhead. The massive bowls were already turning on stainless and copper gears, and the hissing of the steam machines prohibited conversation. The walls were light red brick and extended upward twenty feet. Above that, extending to the dome ceiling, were stainless steel panels. The entire room had the shape of a huge octagon.

The glass dome ceiling which used to admit the daylight, now gave the workers a glimpse of the ever-dismal gray sky. The exhausted, pitiful workers finishing the night shift were dressed in stained white pants and formless white tunics. They were covered in flour and dried dough, and they smelled sour and sweaty from hours and hours of work. But they smiled and glanced at each other and grinned as the tiny scruffy dog flew past their legs. They grinned and nodded at each other as they saw the black derby fly past the front of the workline. Her freedom was something they were not given, and the twelve-hour night shifts were difficult. They knew that when they saw Pebby come, it was almost time to end the shift; for clocks, despite the clockwork town, were not permitted in the factories. Contraband such as a pocket watch was punishable by death. But they could always rely on Pebby and her expert sense of time. They said among themselves, *you kinna set a watch by'er!*

Flying through brick tunnelways and arches, the tinydog made her way through the bowels of the factory, turn right, turn right, turn left, one more turn to the left. Screeching to a halt in a massive octagon-shaped room of white tiles, she quickly found cubicle twenty-two. A small unused square of soft, white towel lay on the floor; a similar pallet in each of the thirty-three cubicles served as a bed for each dog. In other cubicles, dogs of varying breeds were slipping into their geared vests. None, however, was entitled to sport the velvet black derby with the rose-violet flower, awarded only to the fastest and the best delivery dog of the bunch, the Chief Delivery Dog.

Pebby arrived dressed, so she backed into the small wooden red wagon that was parked in her cubicle, number twenty-two, and snapped the hooks on her vest into the gear assembly on the wagon. Taking a quick drink from the common fountain, annoyed that there was no kibble left in the trough, she trotted out of the cubicle, out of the room with its high octagon ceiling, and took her place in the line just outside the open triple doors to await the loading of her first delivery.

Automatons stood watch as fresh, hot baked goods in crisp white paper bags were readied for each dog's wagon. Cog-wheel armature raised, scowling metal faces, they watched for any irregularity in distributing the food. Misappropriation of rationed food was dealt with harshly. Automatons were given the right by the Council to steam-extinguish on sight any living thing that was interfering with the assignment of the bakery rations.

While steam wagons delivered rations not only to the Council, but also to the factories for distribution to the workers, the Council permitted business owners and managers of the factories to order food-by-tokens. Wooden chips entitled the owner to directly purchase items from the factories and stores, and it was the delivery dogs that made this interchange possible.

Nose raised to the sky, Pebby took one last sniff of the morning air. The gray fog settled in as the pretty pink streaks of the morning sky disappeared. The air, even now more acidic, burned her tiny nostrils and made her coat smelly. She shook her coat and ears in place and steeled herself. There wouldn't be another break for a very long time. Her workday had begun.

CHAPTER 3

The Messy Desk

Next door to the Imperial Dry Cleaners, Phillip dropped his brown canvas backpack on the floor in the room he used for his office. His desk was littered with wrinkled paper, food wrappers, half-empty water bottles, and half-eaten cracker packets. The trash can beside the desk was overflowing with crumpled paper airplanes he made yesterday in an effort to keep himself busy while he waited for his mother to finish work. Today was a half day of school and he was here unusually early.

His mother had fixed up a desk and bookshelf in an empty utility room so he would have a place to do homework when he came to her office after school. To his amusement, mops and vacuum parts that had previously hung on the wall had been taken down and replaced with maps.

Maps. Did she really think I was ever going to look at them? Silly, Mom. REALLY silly, Mom! Just another dumb idea!

He chuckled and shook his head at the thought of her ridiculous efforts to make him believe he was going to get any work done here. She had bought a globe, and decorated the desk with pencil cups and a stapler. Plain and graph-lined paper were neatly arranged in a stacking tray. As he looked around at the accessories, he felt just a little bit guilty, but not guilty enough to get to work.

Flippantly, he took apart his stapler and scattered staples all over his desk, not bothering to put it back together. He unzipped one section of his backpack, which spit out cellophane from the last pack of crackers he had eaten. Crumbs spilled over his books and littered his papers. He tossed his workbooks on the desk, knocking over the pencil can in the process. He pushed all the spilled contents into a messy pile in the corner of the desk near yesterday's pencil shavings. He took apart one of his pens and shot the spring into the trash can.

He couldn't concentrate today. He wished he could. He wished he was more like his older sister Claire, who could have her math homework done ten minutes after the teacher gave the assignment. He knew beyond any shadow of any doubt, that she was his mother's favorite. *Who wouldn't love Claire? She's everything I'm not.*

Claire would boast that she had her homework done, and would enjoy free time in the evening. Phillip *never* had free time in the evening, which dismayed his mother considerably. He sighed and shook his head. *Who wouldn't love Claire, Miss Pitter-Patter-Perfect!?* Phillip always felt like she was running ahead, leaving him in the dust. *I just can never catch up to Claire. Claire, Claire!*

Phillip usually delayed doing his homework for so long that he ended up sitting by the kitchen table for most of the evening, head in his hands, trying to decipher math. His mother would sit next to him quietly finishing her own paperwork while monitoring his progress and answering his questions. *Boooring. Math is booorrring,* but his mother would not let him off the hook as far as his school assignments. His mother never had to tell Claire to finish homework.

Claire! That was a whole different story. Claire was bubbly and happy. *That's because*, thought Phillip, as he felt himself get irritated, *she doesn't have a care in the world! Claire doesn't care about math, BECAUSE CLAIRE IS GOOD AT MATH!* Phillip could feel himself clenching his teeth and raising one eyebrow, as he did when he was horribly perplexed.

Claire seemed to get good grades automatically without a bit of effort. She would toss one of her two mean, vile cats over her shoulder and grin as she marched off to play video games. Phillip would struggle behind a mess of homework papers piled high on the kitchen table. Spinning his office chair, he pulled up to the desk. His mind was not on his math lessons. As he picked at the black repair tape on the chair cushion, he tried to force himself to stop thinking about Claire and her extraordinary natural abilities.

Oh! I hate her cats! Nasty Smellies! They were sneaky, slinky, ferocious creatures, devoted only to Claire. They hissed and fussed even if he was in the same room. He devised ingenious ways to torment them, working stealthily, and he laughed to think just how clever he was. When he could, he would give each of them two quick sprays of his mother's plant mister. POOF! POOF! Cold water right in their simple little faces. Another favorite torment of his was to dump their kibble back in the master container so that their bowls were empty and they screamed for food. What those cats needed was a good dog to chase them away, yes indeed!

Wait a minute... ya know, he thought to himself, *I don't have a pet that belongs just to me. I wanted a hamster, but MOM said, 'no, no, no! A million centuries of NO!,'* bobbing his head to imitate her sarcastically. But that didn't bother him terribly, because he really didn't like hamsters that much anyway, he just wanted to see what she'd say. How did it happen that Claire had the Smellicats and his mother had Moushka, her oversized Husky? His mind drifted back to this morning when he had seen the tiny scruffy dog. She was so cute and so lively in a comical sort of way, with her little bob-cut of her silvery-gray hairdo, long, silky ears sweeping the ground as she sniffed the grass. *There's something special about her,* he thought, but he couldn't figure out exactly what that was. Her big brown eyes looked too big for her face, and when she stared at him tilting her head, she didn't even blink once. Her short, curly black coat looked like a little jacket, contrasting with her silvery-tan hair and ears.

He just had to get another look at her! He was thinking about her so hard that he pulled the crushed sandwich he had grabbed from the break-room refrigerator out of his pocket, and gobbled it down. He swept the crumbs into his trash can and hid the traces of his crime. He knew that he had just eaten his mother's lunch and it was only late morning. Just a tiny bit remorseful, he decided to get some math done because, sure enough, she would be coming in to check. He, of course, would deny ever seeing her sandwich, and most certainly deny ever even touching it, let alone eating it. *I will outsmart you once again, silly mother!* He chuckled to himself and pulled up *Revolutions of the Ages* on his computer screen.

Today was a busy day for his mother, a doctor, with an office full of patients complaining about this or that. His mother always concentrated when she saw the patients, and she hated to be interrupted. He heard her heels clack as she marched up and down the hallway, going into each exam room, immersing herself in the problems of each patient. He grinned. He enjoyed hearing her dart in and out of the rooms, which kept her quite busy *and off my case*, he thought, as he chuckled and immersed himself in his newest computer game. *She's too busy to catch me!* It did not bother him one bit to sneak behind her back and play computer games instead of doing homework.

As usual, he was still hungry. His mom kept food in the office kitchen, so after a battle or two he wandered there.

"Phillip?" he heard his mom call, "why are you in the kitchen? You need to work on math first, then get a snack later!"

Sheeesh, she's on to me.

"Just getting a water bottle, Mommm," he called out defensively as he made his way back to his desk, with not only a water bottle, but also a newfound turkey sandwich stashed under the crook of his arm.

He heard his mom going up front to give instructions to the nurses. It seemed as though she never stopped walking from one end of the office to the other, always on the move. That was one thing about her that got on his nerves, but not the only thing. She would walk past his room quietly, then drop in to surprise him and make sure he was working on math. She was in the hall now talking with Jaceena, her nurse and office manager. Jaceena. *Miss no-nonsense, take charge bossi-man, always on my case,* thought Phillip. Jaceena, at exactly five feet tall, was clicking her heels down the hall headed straight toward his door. Phillip imagined her with eight pairs of eyes and legs like a bionic insect.

The footsteps grew louder, and he thought he could hear her breathing heavily. She was an insular blanket of protection around his mother. Jaceena had worked in the hospital cafeteria when his mother was an intern in training, and the short, vivacious Jamacian cafeteria worker had taken a liking to the tall, quiet, chestnut-haired doctor. His mother had hired her, encouraging her through nursing school. She was not just an employee, she was his mother's best friend. Anything that could harm Abby Weathermore would *never* get past Jaceena!

Jaceena's children were all grown, and Phillip was convinced they had suffered terribly. If she realized that he had eaten his mother's lunch, she would have no mercy on him. He steeled himself for the wrath that he knew would fall on him very soon.

"Phillip? PHILLIP!"

He heard Jaceena calling his name as she rapped on his door. Thankfully, he had turned the lock when he came in. He quickly and frantically ditched the game, changing the screen to a default math work-book page and innocently cleared his throat. He croaked out a quiet, "Yes?"

"Phillip!" He heard her whisper loudly as he imagined her face pressed up against his door. "You have eaten every bit of food in dat' kitchen! Your mom's done and she's looking for her lunch! What's up with you boy, com'on Phillip, open the door, and I mean NOW! Open this door!"

He could imagine she was shaking her long finger with her perfectly manicured nails at him as she had done so many times. He shrunk down as far as he could in the patched, leather desk chair as Jaceena ratcheted his door handle back and forth, now realizing that the door was locked. He could feel the heat of her temper rising, as she jiggled the door even harder. Clearing his throat, again, he tried to sound studious.

"Yes, yes, one minute! Coming, working on math!" He shuffled papers to make noise, and slammed a book open and shut several times, trying to sound convincing. He flipped the lock.

A petite, very pretty, but very angry woman dressed in blue surgical scrubs peered around the corner of his office door. A surgical face mask hung by loosely tied strings from her neck. Her hair was pulled back into a perfectly neat braided bun which was decorated with multicolored beads. Her dainty glasses dropped down to the tip of her nose and she stared over the top of the lenses, pursing her lips and shaking her head back and forth.

With a disapproving "umm, ummm, ummmm," she crossed her arms in front of her, then admonished, just loud enough for only Phillip to hear, almost whispering,

"I've tol' you and tol' you and tol' you, your mother's lunch is off limits, Mister!" She shook a long index finger at him.

He shrunk down in the chair, his face reddened, his eyebrows raised.

"Sorry!" he huffed back at her, sarcastically, and actually not sorry one bit.

As quickly as she had snuck up on him, she was gone. He heard her opening each exam room door, spraying puffs of disinfectant and slamming shut the room doors. She kept the office in ready working order as though at any minute, hundreds of people could storm the front door, demanding to be seen. He heard quick footsteps approaching, and he held his breath for a moment. His mother's wide smile appeared around the door. Her hair was pulled back in a ponytail, her white coat still impeccably neat despite the busy morning. He thought he could smell disinfectant on her, or rather, maybe she just always smelled clean.

"Hey, I'm done with patients and I've gotta have something to eat. Come on, let's go and grab a sandwich!" She turned away, then called back to him over her shoulder. "How'd you like my lunch, Buddy? Still hungry?"

He stood and started packing his bookbag, stuffing the used candy and cracker wrappers to the bottom, ignoring the trash can beside his desk. He shook his head a few times quickly. *Mother.* She seemed to have eyes growing out of the back of her head and knew what he was up to, even when she was in the next room or in the next building. *She is too darn nosy. Real nosy.*

He cringed as he heard her calling him again, this time from the front lobby, as she straightened magazines and tossed wrinkled ones in the trash.

"Come on Honey, I'm done," she sighed, tired from the activity of the morning. "It's my early day, so we can head home and work on math, kinda get a headstart on homework? Won't that be great?"

Oh yeah, out... standing! thought Phillip, crossing his arms over his chest, rolling his eyes, and shaking his head in absolute, total, complete dismay.

CHAPTER 4

The Tuna Sandwich

Phillip and his mother walked out the front door of the office and locked the door behind them. The office staff was working on returning phone calls, and setting up for the next workday. Jaceena was leading the entire operation as if she was working the front lines of a war campaign. At that same instant, Naji Najeem led the tiny scruffy dog out of the front door of his shop. She was wearing a leather vest dotted with different kinds of gears; some copper colored, some silver, some burnished gold. Naji was locking his door and trying to hang his

"CLOSED" sign squarely in the center of the door. The scruffy dog turned, intrigued by the tall woman wearing a long white coat, and the dark-haired boy who had smiled at her that morning. The only people that Pebby had seen dressed in white coats had been workers at the Octagon Bakery.

The woman's chestnut hair was pulled into a neat ponytail. Her shoes had thick two-inch heels, and looked comfortable. She stared briefly at the silver and black mop-top dog and they locked eyes. Naji was impatient, and was tugging on the tinydog's leash but her feet were planted firmly and she would not move. Breaking from his mother's side, Phillip ran to the front door of the cleaners.

"Scuse me, Sir, is that your dog? Who does she belong to? What's her name? Where's she from?"

His mother interceded. Striding and holding out her hand, she introduced herself.

"Hey there, I'm Abby Weathermore, and you must be our new neighbor? Mr. Hambeeb told me he hired you to run his shop. Welcome!" She warmly shook his hand, grasping it with both of hers.

"Most pleased madam, I am Naji Najeem, humble tailor, and this is Pebby, the tiny scruffy dog!" he smiled widely and chuckled.

"Pleased to finally meet you, welcome to the plaza!" she exclaimed, as she smiled widely.

"And this is my son Phillip, who seems to be very interested in your little furry friend there." She continued, "Someone seems to have eaten my lunch, so we're going to Frankie's Deli. Can we bring you something back? Frankie makes a mean tuna sandwich!"

Naji looked surprised. What was tuna, and why would it be mean? He scratched his head.

"Yes, thank you, madam, that would be most kind of you!" He wasn't quite sure what *mean* tuna was anyway. *But if they liked it, it probably was good,* he told himself. "What is your mode of business?" he queried, as he pointed to her front door.

"I have a medical practice. You know, coughs, cold, blood pressure, stomach aches, things like that. Garden variety sickness."

Garden variety? What did she have to do with a garden? Maybe herbs? Naji wondered. Would she know why he had been coughing so much lately?

Phillip interrupted him again.

"Mr. Najeem, what about that dog? Where'd ya get her? Can I pet her?"

"Phillip," Naji said, caught off guard and wanting to speak carefully.

"Right now the dog belongs to me until I figure out... ah... oh, I mean, find out... where she belongs." he stuttered and stammered. "Her name is Pebby, she's three years old, and better watch out Phillip, curiosity can get you in substantial trouble!"

Naji laughed haltingly and Phillip was embarrassed. Seeing that, Naji swooped down and picked up the tinydog and placed her in the boy's arms. Phillip let out a sigh as he wrapped his arms around her and squeezed her tight. Pebby licked his nose, one quick, licky-lick, and Phillip tilted his head back and laughed. He was surprised at how strong she was, but she did not try to wiggle away. Instead, she relaxed, as if sitting in this boy's arms was the most natural thing in the world.

Abby Weathermore stroked the long silky ears. *Very strange*, she whispered to herself as she touched the leather vest and fingered one of the brass gears which adorned it.

"Gears on a dog's vet?" she asked. "And what are these little loops? They look like hooks for a wagon. You're not a sled dog, are you?"

She laughed, and stroked the long ears of the tinydog, letting her lick her hand. She frowned, thinking the dog perhaps seemed somehow familiar, but then again, maybe not. She sighed.

"Well, we better go now Mr. Najeem, thank you for introducing us to your beautiful little friend."

She gave Pebby one last gentle touch on the mop-top, and her eyes traveled again to the vest. She stared for a brief moment and wrinkled her forehead and scrunched up her nose. She was thinking very hard about something. Exasperated, Phillip brought her back to the present.

"He said he's trying to figure out where she belongs Mom, sheeesh!" Under his breath he muttered to himself. *Get it right, will ya?* Luckily, she had not heard that last comment. Lately, it seemed to him that sometimes she didn't know what she was talking about. More and more, she was really getting on his nerves.

As Phillip gently lowered the pup to the ground, Pebby fixed her gaze on the woman and her son as Naji tugged on the leash.

"See you soon, Mr. Najeem," Abby added as she turned to walk to their car. "We'll drop off your sandwich in a few minutes, okay?" She watched the little dog turn her head almost quizzically. Naji nodded.

"Most kind, most kind, Ma'am, thank you. Good to meet you!" He gave a little half-bow, nodding his head ever so slightly as they drove away.

Phillip watched the old man and the dog start out on their mid-day walk around the center. He watched them until they disappeared from sight. He relaxed in the car seat, but was abruptly brought back to reality by his mother.

"How much of your math did you get done, Phillip, and isn't the science project due Thursday?"

He watched the back of her head. If her ponytail started swinging right to left, he was in for it. When she started shaking her head as if to say *no, no no*, then he better watch out. His mother had been getting emails from Ms. Madlin, his homeroom teacher, and they had not been complimentary. She thought Phillip was not applying himself and was snickering in class. He was distracted and most of his work was turned in late.

Victoria Madlin and his mother had hatched a plan to get him re-focused on schoolwork. The plan limited his computer time to one hour daily for work other than school. It included clarinet lessons to help his mind focus, and included pages of copywork. It was monitored daily by both women, catching Phillip in an unescapable crossfire.

The ponytail unfortunately bobbed sideways as his mother shook her head.

"You've got to get right to it when we get home!" she continued, "And I mean, im... MEEED... iately!!!"

She accented the middle of the word like she usually did when her temper was starting to ignite. Phillip had been on the end of it before, and he had lost computer priviledges for seven days. *Seven l...o...n...g days.* He was not anxious for a repeat of that debacle. *Meanie, Meanie, Mother!* He pursed his lips and furrowed his eyebrows into a unibrow, nodding his head side to side as he silently mocked her.

"I have Mr. Ravinni coming to give me a bid on some flooring, so I'll be busy. I want to see you get a good start on science, then read two chapters in *Narnia*, then hit the math hard and heavy." She wasn't yet done. "Then, we will keep working on the spelling. Come on now, let's do a little bit more, no sense wasting time! Come on, 'dulcimer'!"

She nodded her head, expecting him to spell it correctly. She had an annoying habit of keeping his weekly spelling list in the visor of the car and calling out spelling words while they were driving. She expected him to promptly and correctly spell the word she called out. It was a game he half enjoyed and he went along with it.

"**D-u-l-c-i-m-a-r**," he replied hesitantly.

She shook her head from side to side, "Dulci-mer!" This time she said it slowly and deliberately, accenting the syllables.

"**Dul-ci-mer**," and she s... t... r... e... t... c... h... e... d... out the word to clue him in on the spelling.

Hesitantly, he shouted back. "D-u-l-c-i-m-e-r!" There, he had it! But she wasn't done. More words followed in rapid-fire succession, as if she was a soldier in the *Revolutions of the Ages* game firing an assault rifle, and he was the prey. His mind drifted to his video game. He pictured her in camouflage fatigues.

"Arraignment!" she shot back.

"**A-r........r-a-i-n-m-e-n-t**!! he spit out, distracted by the action in the parking lot of the deli, where a mother was shepherding her toddlers and two teenagers were wearing headsets, shaking their heads to the beat.

"Wrong, wrong, wrong, try again!" Her head swiveled side to side, and for a moment Phillip imagined it twisting all the way around like a creature in a horror film he and his sister had secretly watched. He bit the inside of his lip to keep from laughing.

"A-r-r-a-i-g-n-m-e-n-t."

"You got it!" She clapped her hands loudy, applauding his efforts. She only briefly stopped the barrage long enough for him to make a face at her, which she caught a glimpse of in the rear-view mirror.

"Fortuitously!" she called out, laughing as they drove up to the carry-out window. He breathed a huge sigh of relief at the reprieve. That one he knew, and triumphantly he spit it out proudly.

"F..o..r..t..u.i.t.o.u.s.l.y."

His mother turned and smiled the broadest smile she had smiled all day. Bobbing her head, she nodded happily, a huge grin breaking out on her face.

"I'm so very proud of the effort you put into your work this week Phillip," she complimented, trying to encourage him.

"I know you can keep bringing your grades up and be near the top of the class. I know you're really talented, *you* just don't know it yet!"

She laughed that high-pitched laugh that he thought sounded like one of the teenage girls in his homeroom, a laugh that annoyed him royally. *This is not the way a mother's laugh should sound.*

Phillip rolled his eyes upward before he realized she could see him in the rear-view mirror. She was ignoring his childish face-making. *Silly Mother.*

"Three tunas on rye, nix the lettuce, Frankie," his mother shouted into the microphone of the ordering station. She came here so often that she was on a first name basis with the employees. Having waited tables to earn her way through college, she was extra-courteous to folks in serving positions.

"Thanks, Doc!" Frankie smiled at her as he handed back her bank card. "I see you've got the helper today! What's up, Phillip? Helping your mom at the office? How's that clarinet coming along?"

Phillip squirmed lower in the seat, trying to make himself invisible as he turned beet red. *Who is this Frankie, anyway, little paper hat perched on his head, white uniform dotted with food stains, knowing her by her first name?* He hated the way people knew his mother, *because when they know Mom, they know me. Privacy, please!*

"Come on, Phillip," his mother whispered. "Be nice, just say hi!" He slouched even farther down.

"Heh," he said half-heartedly, wondering why she had to tell everyone that he played the clarinet. *Sheesh, can't I have privacy?* She swung the car in a wide circle and headed back in the direction of the office, as her cell phone rang.

"Phillip. You take Mr. Najeem's sandwich to him. I have to run in and sign one more paper for Jaceena. I'll be right over to get you, don't drive him crazy with questions if he is busy with customers... okay? Just give him his lunch, huh?"

She pulled into the parking space directly in front of the office.

"Don't come out holding that scruffy dog either!" She laughed as she walked toward the office. Unlocking the door, she waved a good-bye, smiling widely, and shaking her head side to side as she walked, grinning still.

Well, he thought, *it wasn't funny. I wanted a hamster, and I didn't get one. I wanted a drum set, but she got me a clarinet. I wanted to look at the menu, but she ordered me a tuna sandwich and nixed the lettuce anyway, just because she likes tuna and thinks it's good for me! And why is she always nixing lettuce? No matter what she eats, she nixes lettuce! She has this stupid idea that we get stomach germs from dirty lettuce, so she's nixing lettuce out of my life!!*

He scrunched his face. It perturbed him to think about her annoying habits, and he jumped from the car without saying a word. Never mind her and all her quirks that increasingly annoyed him to no end. He was anxious to see the tinydog again.

CHAPTER 5

The Skinny Boy

Pebby watched the skinny, frail-looking brown-skinned teenager crouched at the top of the loading ramp. One shock of dirty hair kept flopping in his face and he kept lifting his hand up to push it back while balancing a clipboard on his thigh. He was intently checking the list. Deen Diggins was in charge of distributing the bakery goods to the squad of delivery dogs and there was no room for him to make a mistake.

Rubbing his chin, he squinted to make out the words. He would never admit how bad his sight was; he could lose his job, and loading the baked goods onto the wagons each morning sure beat working sixteen hour days in a steamy, hot factory. He was squinting for another reason as well. Reading was not his strongest forte. There had been no formal schooling to amount to anything at the bakery. He cherished the dogs he cared for and his hard work and determination landed him a role as Habitron Master of the Dog Corps.

Behind him, a massive arched doorway framed the glittering stainless steel kitchens of the Octagon. The Department of Distribution stood between the outside world and the inner workings of the spotless, shiny, stainless steam-driven bakery. Rows of stainless conveyor belts were attended by workers in pale tan jumpsuits.

Automatons stood at every conveyor belt, watching and waiting to ensure no food was stolen. Distribution workers were easy to spot in their tan suits; it kept them from wandering into the bakery proper where the bakery workers wore mandatory white uniforms. Keeping the workers segregated by their duties was important. A wandering worker could be easily identified and dealt with swiftly and completely; misappropriation of food was punishable by death.

A twelve-foot-high copper clock adorned the main brick wall and separated the department from the bakery proper. Gears of brass and tin surrounded the clock, spinning, turning silently, reminding everyone that the Clockwork Council was always watching. Small brick archways allowed the conveyor belts to tunnel through, bringing bakery goods bagged and tagged by the white-coat bakery workers. Of the six delivery conveyors, the two to the far left were appropriated to the squad of delivery dogs.

Pebby frowned, squinting her eyes. Disgruntled that two dogs had worked their way ahead of her in line, she quickly took her place. Years of speedy, accurate deliveries have resulted in her appointment as Chief Delivery Dog, the only dog permitted to wear a black derby. Tossing her head around the other dogs, she was only too happy to advertise her status to the other dogs in line.

Linus, an all-white Yorkie mix, was tiny, and half of Pebby's size. Linus was her littermate, and Gleena had taken him too, the day she came to pick up her order of four more delivery dogs. Pebby cried hard and hung onto him with both paws. She was not leaving without him, not under any circumstances. They both would go with Gleena, or they both would go to the Steaming Station, where unwanted dogs were destroyed.

His wagon is only big enough for four bags, but I taught him well. He knows this ol' clockwork town better'n any dog except me, so Gleena can't have an issue!

Pebby set eyes on the first dog in line, old Mavis, a small Corgi. She had been hankering to get the Chief title for the past two years but some of her deliveries were late. She was getting old and she had hip joint pain. She snooted her nose at Pebby and huffed, watching her closely as she pulled her wagon into the loading line.

Pebby shook her derby at Mavis just to irritate her, and make her all the more jealous. *You'll never beat me, you'll get sent to the steam station if you mess up again. LOSER!* Pebby shook her head in a prissy sort of way that left Mavis dejected. It didn't bother Pebby in the least. She was top dog, and she had earned it fair and square, *so deal with it, Mavis!*

Deen gave a short, single shrill whistle, and the first dog in line started up the loading ramp. Mavis's short legs made her wagon so low to the ground that it scraped and dragged at the very top of the ramp. Pebby shook her head. Poised to meet her, clipboard resting on his hip, Deen gave Mavis a quick rub on the top of her head, and looked her straight in her tired, old eyes.

"Alright, Mavis. You head to Weeson's Pharmaco first, then, don't waste time, head to the Stables, to Timorree the Manager. After that, side door of the Shoemador Shop, then 57B of the Gearful Garment Factory. You been to that factory before?" Mavis shook her greying muzzle up and down in assent. "After that, head back here for your lunch break. I think your afternoon load is the Clinic, but I gotta check, okay?"

One single, shrill whistle and Mavis was off, clattering loudly down the exit ramp, her wagon nearly touching the ground. She swerved so as not to hit an Automaton posted at the base of the ramp.

Deen shrugged his shoulders, hoping that the clattering noise did not attract attention. Linus had struggled to get up the ramp, but had made it with a great deal of effort. Pebby watched proudly as he was loaded with four light bags, and given his orders. Pebby smiled as he trotted down the ramp proudly, his little cropped tail straight up in the air. He had come a long way from being the runt of the litter, and Pebby's devotion to him had saved his life. Tossing a grateful glance at her over his shoulder, he set off for the Woodshops.

Seeing Pebby, Deen broke into a wide grin.

"Pebby, I'd know that derby anywhere!" His skin was perfectly olive-toned and his features finely chiseled, even at the young age of fourteen. But the even-toned skin was stretched thin over a frame covered in wasted muscles. He looked woefully underfed. Putting her nose in the air, she gave him her most sophisticated look, but he was not to be impressed.

"Awe, go on, ya know I'm only funnin' ya Pebby, jus' funnin' ya!, And don'cha be puttin' on airs with me!"

She sighed and enjoyed him petting the top of her head. He touched the derby lightly, careful to not disturb the angle at which it sat. Pebby was quite particular about her derby. She noticed his hands were large for his age, and they, like his face, belonged to a much older personna.

"Oh, I almost forgot, I have to give you a grooming token. Gleena says you are a bit shaggy and you have a Council delivery in a few days, so go on an' let Treena trim your coat this week, huh?"

Pebby shook her head in assent, letting him ruffle her long silky ears. They could get pretty dirty flying back during the speedy runs. She knew she was getting scruffy anyway. All the dogs welcomed a grooming session with Treena, who kept the Octagon dogs looking their best. Deen carefully tied a grooming token onto the wagon. It would serve as her voucher, and also as an excuse to miss one delivery session in the next few days.

She rubbed Deen's hand with her nose. *He don't get enough to eat. He looks like the middle season wind could blow him over.*

"Sure would love to have a dog like you, Pebby, sure would," he whispered as he softly petted her ears. Straightening her gear-dotted vest, he continued. Donch'a get tired working? I sure git tired of workin', I do, but no way out, just no way. Haven't seen my Ma all year, and she works main mixer in the bakin' room!"

Several Automatons buzzed by, and started to wheel up the ramp. Their multidirectional wheels allowed them a zero-turn radius and their ominous scowl and penetrating turquoise eyes were only matched in the ferocity by the quickness with which they would raise their gear-guns.

"They're watching us, girl," he whispered, putting his face next to hers. "Now, don't forget to give my regards to Naji. Head first to Five Feathers Falconry, deliver to Jeeson, then to the Hydroponics Center. Lee Anna Loo will be watching for you, and last, to Wymore at the wheat fields, got it?"

She nodded as she outlined the route in her head. She had to make all the deliveries while the food was hot, and then hurry back to the Habitron if she wanted to catch a bit of lunch. It was first-come first-served, and if the lunch food was scarfed up by the dogs returning earlier, she would be out of luck.

"Gw'on girl, get outta here, hurry back! I'll try to save ya' some grub, but you know the rules. Now git!"

He stood up. Giving one short, shrill single whistle, he stepped out of the way while the little red wooden wagon pulled by the scruffy dog in the black derby flew down the loading ramp exit past the Automaton, who was menacingly arriving at the top to see what was taking so long. The morning sun glittered on the brass, tin, and stainless gears spinning silently on the back of the robot. Vicious, pointed teeth of copper glimmered and shined as bright as the polished clock on the wall. The penetrating turquoise eyes could burn a hole right through something.

"Good luck, girl," he whispered, as he glanced at the line of thirty dogs of varying breeds, all pulling small wooden wagons waiting to be loaded. He hustled his empty dolly back inside the Delivery Department under the watchful eyes of the angry robot who was already starting to raise his gear-gun. Deen's stomach growled with hunger, and he stumbled from fatigue as he glanced over his shoulder. The Automaton lowered his blaster and made his way back down the entrance ramp slowly, menacingly inspecting the frightened row of waiting dogs, who shivered with fear.

CHAPTER 6

The New Backpack

Pushing open the door of the Imperial Dry Cleaners, Phillip heard the ring-tingling of the doorbell. He cautiously approached the counter and saw Naji Najeem coming from the back of the shop while he dried his hands. He was walking slowly and he was out of breath. He took a long time to exhale through his pursed lips, and an even longer time to make his way to the front counter. Huge ceiling fans tried valiantly to keep the place cool, but to no avail. The shop was damp and smelled old; nothing had been dusted in years.

In a small, pink crate behind the counter, Pebby lay in a T-bone position, back legs extended out, body flat, and she was snoozing. As Phillip drew closer, she raised her head and looked quizzically as he set a white paper bag on the counter.

"Ahhh, Phillip, back so soon?" Naji Najeem smiled broadly, as he continued to dry his hands on his apron. In the fluorescent light his color was more ashen than it had been in the daylight. He looked tired, as if it took too much of his energy just to breathe.

"What's that dog doin' anyway, taking a nap?" Phillip didn't know what else to say, and for a moment there was an uncomfortable silence.

"Mom sent your sandwich, hope you like tuna-nix-lettuce?"

Phillip rolled his eyes and gave the white paper bag a shake. Naji took the bag gratefully. *What is the meaning of nix-lettuce?* he wondered.

Pebby, hearing the rustling of the paper and seeing the white bag, perked up. The massive fans spinning in the shop had muted the noise at the front desk and the steady hum made her sleepy. She had dreamed again of the familiar sweetberry smells and her delivery wagon; foggy memory of the Octagon Bakery cooled by the same whirring fans, shiny silver fans, spotless fans, keeping the work-room cool for the legions of bakers. The warm, tasty treats packaged in pristine white bags, the cinnamon smell of the hot, buttery, soft rolls, all were in the past now.

She sighed, shook her head from side to side, and she felt tears starting in her eyes. Would she ever see Norwall again? She dropped her head. But here was the boy, come to see her. She wiped a tear away with her paw. *Go away tears!*

Naji was busy making Phillip feel welcome.

"You are most kind to bring sustenance to this old tailor," Naji sighed almost breathlessly, and he coughed a few times. He leaned over the counter to size up Phillip. Neither was really sure of what to say and there were a few more moments of uncomfortable silence. Then, Naji asked the safest question that came to his mind.

"How do you like school?"

He opened the half swing-door that separated the lobby from the working area. Phillip found it quite difficult to come up with an answer as he made his way into the inner workings of the shop.

"My mom says I should try harder, but it's boring, you know, stuff, lots of stuff I don't need to know. Boring stuff. Like commas and fractions, now that's boring, Boor... ring!" He sighed deeply and put his hands up flat against both sides of his face.

"My mom is always after me to work on it, but oh, I don't know, I have better stuff to do, like, well, like my games!" he continued. "Like *Revolutions of the Ages*? Sorry, you probably never heard of that. Hey, what's that dog doing in that cage anyway? Can't she come out?"

He leaned down and poked one finger through the pink wire bars.

"Hey, girl, why do you look sad? Hey, I think she wants out, she looks kinda sad doesn't she?"

"I let her rest in there to take a nap, and maybe she's just a bit homesick," added Naji, before he could stop himself.

"Homesick?" queried Phillip, anxious to learn more about the dog's background. Naji changed the subject abruptly, stammering, trying to take Phillip's attention from the dog, who actually did look sad.

"Do you have any brothers or sisters?"

Throwing himself into a nearby old striped armchair which showed signs of repair and smelled musty, Phillip threw caution to the wind, and spoke to the old tailor in a way that he had never spoken to anyone before.

"Well, we have Claire, Miss Superstar, never miss a beat, apple of your eyeball, the whole nine yards, Claire, Claire, Claire, Miss Pitter-Patter-Perfect!"

Phillip twisted his face into a grimace and made circles with the thumb and forefinger of each hand, forgetting for a moment that he barely knew the kind old man. "Yep, superstar, math wiz, superstar inventor, going to college this fall. Engineering, no less. Got a scholarship, too!"

"Scholarship?" queried Naji.

"Yep, first year of college all paid, all because of one STUPID project she did last year! Can you believe?"

"Project? What was her project?"

"Something to do with, like, I don't know... air conditioning? Who cares anyway? Borrr... ing, you know, something TOTALLY useless. But, she wins, somehow she wins, so Mom is of course thrilled! Whole first year paid for at the university across town. Well, I'm glad she's staying home so she can take care of those nasty cats!"

"So, she's a cat lover?"

Phillip looked up at the ceiling in disgust and shook his head.

"Lover? Nooo, I don't think so, she ignores them half the time. The other half o' the time she is right in their face, all lovey-dovey. But she NEVER cleans out their pan, and doesn't EVER fill the water bowl," Phillip scoffed, and spun his head side to side quickly and emphatically.

"Oh really? How many does she have? Sounds like many cats live at your home," Naji asked as Phillip rambled.

"Two. Two smellies. The Smellicats! Yep, she just takes Mom's expensive water bottles and dumps them into the cat bowl, too lazy to go to the sink. Does *not* bother to clean anything out! Mom would have a fit if she saw it."

"Why don't you tell your mother?"

"Well," Phillip crossed his arms in front of his chest and nodded his head, replying smugly, "I'm saving that little bit of ammo for sometime when I might really need to get something over on her. Know what I mean? Anyway, Mom would hardly ever believe anything about Claire. It's always Claire this, and Claire that, know what I mean? *Claire, Claire, Claire, always Claire!*"

"Yes, Yes?" Naji leaned in closer, and Phillip relaxed all the more. "Tell me about your mother. She takes care of people?"

"Yeah, she's great at it. People love her, and she can fix up nearly anyone with anything," he boasted.

"You must be so proud of the good work she does."

"Well yeah, but she's got this thing, she got us in this dump of a house, forever fixing it up, too. All week she fixes up people, the rest of the time she's fixing up the old mess. Believe me, we're all sucked into it. We're all just part of the crew."

He waved his hands back and forth and took on a sarcastic tone to imitate his mother.

"*Phiiillip*, I need help! *Phiiillip*, I need help! *Phiiillip*, I need help! Help me, help me, help me!" He imitated her, and nodded his head side to side for emphasis. He escalated the volume of his voice.

"I'll hear her calling, and I just yell, '*in the bathroom, Mom*,' to give myself a few more minutes of game-time. Sometimes I get up Saturday and she has the paint brushes ready, almost like she is just *waiting* for me to get up so we can start the projects, you know? So I pretend to be asleep, know what I mean?"

"She doesn't hire persons to do the work?"

"Oh yeah, the BIG stuff like knocking out walls, ripping out floors, sure. But the rest? Well, you're looking at the work crew, sitting right here!"

Phillip jumped off the chair and opened his arms as if he was solely responsible for construction of the Hoover Dam.

"Oh my, sounds like she relies on you a lot for help?"

"Yeah, but sometimes I pretend to have too much homework just to get her off my back about it. Anyway, can this dog come out?" he asked, flipping the latch on the door.

"Sure, go ahead."

By now, Pebby had forgotten her worries about the Octagon and was sitting up, intensely listening to the animated exchange.

"Come on out, girl," he coaxed her, rubbing her platinum mop-top and letting her sniff his hand. He picked her up, and dropped back down in the armchair.

"What are these things on her vest? Kinda look like gears. Hey, I got gears in one of my games, *Star Team Adventures*! It's this neat fox that travels around a galaxy that's falling apart. You fit the gears together and they turn stuff. And what are these loops for, like this dog is gonna pull a wagon or something? Weird!" He laughed almost demonically, throwing his head back, so that Pebby slid from his grasp.

"Hey, wait a minute," but she trotted off, getting a drink from her water bowl farther back in the shop. Phillip followed her, but the shop was small and he made his way through a maze of racks of hanging clothes. Naji lost sight of him as he scurried away.

"Phillip, be careful, there are many things in the way and you might get hurt!" Naji cautioned.

"Hey, what's all this stuff?" Phillip asked, frozen as he passed the door to the supply closet which had been left open. He could see some old tables, vases, picture frames, and books, which, unknown to him, Naji had collected during his walks around the complex.

"*Cool...* What's all this stuff doing in here?" He thought he recognized a small utility cart his mother had discarded in the office trash.

"Oh, oh, it's nothing, just stuff from the owner's house, here, come here," and Naji nearly tripped on a backpack he had traded from a patron who wanted a gilt mirror Naji had retrieved from a dumpster.

"Look, this bag is new. What do you think, would it suit you, Phillip?" Naji said, trying to distract Phillip's attention away from the messy collection. Phillip turned and raised his eyebrow.

"Whoa, camouflage. That's really cool. I can have it? You aren't kidding?"

He took the backpack from Naji and started to open all the zippers. It was a large pack, similar to one used in the military, and Phillip had seen soldiers wearing these in his computer games. The backpack had so many side pockets and hidden flaps that it was impossible to explore them all.

"It is yours now, use it to keep your school papers in order. You know, Phillip, I was in school once, and keeping your things in order is the first step to being a leader," the kind old man continued.

"Yeah, I guess. My mom is always telling me I can do better if I just try, ya know?" Naji ignored Phillip's rants. "She's pushy, too darn pushy!"

Naji proposed a deal. "How about a trade? I have something you might like, and above all, I enjoy a trade. After all, what is a trade, but both parties getting something they both want?"

The tired old man gently adjusted the straps, fitting the backpack carefully onto Phillip, who had not forgotten his interest in the tinydog. "How about this: you keep your papers organized this week, and try to keep up with your assignments, and I will trade you a day with this tiny champion? How does that sound?"

"Wow, wow! Wait till the guys at school see it! It's just like the one in *Destiny Fighters!*" He fingered the shoulder straps. He had not noticed that Pebby was watching intently. "You mean it, really? That I can watch her for a day? By myself? Walk her and feed her and everything? Really?" Then the short blurts of the car horn made him look up.

"Oh," he resigned, his shoulders dropped. "That's Mom. I gotta go."

Sweeping up Pebby in his arms, Phillip carried her through the shop, through the maze of racks of clothing to the front of the store, while Naji followed along. Phillip did not want to put the tinydog down. She just seemed so perfect, as if she already belonged with him.

"Gotta go, girl. Hey, maybe I can come over and walk you sometime? Would ya like that?" Phillip rubbed the tinydog's head tenderly. She sniffed his hand one more time, and appeared to nod her assent. He sighed. They locked eyes, and Pebby tilted her head as if she wondered about this vivacious, funny boy. More than that, she wondered about the strange feelings, as if she almost would miss him when he left. These were new feelings she had never experienced before. She had never belonged to anyone. The life she lived didn't have any room for that.

"You sure are something. Gears. On a dog vest? Gears?" He rubbed her head and ran his hand over her long ears. The car horn sounded again.

"Well, that would be the boss," he emphasized resentfully. "See you guys. And hey, thanks for the backpack!" Seeing the white paper bag still on the counter, he picked it up, handing it to Naji.

"Hope you like the sandwich, nix lettuce, of course!" He rolled his eyes and shook his head. Naji nodded his head. Neither of them noticed that the rustling of the white paper had made Pebby startle. She gave a few short, shrill barks. Naji reached down and rubbed the top of her head. "It's okay girl, not this time. Not needing any deliveries." Then abruptly he stopped, catching himself. "Return soon, and be safe in your travels, young man. Remember, organization is the key to being a leader. It is the first step!"

He raised his index finger in the air to punctuate his statement. Pebby was nodding her head, as if she understood and was in agreement. After all, she hadn't been Chief Delivery Dog of the Octagon for nothing. Phillip shrugged his shoulders and raised his eyebrow, not quite understanding the meaning of it all. He gave a short wave goodbye as he headed out to his mother's car, the ring-dinging of the door chime heralding his departure. He could not wait to show his new backpack to Claire.

CHAPTER 7

The Mechanical Bird

Right. Com'on, right. Two rights, then a left. Another left, then straight down. Go, go, and GO! Last turn, left! She had been here before. Five Feathers Falconry was on the outer rim of the town in order to accommodate the squawking of the birds. It gave the falconers access to acres of woods behind the falconry, where they could test their mechanical prototypes. Pebby pulled to a careful stop as she came to the rusty metal gate. The acid of the air caused the metal to rust, and orange sprouts decorated it like a tree fungus. A small, decrepit, one-person wooden guardhouse stood to the side of the gate. An Automaton stood at the tiny wooden shelf of a desk peering at her through the glass window. The road to the falconry was poorly maintained and dusty and Pebby sneezed several times. She waited for the Automaton to register her and allow admission to the premises. Her coat was nasty, dirty, and covered with dust.

Stink'in Automats! she thought, as she held still while he scanned her. The gears on his back whirled faster and faster and transmitted information back to the Integrative Center of the Council, known as the ICC. The information was cataloged by indentured workers keeping track of every movement in the town. Every hour, Council Representatives monitored the recordings and sent teletype directions in code back to the Automatons. The Automaton knew exactly where Pebby had come from, and how long it should take to deliver her goods to Jeeson, the Falconmaster.

The rusty metal gate creaked open automatically, controlled by a series of brass and tin gears on the right hand side. She followed the winding gravel road which was painful on her soft paws. The stone edifice was a cylinder, reaching high in the sky at least two stories. On its top, she saw massive gears of copper and brass rotating slowly, horizontally spinning opposite of the one below it. They were spaced several feet apart and the building looked like it was ready to lift off and fly. Steam pipes rose through the center of the gears, puffing gray-sooty smoke, and a gigantic pair of filigree brass wings was mounted on the roof over the front door.

As she made her way to the front porch, she heard the flock-calling of the birds from within. A long, dainty metal chain hung down to her nose level, and she grabbed it with her very straight white teeth. She shook it vigorously. Several minutes after the bell rang, a tall, thin, kyphotic man with sallow-colored skin opened the door. His ink-black hair made him look all the more pasty-white and he looked as if he had not seen a sun in weeks. Jeeson Jevity was wearing a well-worn, black, high-necked shirt, patched black pants, and a huge protective leather glove on his right hand. He motioned her into the Five Feathers Falconry, wagon and all. It took all his effort to close the massive wooden door behind her and he was out of breath. He coughed a few times, and shook his head to clear the congestion.

"Pebby! Right on time! Achoo! Achoo!" he sneezed twice in rapid succession. "Come in and take a rest. Where's my breakfast?" Sorting through the white bags in her wagon, he found the two bearing his name.

"Ah, yes. The best of the Octagon, my beloved sweetberry-rolls." He pretended to kiss the bags with a loud smooch. "I know, I know, hot and fresh! Bless you, bless you! Here, let me get you some water."

She watched him walk, and he seemed almost to stumble a bit. His legs were thin, and she was suprised that they could bear the weight of his body.

He had never invited her inside before, so hesitantly, she unsnapped her vest from the wagon. Her inner clockwork told her she had only a few quick minutes to rest before the Automaton would come careening up the drive to see what was taking so long.

Jeeson grabbed a dented tin bowl off of a long lab counter and filled it with water from a five-foot bubbling glass cylinder. She was thirsty and she lapped appreciatively. This was special water usually reserved for endangered species and priviledged Council members. *So, this is what fresh water tastes like,* she thought, as she remembered the slimy common trough at the Habitron.

Drawing in a deep breath, she stared in awe at sixteen cages housing the most majestic creatures she had ever seen. The birds were so large and so brightly colored, that she could not believe her eyes. There were deep-coral birds with ink-jet black eyes and beaks, bright yellow birds with green and red tipped wings and pale pink beaks, and pure white birds with huge plumes on the tops of their heads.

There were deep-aqua birds, and two birds who were a deep-indigo color she had never before seen. There were two of every kind, paired side by side in separate cages.

Reaching into one cage with his gloved arm, Jeeson brought out the most beautiful snow-white bird Pebby had ever seen. He was three feet tall, with long, pointed, gray tail feathers, a majestic gray plume, and a massive black beak. Pale aquamarine circles surrounded both his enormous black eyes and he lowered his beak submissively to allow Jeeson to pet him. The falconer placed him on a large contorted tree-branch perch in the center of the room. Stretching and flapping his wings once or twice to his six-foot wingspan, the bird settled on the perch as Jeeson lovingly rubbed his head feathers.

"Good boy, good boy! Pebby, meet Romeo. Romeo, meet Pebby! See, Pebby, he's not afraid of you!" and he cluck-clucked to the bird lovingly.

Afraid? That bird is four times as big as me! Amazed by the size of the bird's massive beak, Pebby watched with interest as Jeeson gave him a piece of warm roll. The enormous bird first took the bread in his beak, then carefully raised his claw and held the warm bread with his raised foot, nibbling the treat gingerly.

"You see, Pebby, the air is so bad for the birds that they keep dying. No one knows what has gone so wrong with our air, but the birds are dropping from the sky every day and dying, and nothing we do seems to save them. The bellows in their lungs cannot stand the poisons in the air, so the Council has permitted us to keep two of every species inside with controlled filtered airflow, to save them from extinction. What was once a hospital for these majestic creatures has become a sanctuary for the few that we are able to keep alive."

She was watching and listening so intently that she didn't hear a door open in the back of the room. A thin woman wearing a spotless white lab coat approached Romeo and stroked the back headfeathers of the enormous bird. Pebby noticed that the bird did not startle, but appeared quite comfortable, and he let the woman scratch his head. In fact, he seemed to enjoy it. The woman sported an enormous twisted bun of thick, black hair, and her long nose made her almost look like a bird herself. Her eyes were coal black.

"Oh, this must be the little dog that always brings our breakfasts!" She leaned down and let Pebby smell her hand as she broke into a wide smile. "The days you bring rolls are the very best mornings, did you know that?" Pebby nodded.

"Pebby, meet Norra, Norra, meet Pebby!" Jeeson laughingly introduced them. "Norra is an engineer, Pebby, and she is in charge of designing a mechanical bird. She studies the birds' flight patterns, mannerisms, and how the wings transport the weight of the birds, etcetera, etcetera, etcetera, and she tries to reproduce those qualities in metal! Her lab is out back, and the Council expects she will produce a flying mechanical bird sometime this year!"

Jeeson spread his arms like imaginary wings, and proceeded to imitate flight, weaving this way and that as he wove around the bird cages, trying to get Norra to laugh. She softly chuckled.

"Well, we hope so, right Jeese?" Norra added, not wanting to think of what would happen if she could not produce what the Council wanted.

Norra gave a nod with her head toward a twelve-foot stainless steel door.

"Come, Pebby, look!"

Pebby quickly followed Norra's quick steps through the stainless steel door, and watched as Norra pulled it shut behind her. The airlock seal of the door hissed like a giant, nasty cat. This was no mere workroom, it was a complete laboratory with a massive high ceiling and a dome skylight. The gray sky could be seen overhead, as could the smoke from the steam pipes supplying the falconry with energy. Four tables with black granite tops stood in a line, like soldiers ready for battle. Lab sinks were interspersed between hundreds of beakers and flasks which littered the counters. Gears and metal pieces were littered haphazardly over the counter-tops.

Multiple filigree birds in various stages of completion rested on wooden perches. Pieces of wings with delicate metal filigree designs lay discarded, some of them on the stone floor. There were signs of trial and error, with a blackboard lining one entire wall. It was covered with numbers, some of them erased, some of them circled. It was obvious to Pebby that someone had been working very frantically to create a mechanical replica of the falconry birds.

At the last table, head bent over a golden filigree wing, and perched on a high lab stool, was a dark-haired young man. He looked to be no more than twenty, with jet-black eyes and thick, jet-black hair like his mother Norra. His face, partially concealed with his safety glasses, was asymmetric, but attractive nonetheless. He was intent on his work and appeared to be heating the metal and stretching it into a thin wire. He briefly glanced up at his mother. Pebby noticed that he did not smile.

Perched on the left side of him was a four-foot high contraption which faintly resembled a bird. The copper body was welded together in odd-shaped pieces, and the three-toed claws balanced the contraption perfectly under the egg-shaped body. The head was aerodynamic and pointed, the copper beak curved. This bird would have no need for cracking open nuts. This bird would carry information to the Council; this bird was being developed as a weapon of control. The slots which were to hold the wing structures were empty, and four-foot mock wing prototypes lay on the bench. Norra picked one up and held it with both hands as she showed it to Pebby.

"You see, this is what they expect of me. To design a mechanical bird, one that can fly, one that can collect pictures for the Council, and one that does not need food and love like the creatures you see in the cages." She rubbed her eyes, which were filled with tears. "I don't know if I can do it, but I try, I try." She heaved a sigh.

"You see here with me, my son Noah, so skilled at metal-workings. They have allowed us to keep him with us instead of him slaving in the factories. But, I don't know what will happen to us all, if we cannot produce the mechanical bird. The birds you see there are the last of their species. The Council lets them live in filtered air and drink the purest water so I can use them as models. Silly, huh? Why not just protect the environment and let them live free, as they have done for generations and generations? It doesn't make sense, does it?" she asked Pebby as if she expected a reply.

Noah looked up, but continued working. He flipped his safety mask up and rubbed his eyes with both fists.

Norra chided him. "Noah, you've got to get some rest! You've been working on that wing since late last night. Come, son, have a sweetberry roll. I will make you some tea, no? You should go to bed already and get some rest!"

"One second Mum, I think I'm on to something, something with this wing and its angle of attachment, give me a minute, hold on, hold on."

Pebby noticed that he pumped a contraption under the lab table with his foot, and started to stretch the metal. Sparks flew out, but unafraid, he didn't move. He worked silently and intently, as if his mother's life depended on it.

"There, got the curve, excellent!" Picking up a burnished copper gear, he flipped his goggles up to the top of his head and gave a wide smile.

"Not your problem, Mom. I am on the wing, did'ja forget?" He laughed now, standing up and walking quickly over to Pebby. He crouched in front of the tinydog and held her face tenderly. "You are our only link to the others, you know? We canna' go into town, at least not without the Automaton, only once a month at most, to stock up ye'know."

Pebby nodded her head in understanding. "Wait! I know ye gotta' go. How about a beautiful sweet feather for your hat? Com'on, no?" Pebby slid the hat down her nose with her paw. For the first time, she saw him smile.

"Excellent! I have the sweetest indigo feather from Ammarana, who is, without any doubt, my very favorite. Here, let me fix your hat." Taking the velvet derby in his hands, Noah carefully attached an indigo feather to the satin band. Norra smiled as she watched him. Placing the derby back onto the little dog's head, Noah watched as Pebby positioned it just so with her paw.

"Hurry now, you have to stay on track or they will be coming for us all! Now, *hurry!*"

Pebby knew she would have to go full throttle speedy to make up the time. Scampering past Romeo, who still sat majestically perched, she watched as he stretched out his wings. Pebby was heartbroken to think birds like this one were suffering and dying from the skies because of grayfog.

Jeeson quickly opened the front door, and watched as she attached her wagon. The Automaton was just starting to exit the security booth and the gears on his back were whirring and spinning wildly. Steam was puffing from the steel pipe on it's head. It tottered a bit on the gravel road as it made its way up the driveway. Pebby kicked up her heels, and darted past it without giving it a glance. *Stinkin' Automat! Go, go, a...n..d.....GO!*

"Be safe, little friend," Jeeson whispered softly as he gave one last quick wave. He quickly slammed the heavy wooden door. Peeking out through a tiny crack, Jeeson put his arm around Norra. Thankfully, the massive robot suddenly made a one hundred eighty degree spin, stirred up gravel dust, and headed back to the security shed, scowling disdainfully.

"Do you think she'll notice it?" Noah asked, munching on one of the Octagon pastries, coming up behind them and sighing in relief at the retreat of the Automat. He wiped the sticky icing off of his face with his shirt sleeve.

"No," replied Norra wistfully, wiping the last trace of icing off of his cheek, "I don't think she'll notice it, not at all. I'm not so worried if Deen sees it. I think he's ready to join us. He's getting old enough now."

She hoped with all her heart that Naji would soon see the small scrap of paper that Noah had hidden in the tiny velvet derby. He had positioned it so secretively, so carefully under the feather he had placed, all under the watchful eye of his mother.

CHAPTER 8

The Orange Bug

Phillip was smirking to himself as he stared at the back of his mother's head from his position in the back seat of the car. *Good things come in threes,* he thought, glad his mother was preoccupied with the car radio. First, a new camouflage backpack was lying across his lap, second, he had so far this day avoided doing any homework, and third, his mother seemed to be in a fairly good mood. She was humming to the music, despite the fact that he had eaten her lunch, forcing her to buy sandwiches at Frankie's Deli.

Phillip relaxed, closed his eyes, and savored the moment when he would show Claire the new backpack. His mind drifted to the tinydog resting quietly in her crate, and he wondered where she went when the shop closed. He replayed the promise of the old man over and over in his mind.

"You keep your papers organized this week, and try to keep up with your assignments, and I will trade you a day with this tiny champion! That's what a bargain is. Each one gets something they really want, and I want to see you a leader, Phillip, yes, a leader!"

Over and over, the promise of the trade intrigued him. He could imagine the thrill of walking her in the neighborhood as well as setting her loose on the household cats. He was abruptly brought back to reality by his mother, who had switched off the radio when the song ended.

"How much of your math did you get done today Phillip? Isn't the science project due Thursday?" The ponytail bobbed back and forth as his mother shook her head. She saw him shrug his shoulders silently in the rear-view mirror, as he sunk down further into the seat. The tone of her voice started to rise.

"Well," she huffed, "you've got to get right to it when we get home, Phillip." She wasn't done yet. "But first, you'll need to clean up your room, I saw tons of stuff on the floor this morning. Can't you throw paper in the trash? You know, I don't mind running the sweeper but I don't have time to pick up candy wrappers and garbage off the floor. Can you collect all your shoes, too? Please?" She jiggled in the seat trying to get a full view of him in the rear-view mirror as he struggled and wiggled to avoid her gaze.

"So, cleaning and homework first, before any *Revolvings of Ages*, whatever that game is. Come on, let's not waste time now. We're home early today, so let's make the most of it!"

Revolutions of the Ages, not Revolvings, get it right will ya? he whispered under his breath.

She smiled a sinister smile and looked as if she was ready to slap a paint roller in his hand the minute he was finished with his homework. He might have to feign a stomach ache. He felt his life darkening, his plans to play *Revolutions of the Ages* ruined before he even got started.

"Mom, kinda feels... my stomach's going in a bad way? Like when I got sick before, maybe I need some snacks to get it quiet? Maybe a tiny rest?" He rested his arm across his stomach and shook his head back and forth as if pain and pressure were building. His mother smiled widely but did not say a word.

The afternoon clouds were moving in over West Margate, a neighborhood lined with canopy oaks. Phillip stared out the window at threatening rain-clouds as they carefully maneuvered the winding road, the bending oaks making a tunnel-like entrance to his street. No two homes were the same, and they reflected the individuality of the owners.

A few ladies in neon athletic suits were jogging down the shady road and his mother waved to a man and woman walking a German Shepherd. As she rolled her window down to shout a greeting, Phillip huffed and crossed his arms over his chest and shook his head.

"Mom, it's gonna storm, can we please just get home? I got work to do!" He tapped his foot impatiently, forgetting the fact that he had wasted several hours at the office playing with his desk tools and snacking. As they rounded yet another curve, a small park appeared on his left as if out of nowhere. Aside from the picnic tables and swings, there were benches set on the edge of a fresh-spring lake, and a small covered pavilion where he had enjoyed his last birthday party. He remembered the neighbors making a fire in the stone firepit in the fall, and thinking of the marshmallows reminded him that he had not yet eaten his tuna sandwich.

One final curve in the road and they were home. The sprawling red-brick ranch had a semi-circle driveway of beige-colored pavers which were variegated and occasionally dotted with orange rust stains. Clumps of grass were growing through some of the bricks in the driveway, which made it look slightly messy. A sidewalk of more pavers led from the driveway through a large archway to a courtyard. Three tall, identical windows, arched at the top, decorated each side of the front of the house. French-blue shutters had recently been painted, and the color softened the red brick. Years of dark shade had spotted the red brick with black mold stains, which, a little at a time, they had cleaned with a monster pressure washer. Now, as Phillip jumped from the car, he realized how much better the house looked since they had first bought it.

As he passed under the brick archway he tossed his new bag onto one of the white wooden rockers. He dropped into the other rocker to smell the sweet smells of the herbs in the small courtyard garden. There were tall ferns in pots as well, and small square flower beds strewn with pretty blooming flowers. Phillip had helped his mother plant the beds in the courtyard. Some of the flowers were wilting in the Florida heat and Phillip begrudgingly turned on the hose and watered the plants before his mother even asked him to do it. Wasn't he a big help with the flowers?

Phillip had already forgotten the names of most of the herbs in the garden. He turned the hose on high and shot water at the delicate plants, pretending he was a soldier of fortune in his *Revolutions* game. He didn't seem to notice he was blasting the delicate herbs and breaking their stems.

He thought about his annoying mother. He got quite irritated when his mother pinched off a sprig of an herb and waved it under his nose to make him guess the name of the plant. Uh oh, Mom is walking in from the car. She had taken a minute to grab her bookbag, and if he looked busy, she might not give him any more chores. He threw the hose on the ground, and as the trigger hit the ground, it shot a cold spray directly in his face.

Spitting, and wiping his face on his sleeve, his attention was drawn to a black and orange cricket sitting pretty on the arm of the wooden rocker. He grabbed a used zip-plastic bag out of his lunch box, and with lightning speed, inverted the bag over the cricket. Sealing the bag, he slid it into his pocket. He snickered. There would be treats galore in store for Miss Pitter-Patter-Perfect.

CHAPTER 9

The Mysterious Widget

S tepping inside, his new backpack and his old lunchbox were clutched firmly. His old backpack slung over his shoulder, Phillip was greeted by an eighteen- pound, fifteen-year-old tuxedo cat who gave a nasty, welcoming HISS and sauntered away.

"*NASTY!*" he muttered under his breath. That overweight, angry cat belonged to Claire since she was five years old, so the cat was actually older than he was. The cat would swat and hiss even the most gentle visitors, and it harbored an especially harsh and undying resentment toward Phillip from the mean tricks he had visited on it. The cat had a hiss-story. Way before he was born, his mother and sister had taken the cat to Washington D.C. where their mother was attending a conference. The hotel staff had called his mother during her meeting, complaining that they could not clean the room because the cat was hiding under the bed, growling and reaching her paws out to swat the maids. Now, she lumbered around the house, but generally patrolled the front door, guarding her territory with a mean, vengeful stare and a frequently upraised swatting paw.

Effortlessly, Phillip pulled out a ladder-back chair and dropped two backpacks and an unzipped canvas lunchbox on it. His sister materialized out of nowhere.

"Hey Buddy! Wheeeeee! You've joined the army?" Dancing a few dance steps and snapping fingers in the air calypso-style, Claire grinned widely and headed for the refrigerator. Medium build, with pretty facial features, her figure was a beautiful near-perfect hourglass. She could not have cared less. This particular afternoon, her laboratory safety glasses hung loosely around her neck. She was wearing an old t-shirt spotted with battery acid burns and dime-sized holes. Grabbing each door handle, she flung the refrigerator doors open as though they guarded a secret kingdom. Claire basked in the golden glow of LED lights as she surveyed the contents.

Grabbing a cheese stick from the meat drawer with one hand and reaching for a cold leftover chicken leg with the other, she flung her long dark ponytail back as she watched Phillip start to unzip the military camouflage backpack, not bothering to look up at his older sister.

The black-and-white nasty tuxedo cat pounced on the crumbs that rained down as Claire munched hungrily on the leftovers. Standing, eating between the wide-open refrigerator doors, she breathed in the cool air, relishing the coldness. The kitchen was hot, and she inhaled the fresh, frosty air. Their mother was known to be frugal and set the thermostat higher than they would like. If they left a room for more than five minutes, she was likely to turn off the light.

"Get a plate, will ya? Man, Mom would scream if she saw you." He watched her bounce the doors shut with her hip and head for the sink where she washed her hands for at least three minutes, lathering soap all the way up to her elbows. Her mouth was still so full of food she could not speak, but she chewed and gulped, until she was finally able to croak out a few words.

"Look, if I wanted the food police here, I would've called them, so back off, BUSTER!" She threw her head back and laughed playfully. 'Buster' was her pet nickname for Phillip, and he hated it. That fact alone encouraged her to use it even more.

"Hey, aren't you supposed to be starting your homework? What's goin' on with Mom? Any word on the weekend? Are we on paint, yard, or cleaning?"

She opened the refrigerator once again and grabbed a bottle of ice tea, which she raised in the air and chugged so fast Phillip thought she would choke. She wiped her mouth on the sleeve of her t-shirt, then turned and peeked through the kitchen window blinds.

"Well, well, well, what is she up to? Who's she got out there now? Oh, it's poor, little Ravinni. I bet she's trying to talk him into an even bigger discount. 'Course he takes so long to do anything, he half-forgets what he's charged, poor guy. Oh, my gosh! He's pointing to the dumpster on the side of the house! That thing is already overflowing. Yes, yes, yes, he's motioning like it's going to be taken away, but ohhh, no, no, no! Looks like he's motioning that another one is coming!" She called the plays with the precision of a play-by-play sportscaster, almost whispering, not caring that Phillip was ignoring her. She continued, talking to no one in particular.

"Well, no matter," she shrugged her shoulders and turned around to face Phillip, noticing for the first time that he was pulling the inner linings out of every opening of the new backpack.

Grabbing the fat tuxedo cat and draping her over her arm, Claire dropped into one of the kitchen chairs.

"Hey, let's see the new backpack. When did you guys go shopping? And how did I manage to avoid it?" Petting the cat and stroking its ears, she was oblivious to the fact that her shirt was getting covered in cat fur.

"Hey, c'mon, where'd you get this backpack? Did Mom spring for it?" Claire asked as she grabbed at the backpack which Phillip quickly whisked away from her.

"Hey, man, wash your hands man, wash your hands, you got chicken grease and cat stink!!" Phillip pulled the backpack even farther out of her reach protectively.

"No seriously, where'd you get it, it's kinda neat. I like the leather on the bottom."

"New guy running the cleaners next to the office. He's got a dog, outstanding, but kinda weird though, wearing a weird vest all covered in metal gears. Navi's his name, something like that. No, I mean Naji, yeah that's it. Naji. Naji Najeem to be more *pacific*. He asked about you. I told him how you won with that air conditioning project whatever, and he was interested."

"Not AC, you dweeb, it was steam. Just steam, just purifying the water in turbines, stomping out viruses and bacteria... All in a day's work, right, Buster?"

She laughed, grabbing a shortbread cookie from the always full cookie dish on the counter. Watching her bite into the sweet treat, Phillip reached for one as well. One thing you could be sure of, there were always home-made baked treats in the kitchen. Claire was partial to the cookies, while Phillip loved the cinnamon-and-sugar muffins decorated on the top with raisins. His mother sometimes put the cinnamon and raisins on top to make a face. Once, when he had bombed his math test, she decorated the muffins with a frowning face instead of a smile, which both annoyed and embarrassed Phillip.

"There's stuff in here," Phillip muttered quietly to himself as he pulled each pocket of the new backpack inside-out and discovered tissues, pencils, and scraps of paper. He opened each zipper carefully in turn and explored each pocket. In the tiniest pocket, deep inside the bag, he felt something hard. His fingers closed around something metallic and he could feel its raised designs. He held it in his hand for a moment and raised his eyebrows quizically.

"Why are you interested in someone's old junk? Just take that thing over and dump it into the trash, man. You don't know what you're touching, you don't know where the stuff came from." Claire focused on her phone, the light illuminating her face. She never looked up at her brother, who continued to search every pocket of the pack.

"Yeah, who knows where the stuff came from?" Phillip peeked in the bag and turned the metal object over and over in his hand. He wasn't going to bring it out of the bag where Claire might see. Nope, this is none of her pesky business.

He brought it up closer, but still kept it inside the bag. It was tarnished, and appeared to be in the shape of a hexagon. He thought he saw gears in a pattern similar to what he had fingered on the scruffy dog's vest, but he couldn't be sure. Some of the metal gears were pointed, and pricked his fingers. It looked as though there was lettering on the widget and he dropped it back into the pocket of the backpack quickly and furtively. He was, in no way, going to show it to Claire.

CHAPTER 10

The Persnickety Pets

C laire stood up, crammed her phone into her pocket, and opened the refrigerator again. Next in her sight was a small bowl of left-over mac n' cheese. This time however, she ate it over the kitchen sink where she once again peered out through the slats of the blind to watch her mother. Abby Weathermore was still talking animatedly to a white-clothed workman.

"Oh boy, that definitely is Ravinni. She'll be out there for another hour trying to talk him into an even bigger discount, which means, who knows when she'll start supper? Might as well stay in the lab." She sighed, and shook her head.

"I am totally over the dust, and totally over the painting and mess. Whatever were we all thinking? It will take us another whole year to finish the T.V. room and Mom's bedroom, never mind her bathroom. That Dumpster monster on the side of the house has been there so long that my friends keep calling it 'Claire's garbage pit'. I am totally over living in mess!" she fumed. She turned from the window, totally irritated by her mother.

Phillip ignored her ranting. He turned his attention to the well-worn brown fabric backpack he had carried the last two years. He had refused to replace it, despite his mother's pleadings. Unzipping all the compartments, he swiftly, without thinking and before Claire could intercede, raised the upside-down backpack high in the air, and shook out the entire contents beside one of the kitchen chairs.

Books, loose papers, crumpled candy wrappers, small notebooks, and a used juice carton fell to the floor in an avalanche of trash. Both cats scattered. From the front living room, Freddy the African gray parrot, an expert in imitating sounds, started to make explosion sounds: *Poof, Whoosh, Bang!* He chattered noisily, hiding behind one of his half-chewed wooden toys.

"What the heck, Phillip!" Claire spun around.

"What's goin' on?" She shook her head side to side. "Whatever were you thinking?"

Giving a loud "aHAAA" as if he had just discovered the secret to success, Phillip set his new backpack on an adjacent chair and proceeded to lecture Claire.

"Watch, and learn!" Phillip raised his eyebrows and crooked his finger at Claire, as he had seen Jaceena do so many times. "I am done with this old thing, ... and,..."

Hearing a car door slam, Claire once again peeked through the window blinds and saw their mother walking toward the front sidewalk. She was carrying her laptop case and a small rectangular black case.

Before Phillip could sort the trash, a large bug of unknown origin crawled out from under the pile of stuff, which included crumpled wrappers from lunch crackers, used soda straws which had once served as paperball shooters, Bandaids, used dirty erasers, and crumbs.

Screaming, Claire grabbed onto the nearby counter and hoisted her feet. Phillip danced and danced, and stomped the insect which was now lying on its back, stunned but still wiggling his legs.

"I call that my roach-approach!!" Phillip raised his eyebrows, laughing and waiting for Clair to react. React she did.

"Pick it up... Pick... it... up! GET IT OUT OF HERE NOW!!!"

Alarmed, Freddy screeched even louder. Still laughing, Phillip quickly dashed to the kitchen sink, grabbed a paper towel, and mercifully carried the stunned insect to the front door where he collided with his mother. His face was red from laughing so hard. He was out of breath.

"What's going on, what are you doing with that towel? I thought you were supposed to work on math? What've you got there? What's so funny, and why is Freddy goin' crazy?"

The African gray parrot was still making explosion sounds interspersed with a screeching high-pitched alarm.

Phillip shook the bug into the herb garden and laughed.

"Just a little bug we found in the kitchen, no worries, see, all taken care of!" He smiled smugly and ditched the paper towel thoughtlessly on the front sidewalk. He turned and headed back through the front door. Then, he remembered the mess he had made in the kitchen. Quickly, he came up with an excuse.

"Mom, Claire was helping me kinda organize my stuff, you know, my papers were a mess, and she gave me some files....so I could, you know, keep my stuff in my new bag?"

"Well, whatever, I'm glad she is helping you. You guys should work together more. How about it?" She put her hand lovingly on his shoulder. "Now, first pick up that paper towel you threw on the side-walk, and get to your homework!"

She continued, "Claire can be bossy, but she has good ideas for being organized in school and *you* have the greatest imagination I have ever seen. You guys, together, are unstoppable, right?" She smiled, shaking her head up and down, bobbing her ponytail.

"Oh, here, you left your clarinet at the office. How about playing that for me after supper?"

He shrugged. "Sure Mom," anxious to say any-thing at this point to get back to the mess in the kitchen before she spotted how bad the trash from the backpack really was.

Trailing through the front door behind them was a kyphotic, silver haired man who looked to be about one-hundred-years old. His hands were gnarled and he held the dirty tablet pinched between his thumb and the rest of his fingers.

"Come on, Mr. Ravinni, come through the kitchen. You remember my son Phillip?"

The old man, dressed totally in white painters clothes spotted with paints and stains of every color, waved a dirty, lined little tablet.

"Of course, of course, I remember, he's the one, helped you pick the tile for the bathroom, no?"

Phillip, anxious to pull away and get back and clean up the disaster he had made in the kitchen, agreed.

"Oh yeah, it was me all right, wasted...," then he quickly corrected himself.

"I meant spent, yes, gladly spent most of a Saturday figuring out the tile?" Changing the subject quickly, Phillip continued.

"Mr. Ravinni, how long will the dumpster be sitting on the side of the house?" The guys had made fun of it, occasionally calling him "Dumpster Dash."

Mr. Ravinni laughed and used his sleeve to wipe his nose, much to Phillip's disgust.

"Well," he laughed, "you see, I am old, and you see, it takes t... i... m... e," he said very, very slowly, spelling the letters of the word, as if to drag it out even further, stretching his hands out as if to show the months and years it would take him to complete the house.

"T... I... M... E..." and he stretched the spelling of the letters out so slowly that Phillip saw his mother raise her eyebrow and quickly shake her head as if to say "stop" behind Mr. Ravinni's back.

"Mr. Ravinni, you remember Claire?" his mother interjected, now seeing the pile of Phillip's belongings and bits of trash on the kitchen floor.

"Well, well, well, what's happened here?" she added softly under her breath, forcing a smile all the while.

Claire had settled into one of the ladder-back chairs with her face buried in her phone, trying to catch up with her friends. The only reason she hadn't scurried back to her lab was her eagerness to see Phillip have to account for the pile of trash he had dumped on the floor. Nothing finer than seeing him on the hot-seat.

Her mother ruffled her hair and planted a kiss on the top of her head.

"How's my favorite inventor?" Smiling contentedly, her mother continued.

"You guys keep working together, I like that! Claire, so good that you are helping him get organized!" She forced herself to ignore the pile of refuse that littered the kitchen floor, which she usually kept immaculate.

"Did anyone have a chance to walk Moushka?"

Claire and Phillip looked sheepishly at each other. Then, they both glanced in one corner of the kitchen, where a large dog crate housed a huge, fluffy dog lying on his side, snoring. All the commotion had not, to this point, bothered him one bit, nor had it interfered with his afternoon nap. He had only raised his head once when Claire opened the refrigerator. When no scraps of food were forthcoming, he went back to sleep.

When Moushka heard Abby Weathermore's voice, he stretched and yawned. He was old, but he still enjoyed long afternoon walks.

"Nope? OK, well, you guys keep working together, I will take him, just as soon as I'm done with Mr. Ravinni."

The old, very large and very fluffy dog sat in one corner of the kitchen in his crate, looking dejected and forgotten. But even so, he rose to stand and wag his tail at his owner. Even though the children would conveniently forget to walk him unless they were prompted, he knew Abby would take him out the minute she got home. Opening the crate, Abby

Weathermore rubbed his head and he responsively flopped on his side on the cool tile as he waited for a scratch.

"Claire, can you keep an eye on him until I finish with Mr. Ravinni, then I will take him out?"

"Sure, Mom." Claire sighed. Sometimes family responsibilities got terribly in the way of her inventing. But, Claire loved the old dog and she rubbed his stomach. The old dog had a bad habit that persisted despite many attempts at training as well as a series of dog trainers. He would eat anything paper. Once, he had eaten a quarter of a jigsaw puzzle when they weren't watching. He would eat half of a roll of paper towels. He would eat, much to Phillip's chagrin, any homework pages that he could reach, although the "dog ate my homework" excuse had never worked for Phillip. The entire family took turns monitoring him when he was trolling the house for edibles.

"Don't mind us, you guys, we are headed to the back," their mother added. "I'm so anxious to see what our Mr. Ravinni has planned for my office!"

They watched their mother set her things on a bench in the kitchen and head for the long hallway. They smothered their inappropriate laughter while Mr. Ravinni, hunched at almost a forty-five degree ankle, a massive puff of out-of-control silver hair going every which way, and carrying a used, tattered tablet, crept behind her. He was shuffling his feet and rotating his head from side to side looking for all the world like a mechanical wind-up robot. They looked at each other, covered their faces with their hands, and tried to stifle their laughter. From the front room, the African gray parrot gave a loud "Shuuush!"

CHAPTER 11

The Hydroponics Lab

Pebby ran in a fast gallop, the wooden wagon rattling so bad that she was afraid she would blow an axel. She was running on a gravel road around the outer circumference of Norwall. While the city terrain was generally flat, the outer limits of the city faded softly into a mountain range that was craggy, steep, and treacherous. The road serpentined its way through a massive rock archway, and all over the mountains, green hardwood trees and patchy conifers covered up and shaded the underbrush. Some of the trees looked as if they had been swept by fire.

The tops looked burnt, another casualty of the acid gray sky that was scorching Norwall. Under the trees, what underbrush that remained was brown, withered, and dying as well. Even the occasional drenching downpours of rain could not save them. Between the shade from the remaining trees, and the covering of the three suns by the gray sky, the short vegetation didn't stand a chance.

Almost there, keep up the pace, almost there! She paused. Ahead of her stood a tall archway tunnel of rocks. Emerging out the other side, a massive mountain of rock housed a structure set into the mountain. A honeycomb network of windows protruded as a round dome which comprised the front wall of The Hydroponics Institute. Four-story-high vertical gears turned on each side of the building, bounded by massive twin waterfalls. The sister waterfalls appeared to be turning gears which rotated slowly, like giant waterwheels, delivering the mountain water into the facility and providing the steam energy to run the habitat. The waterfalls poured into a stream which flowed away from the Institute, making a pleasant sound of rushing water.

Pebby stood for a minute, enjoying the sounds of the waterfall and breathing in the clean, misty air. Of any place in Norwall, the Craggins was the place where the air was cleanest. Taking in deep sniffs, she noticed that the water in the river was dark green. All the fish had died long ago, and the river itself had a sickening foul odor. The majestic waterfalls of the mountain water were clean, and it was rumored that the mountain water was reserved only for growing the produce of the hydroponics lab and supplying members of the ruling class with fresh, pure mountain water.

Trotting down the road leading to the entrance, she knew she had to make up time. She also knew that Lee Anna Loo would never complain about her tardiness. Through the glass honeycomb dome of the building, Pebby could see massive plants. They were larger and more healthy than she had ever seen on the mountain. Light water-vapor covered some of the windows and two copper pipes emerged from the top of the honeycomb, spitting out dirty gray smoke.

She approached the door, which was a series of massive round gears of copper, tin, and steel. Nearby stood the Automaton guards. They scowled at her, one of them raising a gear-and-cog-driven arm which clicked and beeped, sending radio frequency blips to the Verification Center. A reply of three long and one short beep confirmed her authorization to enter. *Stinking Automats!*

Whirring and spinning, monstrous gears opened gigantic doors to admit her, then closed rapidly behind her. Pebby pulled the wagon into the lobby where the floor and walls were white tile. Stretching as far as she could see overhead was a honeycomb dome of glass. A middle-aged, dark-skinned woman in a white coat greeted her. Her long, black, curly hair was tied with a white ribbon, and her ponytail was wrapped in a hairnet. Multiple gadgets and measuring devices stuck out from her pockets and her shoes were flat oxfords with thick rubber soles. Her glasses were black-framed, thick, and much too large for her dainty face.

"Pebby, darling girl! How are you my dearest child?"

Lee Anna Loo ran to greet her, opening her arms expansively. Pebby raised her nose and looked up at her, while Lee Anna scratched her head and softly petted her ears.

Lee Anna Loo had, over the past few years, asked Pebby to come be her dog. At times it was tempting, but Pebby had refused the offers gently, remaining steadfast in her devotion to her freedom. *I got the run of this clockwork town.*

She smiled at Lee Anna Loo. It was certainly very tempting, as this giggling, wacky but brilliant scientist was in charge of the facility that grew food for the workers and the Council. Lee Anna Loo ruled the Institute with perpetual sweetness, kindness, and concern for the workers who gladly carried out her bidding. Behind the reception desk, a wall of glass separated the lobby from the laboratory, and Pebby watched with interest as several hundred workers dressed in green and white prowled around the plants growing on trellises, supported by cross-strings so their fruit would not pull over or break the precious plants. In the hydroponics laboratory, the environment and air quality was tightly controlled and continuously monitored.

Pebby could see green vines twirling from the white water troughs to the two story ceiling, which was fitted with solar light.

"Like my new lights? Sky getting so dark, we had to make the sunlight ourselves!" Lee Anna laughed.

" 'Course you know, they're expecting me to produce a plant that does not need sunlight. Find a way to circumvent photosynthesis, they say, HAAA! on them, I say, HAAAAA!!! Good luck with outsmarting the Calvin Cycle!" she sighed.

"But I keep on tryin' I do, keep on tryin' like it's my fault the skies goin' dark? You thought any more about stayin' with me? You could have the run of the place, ya know. I know only the Council is allowed to have dogs, but I got some mighty high friends in mightly high places, so I'm sure I could swing it, if you'd be willin'?" She pet the scruffy dog lovingly and rubbed her ears.

"Just hate to see ya workin' so hard. Here all you have to do is patrol the rows and chase the vermin away!" She laughed.

Her face was nicely framed with beautifully meticulous black braids, which wound tightly around her head. To Pebby, she looked almost doll-like, with finely chiseled features, high cheekbones, and a strong chin. A million freckles dotted her face. Carefully, Lee Anna Loo lifted her bags of bakery goods out from the little wagon.

"I sure do love these raspberry rolls, ya know I do, hot and fresh, just like Mamma likes them! Com'on Pebby, take the wagon off and stay awhile?" Lee Anna loved the little dog, and wanted badly to keep her. Biting into the soft, warm roll, she tasted the raspberry inside. It was still hot, fresh, and a bit runny.

"Here, have a little bite! Come on, just a nibble?" And she dropped to the floor and sat just beside the scruffy tinydog on the cold, hard tile, her white lab coat spread out around her. Lee Anna Loo lovingly watched Pebby bite a small piece of the raspberry roll carefully, taking care not to nibble fingers. She gave a quick licky-lick, washing the stains of rasberry off of Lee Anna's fingers. Her internal clock was ticking; *Gotta Go... go... go... and... GO!* Pebby started forward to turn the wagon.

"OK, I get the hint, no more love-time today, guess I'll have to talk to the plants!" Laughing again, Lee Anna straightened the wagon behind Pebby and gave her one last pat on the head.

"Don't forget to say 'hello' to Najeem! I'll stop by and get some more lab coats on my next Furlough Day!" Lee Anna gave Pebby one more hug, then straightened the wagon. She pressed the button to unlock the mechanism of the massive airlock door and waved goodbye, giving a little sniffle as she shook a white handkerchief.

Pebby would miss her, but she would see her again on Furlough Day. She knew that when you were a manager, you could, when permitted by the

Council, shop, pick up supplies, and see other up-per level managers. Other than that, people like Lee Anna Loo were required to remain at the facilities they managed, with their interactions limited to the indentured workers who lived in the Habitrons. Their rooms were tiny cubicles furnished with a single bed, a small dresser, and a straight-back chair. All the rooms were the same. Painted a soft white, hooks fastened to the wall served as places to hang clothes. Each person was given a small, round bucket to hold personal items while they walked to the shower room located at the corner of each hall-way.

Each worker had two uniform jumpsuits of lime green, and two plain dark brown shirts and pants sets to wear when they were not working the six-teen-hour shifts. Everyone was assigned the same white with blue-striped knee-length nightshirt, fashioned from heavy cotton grown in the hydro-ponics lab.

Some workers graduated to mid-level manage-ment, but in general, most workers spent their life working the various habitats, tending to the thou-sands of plants growing in pots of specially treated water. The workers were responsible for harvesting the crops, packaging the foods, and shipping to the proper destinations. The most perfect of the harvest was reserved for the Council. Everything happened under the watchful gaze of Automatons, stationed at key points so as to guard the entire enterprise.

As the stainless steel and brass doors opened, cool misty air rushed in. Throwing one last look over her shoulder, Pebby heard one last soft good-bye as the gears slammed shut. The Automats at the entrance scowled in acknowledgement as she took off for the grain fields.

Circling the city on the outer border, she ran in the shadow of massive airships which monitored movement on the roads. She could see a large fan wheel and steam bellows powering the flying structure as two Automatons aimed cog-wheel blasters at real or imagined targets.

Wymore, head grower of the grain fields, would not put up with her being late, nor would he accept any food that was not hot and fresh. He would, without a second thought, talk to Gleena and bitterly complain if the food was late. He had done it before, but Pebby brokered no hard feelings toward him. Still, she sped up her run, and panting now, made her way to the flat, open lands of the wheat fields of South Norwall.

The Laboratory

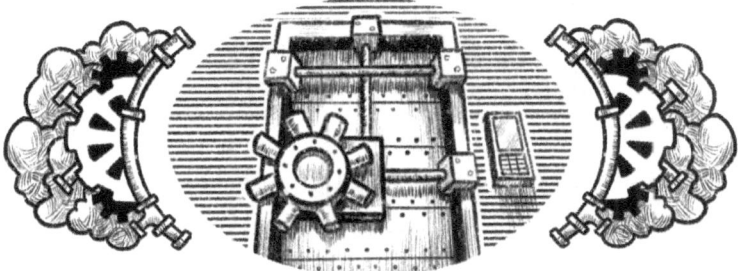

The house they had all fallen in love with was massive and old. It was in a state of utter disrepair, but they considered themselves fortunate to buy it at such a deep discount. While the basic structure was solid, the painting, flooring, and fixtures were out of date and badly in need of repair. The landscaping was overgrown and woody, and the main facade covered with serpentine vines and mildew stains. There were various twists and turns in the floor-plan, and rooms with unusual features reflecting the character of each previous owner. As time passed and the different owners modified the original floor plan, the house grew enormous. Visitors often got lost in it. The Weathermores deemed it perfect.

There were sliding bookcases hiding one room from another, doors with unexplained multiple locks, and rooms with unusually high ceilings. Some of the rooms were in strange shapes rather than squares or rectangles. Down the long hallway that led from the large galley kitchen, tall arched windows looked out on a garden area. The filtered sunlight criss-crossed through the windows, and at the end of the hallway to the left, was a sunroom with curved windows on the back wall which looked like it had been constructed as a solarium. The floor was gray-slate stone, and Claire had immediately claimed this room for her lab.

She had installed a series of complicated locks on the door, with the main lock coded with numbers that she alone knew. Her mother had, against Claire's objections, forced her to put the combination and duplicate keys in a sealed envelope, which remained hidden in her mother's underwear drawer. Claire had made her mother swear that the envelope would only be opened in case of dire emergency.

To the right of Claire's lab was a large den, decorated with comfortable couches and a large screen

TV. Beside the den a smaller hallway led to an octagon-shaped office with sixteen foot ceilings and clerestory windows. It was this room that their mother claimed for her home office. Inside this unusually shaped room, massive sliding oak bookcases led to a guest bedroom and bathroom. Moving the heavy bookcase was a chore, especially after they had filled it with their favorite books. They left it partially open so they could squeeze through sideways. The sunny bedroom behind the door was equipped with large arched windows looking out on the side yard. It was painted the lightest shade of blue-green, and was home to a wrought-iron bed that Abby had owned in medical school. It was a quiet and peaceful refuge, and sometimes Abby would stretch out on the four-poster bed for a nap.

It was here that Mr. Ravinni had finished working several months ago. Now, he was ready to start renovations on Abby Weathermore's office. Mr. Ravinni was extremely hard-of-hearing, so Abby Weathermore was shouting.

"What about this? It looks like real wood, what do you think?' Her voice was so loud it echoed in the octagon-shaped room. An expansive, black wrought-iron chandelier with candle holders on its upturned ends hung down from the center of the room. Dusty cobwebs floated from the upturned ironwork and danced in the breeze from the air-conditioning unit.

Phillip and Claire, still lounging on the kitchen chairs, looked at each other and tried to control their laughter. Phillip had his head down as his body shook uncontrollably with spasms of giggles. Claire, hand clasped over her mouth to stifle her own laughter, continued to slump over her phone. She was terribly interested in the group chat of her engineer friends who had their own private server. Her sides shook with laughter and her thumbs moved at lightning speed, as her mother continued to shout instructions to Mr. Ravinni.

Breaking from the phone for a few seconds, Claire struggled to get a few words out through her stifled laughter. She heaved a deep breath and whispered, "Here, Buster, take the key and go to my lab. File cabinet on the right as you go in the door, open the TOP DRAWER ONLY, and get out an accordian file. Then go in the BOTTOM DRAWER and get a pencil box. Think you can remember that Buster-Boo?"

Laughing again and trying her best to hide it, shaking her head, she turned her attention back to the small screen which illuminated her face. Her hair framed the phone like a curtain. The stove could have caught on fire and doubtful she would have noticed. Meanwhile, Moushka was stretched out on the kitchen tile pondering the pile of trash and figuring out what might be tasty. He eagerly awaited his afternoon walk with Abby, who would give him time to enjoy the park.

Without taking her eyes off her phone, Claire lifted the lanyard that she always wore and handed it to Phillip.

"Count this as your lucky day, and the *only* day you will ever set foot in my lab, OK?"

Not bothering to answer, he grabbed the key and headed down the hall. He could still hear his mother shouting her instructions to Mr. Ravinni. As he passed the door, he could see Mr. Ravinni looking quizically around the room, holding up one of the tiles which looked like bleached pine wood. He enthusiastically shook his head up and down, and Phillip thought he looked like a bobble-head.

"I like, I like, very much I like!" Mr. Ravinni said slowly as he lifted the tile several inches from his eyes so that he could see the pattern." Now, I take measures!" He proceeded to use a stick-like device, his bent frame pushing a small wheel around the octagon shaped room to measure the distance. Phillip fiddled with the key, trying it in one of the six locks. *Sheeesh!* Finally the door clicked open and he strained to pull it outward.

He found the file cabinet straight away, and grabbed the accordian file and pencil box. He froze and marveled at the long wooden workbench, where soldering pens, wires, electrical outlets, flasks, and beakers were surrounded by nuts, bolts, and several small motors. A large, lined journal lay open on the workbench. *So here's where she spends all her time. This is OUTSTANDING! Why does she get a lab? I want one too!*

The tree outside shaded the large windows, which, for some unknown reason, reminded him of the orange and black insect that was still in his pocket. Trying to resist what he knew he just *had* to do, he raised one eyebrow and smiled as he gingerly unzipped the small plastic bag which still had cracker crumbs in it from lunch. He placed the bug on top of the lab journal.

"You know what to do," he whispered gently. He smirked as he prodded the insect onward, softly closing the door and heading back to the kitchen. He hurried back up the narrow hallway to the kitchen where first, he picked up the garbage littering the floor, disposing of it in a large black trash bag.

He collected all his writing implements, separating pens from pencils, and placed them neatly in the new pencil case. He stored the rest in labeled zip-lock plastic bags. He discarded worn erasers and stacked his papers into a neat pile.

He took out the accordian file Claire had magnanimously shared with him, and started sorting the papers according to the school classes. He tore all the scribbles off his tablets, unfolded the organizer, and discarded old papers. He loaded the items into the new camouflage pack. Once again, he felt the piece of metal in the bottom of the front pocket, and this time, curiosity got the best of him. He stealthily took it out just to peek at it. Hearing his mother yelling her goodbyes to Mr. Ravinni, he knew he only had a moment. She would be all over him if he wasn't working on math.

Claire continued to be transfixed by her phone, although she had moved to the floor where she was petting Moushka with one hand and furiously messaging her friends with the other. Turning his back so she could not see, he lifted the widget from his new backpack. It was like nothing he had ever seen before; the widget had a large semi-circle gear at the top, ornamented by two interlocking gears and a flat arch of brass in the center of the fob.

Najeem's Tailor Shop
1426 Wenderling Way
Norwall

Raising his eyebrows, he entertained for a fraction of a second the thought of sharing his find with his sister and his mother. Deciding otherwise, he crammed the widget quickly into his pants pocket. Hearing his mother approach the kitchen, he threw himself into one of the straight-back chairs, flipped open his math book and grabbed a pencil, smiling smugly all the while.

CHAPTER 13

The Fireplace in the Park

Abby Weathermore had accepted three tenets. First, that her children were very different from one another; second, that getting her medical practice off of the ground was a lot more work than she had expected; and third, that renovating the old house was costing quite a bit more than she had anticipated.

As she headed to the neighborhood park with Moushka prancing along happily on a long lead, she exhaled deeply, relishing the time alone with her thoughts. Under the canopy of trees, Moushka wanted to explore and he pulled hard. Trying to keep him from going too far off the path, she felt the old familiar pain in her right ankle. It had been fractured when she was Phillip's age and it had never healed quite right. Some days, it caused pain with every step she took. Other days, it was only a manageable nagging ache. The pain never really went away, but somehow she had learned to live with it.

Still, she worked long days, and came home to a house that needed constant work. They were trying to do some of the work themselves to save money. They had, over the years, laboriously painted walls and trim, replaced doorknobs, fixed cracks in the walls, and cleaned up debris in the yard. Many nights after the children had settled in bed she would wrap her ankle in ice and elevate it to bring the swelling down.

They would hire people to do the heavy work, like the floors. By sheer luck, they had discovered Mr. Ravinni and hired him to do the more complicated renovations. His work was exceptionally good, and unbelievably cheap. He was, however, exceptionally slow, which most homeowners would not tolerate. His snail's pace work efforts gave Abby time to save the money to pay him as he slowly completed each project. Remodeling a house with two very opinionated and stubborn teenagers was quite a challenge. Abby not-so-fondly remembered discussions at the paint store when the three of them debated the color design selections for the house.

Abby had fallen in love with the circular skylight in the foyer, which was at the top of a white dome. Regretfully, the previous owners had painted the dome white and had thrown handfuls of gold glitter onto the wet paint. She laughed to herself remembering how she had perched precariously from the top of a ladder while the children swung the massive glass chandelier to the side so she could sand off the glitter. They had painted the dome sky-blue, and it gave the illusion that the foyer opened to the blue sky.

While they had loved the foyer, it was the huge stone fireplace in the kitchen that had cinched the deal for the Weathermores. They liked nothing better than throwing a log on the fire and watching the flames dance after a long day at work or school. The golden glow made the kitchen their favorite place to congregate and it was the center of action in the sprawling house. They had refinished a long rectangular harvest table they found cheap at an auction, and matched it with eight ladder-back chairs. It was not unusual to find one of them using the table to work on a project, and they had all but given up hope of keeping it uncluttered.

Abby Weathermore was proud of her children and she cherished their individuality. She laughed to herself. Claire was brilliant, but often forgetful and unfocused. Everything came *so* easy for her, that sometimes she was not as disciplined as she should be. Her mind moved in a million directions, often at the same time.

Phillip, on the other hand, was a work-in-progress. He had made great strides in school, but still was an expert at avoiding what he did not like to do. He could be devious and cunning, but she knew it was not in a malicious way. He royally enjoyed thinking that he was pulling the wool over her eyes. She hoped that learning a new instrument would help him focus. And more than that, she hoped that he and Claire could learn to work together. That, more than anything, was her hope; that they would stop the bickering and support each other. She hoped over time that they would learn to always be there for each other.

The walks with Moushka helped her keep a sense of calm and gave her the energy she needed to keep up with her hectic schedule. Moushka was getting old but he still could out-pace her. Slowing down now, they wandered to the dock, where the lake mirrored the blue sky and ducks motored around. Dropping onto a bench, she stretched out her back. Moushka sprawled on the ground beside her.

"We aren't as young as we used to be, are we Moush?" She rubbed his head affectionately. Her ankle was starting to throb now; walking the uneven ground was particularly difficult. She would need to ice it when she got back to the house.

She looked at the scenery, petted the fluffy dog, and rubbed her ankle. Well, they just needed to keep building the practice, finishing the house, and focusing on the children's schoolwork. That was it; it was just that simple. She needed to keep doing what she had been doing the past few years, even when it was hard. There was no other way now, they were committed to the house and the business. Stretching her arms high above her head and glancing at her watch, she wondered how Phillip was coming with his homework. Reluctantly, she knew she better head home.

They sat for a minute on the circular stone firepit close to the water while she re-tied her shoe. She rubbed the sore ankle, and Moushka sniffed it as though something was not quite right. His cool nose felt good. Then, suddenly, startled, Moushka growled under his breath. Something was wrong. He didn't like the smell of the firepit; he seemed spooked. He was very protective of Abby, who had raised him from a pup.

"Hey, no pulling! Wait!" He pulled so hard, she stood up, and for an instant, winced as she put weight on her ankle. Moushka continued to pull her. Nearly falling off balance, she righted herself.

"Wow, what got into you?" His ears perked up, as if distant sounds were calling him, and gently, he tugged her toward the house.

"Well, I guess you're tired Moush, I'm tired too, long day. Let's do something easy for supper, huh?"

She was so busy watching her steps on the uneven terrain that she did not notice the big, fluffy dog glancing back nervously toward the fireplace. It was as if he heard sounds that frightened him. Pulling her thin athletic jacket around her, Abby shuddered and tried to ignore the chills running down her spine. *Ankle hurts, ankle hurts, need to ice it down.* She hurried to try and keep up with Moushka, who was pulling her very hard away from the pit and back toward the house.

Danger in the Wheat Fields

Pebby's wooden red wagon clattered as she ran up the hill. It was a gravel road, somewhat steep, but with a majestic summit view of the wheat fields of Norwall. Wheat, being the last food-crop to survive the increasing pollution from the gray-skies, was heavily guarded. It provided the main ingredient of the production line at the Octagon. The food produced was the mainstay of the population's diet, supplemented by fruits and vegetables grown in The Hydroponics Institute.

As Pebby took in the acres and acres of fields, she saw a steam harvester machine travel up and down the rows while cutting and gathering wheat. It loaded it onto steam-driven snail wagons to take it to Moniker's Mill. She could see the copper and brass gears spinning as they moved the bulky harvester. A stainless steel pipe on top of the dull tin box puffed black, sooty smoke.

The big wooden wheels of the harvester thumped as they made their way over the rough ground, the tin box dangerously off-balance. Pulling up to the snail wagon, the harvester unloaded the wheat onto a flat-bed trailer pulled by the gigantic copper snail. Pebby squinted, trying to focus on a petite, olive-skinned girl with braided dark hair perched at the helm of the snail steam-powered trailer. It looked to be Wascilla Wymore, daughter of Wymore, manager of the wheat fields. The fourteen year old known as Wassy had a bad habit of picking up Pebby and squeezing the stuffing out of her with suffocating hugs. Wassy never stopped chattering, and although very bright, she could be overbearing. Pebby always avoided her if at all possible. Wassy had been trained by her father to be one of the best drivers of the snail steam wagons that ferried the wheat to Moniker's Mill. The Automatons had become so accustomed to her scrunching up her nose and making faces at them, that they mercifully left her alone.

Pebby waited at the knoll of the hill until she saw Wassy pull away with another load of wheat, likely on her way to Moniker's Mill. The tinydog's sensitive nose burned from the sour-smelling, dirty air, and she shook her head. In the distance stood a small two-room stone cottage occupied by Wymore, manager and guardian of the wheatfields. It looked like one-half of a gigantic egg, sitting on the rocky ground. The cottage itself was made of small stones and cement, with a distressed-copper canopy over the front door. A twisted copper pipe extended up from the chimney into the gray sky.

Pebby slowed her trot down the hill so as not to pick up speed. The wagon had no brakes and could easily get out of control on the hill. She could feel the wagon touching her back legs as she deliberately slowed her gait, trying not to skid on the gravel. The road led directly to the house, and Wymore, who had been curiously watching her from a side window, huffed a bit, then hurried to open the heavy wooden front door.

"Well, well, well, aren't we just a bit late? Those rolls better be hot and fresh, Pebby," he intoned, and although he sounded gruff, he didn't really mean it.

His features were rough-hewn and he was a heavy-set man, despite the paucity of his diet. The years of overseeing the growing of the wheat fields had taken a toll on him. His skin was deeply tanned and spotted with sun-spots. He looked much older than his fifty-eight years.

Grabbing his white paper bags from the wagon, he gave her a quick pat on the head.

"Com'on in, I know I'm your last delivery before lunch, so come in and take a load off, won't cha?" He grabbed a Cinni Roll out of the paper bag with his still-dirty hand. He stuffed large bites into his mouth, half-talking, half-chewing.

Unclipping her wagon, she nosed her way into the house. A small fire was burning in the fireplace and a kettle could be seen over the fire. Strange smells wafted from it.

"Now, don't give away me secret! I have the best stew this side of the fields, and no one the wiser. The nasty Automats standing on the field got no idea'r I'm cooking right under their noses, that is, iff'in they even have a nose?" He threw back his head and laughed.

"Stinkin' Automats! Right, Pebby?"

She buffed his leg with her head, knowingly agreeing with him.

"Com'on, I'll git you a bowl, try it!"

Carefully pouring a generous amount into a chipped ceramic dish, he set it kindly in front of the tiny scruffy dog who lapped it up quickly. The stew was truly delicious.

"See, when the Automats ain't looking, I stick plants in me pocket, and then, I sort 'em later. Specially mushrooms, they're the best! I kind'a know which ones taste the best, and also which er' the poison ones, so I boil 'em, even though technically I'm breakin' rules, I make me own stew. Got roots, and 'shrooms, and leaves, and presto!!! Me own stew! Wadda' you think?"

Seeing the empty bowl, he quickly picked it up. "It's good, right? That'll put some more meat on those skinny bones, right?" He rubbed her head gently this time, and she enjoyed the affection, the full stomach, and the warmth of the fire.

"Ya know, there was a time when we could do what we wanted. A time before the Automats. You're too young to remember it girl, but I remember it, and I know Naji Najeem for sure remembers it. Me and Naji goes way back. Why, we's go way back to when Norwall was a democracy, that bein' way before the Council, the Automatons, and the stinky skies. Yep, before the rules about eat'n, and what we're allowed to have. I'm sure Naji remembers those days, gosh, that man can eat!"

Pebby thought back to Naji and the meager rations on the shelves in his apartment above the shop. There was never any meat. They had meat only once on the solstice, and never again since. Naji had given her his ration, feigning stomach upset. Their diet now was supplied by the Octagon Food Administration Department, known as OFAD, along with their allotment from the hydroponics lab. That was all. That was it, but it wasn't enough. It was barely enough for them to survive. Wymore shook his head.

"Things surely have changed, Pebby, never enough to eat, and the robots wanting to steam ya for take'n bites of food? Listen, they separated us, and they keepin' us down, and they keepin' us inside."

Whispering now, he held her little face in his hands and looked straight into her eyes.

"We'll take it all back, sometime, Pebby, we'll take it back, and then our bellies will be full! Naji's the one, Pebby, Naji's the one! He's got the book smarts to lead us, don' he?"

Pebby was not sure what it all meant. Distracted, they had not heard the whirring of the Automaton fast approaching the front door of the cottage. Pebby was way past her scheduled visit time and an alarm had sounded. They had been so distracted by the stew and the warmth of the fire, that they had forgotten that their time was strictly regulated.

"Quick!! Hook yourself up!" Wymore whispered as he ran to the fireside, where he had saved a bucket of water. Dousing the flames, he hid the kettle in a stone alcove up in a high corner inside the fireplace. As the door slammed open, the last bit of embers sputtered as the smoke dissipated.

A scowling robot with a blaster wheeled into the small cottage. Dragging dirt and pieces of plants stuck to its wheels, it aimed the blaster menacingly at Wymore. The little dog burst out through the doorway, wagon clattering madly, derby perched precariously on her head, with one final, quick glance over her shoulder. She saw the Automat's gears spinning wildly on its back.

Steam puffed from the stainless tube on the back of its head. It rotated now, blaster raised, and fortunately decided that nothing was amiss in the cottage. It retreated back outside to take its place along the periphery of the wheat fields, scowling and showing vicious teeth as the tiny scruffy dog ran full speed up the hill in a cloud of dust, her red wagon bouncing furiously behind her.

Friday Foolishness

The weekend was finally here! It had been an especially good week for Phillip. He smirked as he unpacked and assembled his clarinet. The sun, pink in the sky, filtered light through the trees and high-arched windows into the living room of the Weathermore's house. As was their Friday afternoon tradition, they were assembling in the front living room. Even though they numbered only three, they met formally each Friday afternoon to discuss the accomplishments of the week; the ups and the downs, the good and the bad, and most importantly, the plans for the weekend. Phillip knew that his mother would request a few songs on his clarinet so he was assembling his instrument, trying to be one step ahead of her.

Claire was also involved in music lessons, mainly to appease her mother. She had only half-heartedly paid attention during her violin lessons, and was reticent to practice. She always found an excuse to avoid it. *Perhaps Mom will ask her to entertain us?* Phillip chuckled to himself. *Oh yes, entertain us indeed!* Phillip started to laugh just thinking about her screechy strings and sour notes. It was painful to his ears.

"Mom! Claire! Come on guys!" he shouted loudly, raising his clarinet high in the air and waving it impatiently. He had some surprises for his mother and sister. And these were *big* surprises. He loved their Friday afternoon meetings because more and more, he was finding a natural flair for music. With even a little practice, he was gaining new-found confidence. In fact, he was turning into a rather confident performer.

He belted out a few scales as loudly as he could, and played through his usual warm-up. He expertly unpacked his music folder, which was just recently kept quite neat, and placed the national anthem on top. He proceeded to play with all his might. As the strains of the melody echoed through the house, he heard the *clack, clack, clack* of his mother's shoes on the hallway tile. He heard Moushka trotting along and before he got midway through the song, his mother silently flopped on the couch. Moushka stretched out at her feet, looking as if he was ready for a nap. She smiled broadly.

"And who, may I ask, didn't really want to start lessons?" She laughed and shook her head.

"You are so good Phillip, with just the teeny tiny little bit of practice. Imagine how good you could be if you practiced every day? You sound sooo good!!" She clapped her hands applauding him, and he raised his one eyebrow and blushed.

"Well, Mom,... uhhh... they asked me to play the anthem at the awards assembly. Ya know, it's nothin' really, just one song, it's not like it's a big concert or anything ya know?"

"Phillip," she interrupted him, "that's a REALLY big deal!" Her eyes were wider than Phillip had ever seen them, and she was sitting straight up, straighter than he had ever seen her sit. He thought for a minute she might cry, but she gulped quickly and rushed over to give him a hug.

"Wow." She shook her head back and forth.

He also was hiding the news that he had nailed his spelling test, but he smirked as he waited with baited breath to share the news until Claire was present. Claire arrived, sporting two slinky, scowling cats draped over her arms like a mink stole. Not bothering to find a seat on the couch, she dropped to the floor, trying to hang onto the cats who were making serious efforts to escape. One hissed loudly and swatted at her with a wide open paw. Phillip thought his sides would split from holding his laughter back. Clearing his throat, he waved his arms high in the air, still clutching the clarinet.

"Well, we have some news today, in case, just in case you haven't heard, I have been asked, no, I mean invited, yes, *invited*, to play the national anthem at the assembly!"

He smiled broadly, waiting for Claire's reaction.

"Wow, Buster, that's great! Guess it helped, organizing your stuff?" She laughed, teasing him, gently so as not to ruin his moment.

"And, Mom," Claire continued, now that she had the floor, "I got my schedule for classes, and the voucher that pays for next semester from the Science Foundation!" Claire grinned proudly, feeling that winning the Science Exposition had saved her family thousands of dollars in college tuition. The only requirement was that she had to maintain her grade average of at least 80 percent or above in her major field, which of course, was engineering. She didn't think that this would present a hardship for her. In fact, she was quite confident that she would be one of the top students entering the prestigious program.

"Claire, you know I am so very proud of your winning, not just because it pays for college, but you really had the courage to see it through! Remember when you wanted to quit?" her mother gently reminded her. "You didn't quit. And look where it got you? I'm so proud of you both!"

Phillip smiled to himself and breathed a sigh of relief. His circle of friends had admired his new backpack, and Claire's help with the organization of his papers had impressed his teachers. He found it easier to keep up in class when all his notes were organized and he relished the attention his new-found skills garnered. Now it was time for the rest of his announcement. *Mom's finished oohing and ahhing over pitter-patter-perfect, so now to wow her with my news.*

"Guess who nailed his spelling test? And guess who sailed, and I mean sailed to the top of the pile in World History?" He bowed graciously, and then pumped his fist in the air, still grasping his clarinet.

"Save all applause, save it, save it, there is more to come!" he added expansively.

And with that, he blasted out the "Star Spangled Banner" as loud as he could. Freddy, the gray parrot, looked as though he could fall off of his perch. The music was loud, but he gripped tightly and tried to sing along. When Phillip finished, throwing in a high squeaking note at the end and holding it until his breath totally gave out, he deeply bowed. His mother and sister cheered and applauded.

"Hey Ho, how 'bout dinner and a show?" Claire waved her hands in the air and jumped up, throwing her arms around her brother, giggling at his discomfort. She would not release him, even though he squirmed and tried to free himself. Their mother laughed.

"Easy, Claire, you'll squeeze the stuffing out of him!"

Phillip coughed and sputtered, turning red in the face. Bent over, he was still coughing as though he couldn't catch his breath, but laughing all the while.

"Can we go to a movie and grab pizza?" Claire begged. "I'm too tired to help cook, and there's a revival of *Godzilla*, in the original Japanese with subtitles!"

Phillip was already pretending to heave behind Claire's back. He hated subtitles in movies, and Claire's passion for foreign monster films irritated him. Claire didn't grasp why her mother was laughing. In the background, Phillip was clasping his hands as if in prayer, all the while shaking his head slowly, silently mouthing the words *no, no, no.......* *please no!"*

But the Weathermores generally did things together, especially on Friday night.

"Phillip, why don't you invite McClure along?" his mother asked. McClure was his best friend and had spent many an evening laughing with the Weathermores. Sometimes, they all joked that they should just give him a room at their house.

"Mom, I'm too embarrassed to ask him to see that junk. The special effects are laughable!" Phillip prowled around the living room behind Claire's back with his arms curled, doing his best T-Rex impersonation.

"It's a classic!" Claire pronounced, still not understanding what her mother was laughing about.

"Still, Phillip, you chose the last movie, I think it is Claire's turn. Now, how about a little music, then you can phone McClure?"

"Text, Mom, TEXT!" Phillip's head bobbed emphatically.

"Text? Ya know, like pushing the buttons and sending words on the phone? Text?" Phillip raised both his eyebrows, shook his head, and looked at her with exasperation. *Nobody phones, sheeesh, get it right will ya,* he thought, but didn't say so as not to not hurt her feelings.

Raising his clarinet to his lips, he bleeted out a few bars from his lesson songs while his mother closed her eyes, and nodded her head to the music appreciatively. The concert was short and sweet, and his attention turned to getting ready for the evening with his best friend.

McClure might be his best friend, but they were polar opposites. While Phillip was obsessively neat about his attire, McClure was messy. He often wore the same black t-shirt two or three days in a row. His hair was spiked up in the front, and his pants were frayed on the bottom, his shoes worn and dirty. His clothes often looked wrinkled and worn. Phillip thought that McClure's mother bought them second-hand at flea markets, but he never said a word about it.

While McClure looked disheveled, he was on top of his game as far as his school work was concerned. He was at the absolute head of the class as far as academic performance. He had been the champion in the last county spelling bee two years in a row. He was sharp and witty and astute. He was a math and computer wiz. The recognition he was given at school more than made up for that which he did not get at home. He had confided to Phillip that no matter how he excelled, his father's favorite nickname for him would always be "loser."

He and Phillip had bonded as best of friends. They complemented each other and accepted each other for the way they were; they helped each other. McClure helped Phillip focus on school and Phillip shared with McClure some semblance of a normal family life, with normal ups and downs.

At least they could suffer through the Japanese *Godzilla* together and get a good laugh. They could get pizza near the theater and tease Claire unmercifully, and suffer through the subtitles together. It would give him someone to laugh with, stupid movie, stupid sister.

Phillip packed up his clarinet as he hatched a plan for the evening. He would show Mc Clure the widget that had stayed in his pocket all week. Phillip had done his research. He could not find anything, no city, town, municipality, or country on the planet which was named Norwall. McClure would know what to do. They would work it out together; they always did.

CHAPTER 16

Lunchtime at the Dock

Pebby headed back to the Octagon as fast as her legs would carry her. The low-flying steam ships that cruised overhead typically did not bother her, but today was different. She sensed that they were watching her. She had spent too much time on every delivery this morning. And, they had literally burst in on her and Wymore, cog-gears threatening to shoot and vaporize them.

She needed to get back to the safety of the Octagon. She felt safe with Gleena and Deen. Gleena had a contact on the Council that prevented the

Automatons from harassing the dogs. Maybe she should get her grooming today; Treena Trembly always made her feel loved and cherished and Deen could probably be sweet-talked into reassigning her afternoon deliveries.

Not to mention, several hours of brushing, washing, and grooming would feel good after the morning run. She had circled the outer crest of Norwall, and had scaled the mountains of the Craggins. She had traversed the wheat fields of the southern plains. She had run through the woodsy perimeter where the falconry stood. Roads in the periphery were gravel, unlike the cobblestone streets of the town. She had gotten unmistakingly dirty. She could hardly wait to get her coat in shape again. Besides, it looked bad for the Chief Delivery Dog to be dirty and unkempt. Treena Trembly could fix all that.

She had been scared out of her wits at Wymore's cottage and she needed time to rest and relax. The Automatons had given her a fright and she longed for the comfort of a friend. She wouldn't see Naji Najeem until later. But talk of Naji was on everyone's lips. *He must be friends with everyone, because everyone knows Naji, and they all think he's grand.*

She didn't understand why everyone knew she traveled back to the tailor shop each evening, as if she belonged to Naji. But, she *didn't* belong to him because she had never belonged to *anyone*. She just would *not* belong! Wasn't she free to come and go as she pleased? Anyway, owning dogs was against the rules. She wasn't about to break any rules, not with those stupid Automats waiting to blast people or dogs that got in the way of The Mandates. All the rules that they had to follow, called The Mandates, could mean the difference between life and vaporization. Lucky for her, the Delivery Dogs flew under the radar of The Mandates, and so long as they did their job, the Council had decreed the Automats leave them alone.

Trotting up the delivery ramp, she met Deen Diggins at the top. She lifted her head as he petted her silky ears.

"How did it go? I guess you were on time, didn't hear any complaints from Gleena. Good job girl, good job!" Deen looked even more tired and worn out than he had a few hours ago, but she knew that his shift ended after the lunch-time feeding.

"Go on, take off your wagon," he whispered close to her ear.

"I've been holding the grub a bit, trying to give you time to get back, but I can't hold it any longer, go on girl!"

He watched her trot through the enormous doors to Cubicle Twenty-Two, where she pressed the latches on the sides of her vest and put the red wagon back in place. Scrambling as fast as she could, she headed for the circular feeding trough where massive gears slowly turned a giant turntable. The kibble tray slowly rotated in front of the hungry pups. A small trough in front contained crystal clear water, unlike that which she had seen in the stream outside the hydroponics institute. Delivery dogs were given fresh, clean water usually reserved for the council. With the exception of the snail steam trucks that huffed and puffed their way around town, the delivery dogs were the cornerstone of the food delivery system to middle managers of the factories.

Pebby filled her little belly quickly. She had learned from an early age to eat fast, before all the food was taken by the others. It was first-come, first-served, and she was relieved to see Linus eating his share. His morning run must not have been too bad. Deen usually tried to go easy on the small dog, giving him in-town runs to the local shopkeepers rather than the industries on the fringes of the town.

Finally full, she rested on the worn pallet in her cubby. Deen Diggins and Radon Rodrique, his short, chubby sidekick, had cleaned the cubicles while the dogs made the morning runs. The tile floors were spotless, and the pallets, while worn, were at least fresh. Twice daily, Radon could be seen dragging a white sack around the Habitron, picking up all the pallets, stuffing them in a white laundry bag, and shoving them through the chute to the basement laundry facilities.

In the basement, Habitron workers laboured in sixteen hour overlapping shifts to clean laundry washed in giant, gear-driven tubs. Spinning gear fans dried the laundry with cold air, so that the dogs' pallets could be replaced before the evening feeding. Working in the wash facility was a dreaded job, as the basement was damp, the shifts long, and the work back-breaking. The life-span of the laundry workers was short. Their diet was poor, and the air quality even worse. Sometimes it was years before they would see the outside sky or breathe fresh air.

Poor ventilation and lint particles in the air made them susceptible to pneumonia, bronchitis, and a host of fibrotic lung ailments. When they did become sick, and only if they were nearly unable to stand, they were sent to the hospital ward, where Automatons stood guard at each and every bed, to keep watch and ensure that they did not either try to escape, or attempt to eat unauthorized food.

Stretching, stiff and sore from the morning run, Pebby reached into her wagon and grabbed the Groomerly Grooming token in her teeth. Hurrying to take her place in the front of the line, she presented it to Deen.

"Good choice, Pebby, good choice. I'd say, take a grooming if you can get it! Might as well take the afternoon off and let Treena fix your coat. I'll get Radon to check those wagon wheels. Your morning run was a little rough, I know." He smiled knowingly, glad she was taking the opportunity to take respite.

Radon Rodrique was not only the custodian of the delivery-dog Habitron, but was also the skilled wagon-smith for the fleet. He kept the wagons in top working order, replacing wheels, fixing hitches, and painting them whenever they looked worn. He was in his mid-teens, but looked much younger. He was one of the few children that was overweight, and many attributed it to the fact that his mother worked as a line inspector at the Octagon.

No one would ever admit that Radon and his mother secretly consumed the baked goods which did not quite meet the Octagon standards. Pebby knew that he kept her red wagon in top-notch shape, so what his mother fed him was of no concern to her. The run on the gravel had thrown the wheels out of alignment, and they would clatter noisily, drawing unwanted attention to her. *Better to fix it now, before the Automatons complained, or worse, I blow a wheel coming down a hill. Stinkin Automats!*

"Hey, I think I gave you the wrong grooming token, hold on," Deen reached deep into his pocket.

"Yep, yep, found the right one, make sure you give this to Treena Trembly, now don' go giving it to that mean old Merry McGuttchen, ya know, she'll rip ya head off as soon as look at ye? Right? You understand? Only to Treena. Only, only, only! Now off wich ya!"

Pebby flew down the delivery ramp under the watchful eye of the Automatons, with the grooming token tied tightly to her harness. She did not pause to look at the Automaton whose gears spun wildly on his back as he raised and lowered his blaster menacingly at Deen. She headed to Groomerly Grooming as fast as she could go. Much to Pebby's delight, one year ago, Treena Trembly had been named Chief Groomer of the entire fleet of Delivery Dogs, and Pebby could hardly wait to see her again.

CHAPTER 17

The Saturday Surprise

Saturday morning: PLOP!!! the paint roller slammed into the pan. SQUISH!!! Phillip squeezed the roller against the pan and rolled it back and forth a few times to get off the excess paint. Phillip was dressed in an old scrub suit his mother had saved from her intern days. He looked for all the world like a miniature neurosurgeon, right down to the blue paper shoe covers. It was mid-morning Saturday and the smell of the paint drifted from the long hallway that ran from the kitchen. The nauseating smell wafted throughout the house. He scrunched his face and wrinkled his nose. He felt his stomach rumble when he smelled the disgusting latex paint.

He was sick of the remodeling of the old house, but several things had gone his way so he didn't fight his mother on it. First, and most importantly, she had arisen quite early and she had painted all the edge work. All that was left for him to do was to roll the walls. *White covering white, should be easy enough. Get done quick with this stinky job and move on to Revolutions of the Ages!*

Second, McClure was coming over to spend the day, so there would be no more chores after the painting. And third, she promised to bake the cinnamon rolls he loved. Even though the paint fumes were overpowering, he could smell the cinnamon aroma drifting from the kitchen.

Slap, slosh, push, push the roller, Slap!! Back in the tray, pick up paint. Slosh! Push, push, push. His mother had meticulously framed out the windows and doors and laid down large plastic drop-cloths to protect the new tile. Phillip smiled as he rolled the walls. She was a better painter than the ones they had hired and he prided himself on his work as well.

Once, they had hired a painter to paint the laundry room, and when he was almost finished she gave him his pay and shooed him out the door. Shaking her head back and forth, she reopened the paint cans, recruited an unwilling Phillip and threw a brush in his hands. Together, they spent the rest of Saturday repainting the entire laundry room. He had to admit that it looked much better after they were finished.

As he painted the hall, he heard her humming in the kitchen. *She is the most annoying person I know.* She had hung a collection of wall clocks in the laundry room, some with gears, some with melting faces, some that were small, and some that were huge. He guessed that there were about a dozen clocks on one wall. She was always collecting more old clocks, and as he sloshed more paint, he wondered if she would hang clocks in the hallway. He hoped not; he liked the pristine white walls which accented the large arched windows. He stopped to stare outside at a squirrel sitting calmly under the oak tree. The squirrel appeared to stare back, then sat up and screeched, "chee chee chee!" as it ran up the tree and hid. *Stupid squirrel,* he thought, *stupid, stupid, squirrel!*

Abby Weathermore had completed her part of the painting and moved on to her usual Saturday morning baking. Phillip could hear her in the kitchen, mixers whirring, eggs cracking, and the refrigerator opening and closing as she collected ingredients. She knew Phillip was waiting on his favorite cinnamon rolls. As he rolled long strokes up and down the walls, he could already smell the treats that were baking. His mother had a special cream cheese icing for these, and she would decorate the tops with raisins. She would bake enough so that they enjoyed fresh baked goods during the entire week.

"Mom, you're not giving those cinnies to Mr. Ravinni this time, are you?" he called out, dipping the roller in the pan and shaking off drips.

His mother laughed as she looked down the long hallway with its tall, arched windows that looked out on a pretty green courtyard.

"Are you kidding? As hard as you're working? This batch is all yours! But I might make an extra one for McClure to take home, OK?"

"Yeah, don't spoil him too much, he won't wanna leave... when is his mom bringing him?"

"Pretty soon, I guess, hey, it looks great already! Keep going, it shouldn't take you more than another half hour or so and you'll be done!"

The kitchen timer and the doorbell rang simultaneously. Freddy, the plucky family parrot, sat in a five-foot tall Victorian-style cage in the front living room. He could imitate any sound and he began to mimic the kitchen timer. *Bing Bing Bing!!!* Between the doorbell, the timer, and Freddy, it was impossible to tell which sound was coming from where.

In the middle of it all, Claire made an appearance, having stayed up too late again and now sleeping in much too late . She rubbed her eyes with her fists, as if waking up this late was still an insult to her senses.

"What the heck, it sounds like a five alarm fire here, what in the name of heaven, how can a person get enough sleep?"

"Claire, my darling, can you get the door? I think it's Sylvie and McClure." Abby donned oven mitts to take out the oven-baked rolls and put in another load of cinnamon rolls, her signature recipe.

"Claire, while you are inventing, how about getting to the laundry today? Have some coffee and wake up, dear. You can invent while the loads are washing."

"But I'm not dressed," she yawned sleepily, pouting, rooting through the coat closet for a hoodie to wrap around her. *If people are coming in, at least let me cover up my pajamas.*

Abby heard Freddy blow Claire kisses, then start to squawk alarm sounds as Claire opened the front door. The feisty African gray parrot was better than any alarm system. Once he had actually saved them from a house fire when a pot of chili was left unattended on the stove. That had garnered him an interview with a local television station and made him a celebrity in his own right. They had all laughed themselves silly when "Plucky Parrot Saves Family Home" was the headline on the local news. The little African gray took it all in stride, but continued to closely monitor the home for untoward events.

Freddy had seen McClure and Sylvie visit before and he let them proceed without fanfare. He prided himself in the fact that visitors knew better than to approach his cage. He liked the fact that his sour and skeptical attitude intimidated most guests. Both Sylvie and McClure had been to the Weathermore's house so many times before that they knew their way around, and they knew to keep far back from Freddy's cage to avoid a hard bite. Phillip came out to greet them in the kitchen, and McClure chuckled.

"Cool. Brain surgery, or are you dressed up for Halloween? Hey Mizz Weathermore, can I paint too? I'm pretty good!"

Abby rolled her eyes.

"Are you sure? Sylvie, is it OK?"

His mother shook her head in ascent, then admonished him. "Just make sure you don't step in paint and then track it around the house!"

"Mom," and he pointed to Phillip's feet, shaking his head, "paper shoe covers, really?"

McClure rolled his eyes. He donned another old surgical suit and soon the two boys were rolling as fast as they could, laughing and dividing up the walls to see who could paint the fastest.

"We better make sure it's neat or she'll make us do it over," Phillip whispered.

"Your mom is nice. She's talking to my mom now. Probably talkin' about my Dad and his stuff."

Phillip did not know how to respond. He knew McClure's dad acted strange. *But hey, would I say anything about it? It could make Clure feel bad, but probably that's why Mom won't let me go there.*

McClure was quiet, but his face reddened with embarrassment. Phillip was too kind to say anything about the fights, the moods, and the nasty stuff that hung onto McClure's father like a bad rash. He was glad he could invite McClure over and get him away from his house, knowing that McClure's dad would not be around to spoil the mood. Besides, they were having too much fun.

His mother Sylvie was having fun in the kitchen with Abby Weathermore, and the smell of cinnamon was starting to trump the paint smell. Phillip knew that his mother would see to it that McClure got to enjoy fresh-baked treats. As annoying as his mother could be, Phillip would give her credit for this, that at least on Saturday, the house was filled with good smells and tasty treats. Still, she had been downright annoying lately. He watched McClure sniff at the smells coming from the kitchen.

"You're lucky your mom can bake so good, my mom can't, ya know."

"Ya, I know," replied Phillip, "but you don't know just how *annoying* she can be. Don't let her fool ya! Look how she's got us slaving on a Saturday!" Phillip dipped his roller into the nearly dry pan and fumed in irritation as he rolled the final parts of the wall. McClure nodded his head in agreement and laughed.

"Hey, that widget you showed me last night?" McClure whispered, "I looked up everything, and I can't find any Norwall either. I mean there's not a country, county, or state anywhere on the globe with that name." He pushed his roller up and down the wall, finishing the last of the painting.

"Let's look at it closer in your room. We gotta be wrong. There's something somewhere. We'll look up stuff soon as we're done!"

"Yeah man, let's ditch these stupid duds!"

Phillip slammed his roller into the paint pan, splashing paint onto the dropcloth, and onto his hair, laughing his devious laugh all the while.

CHAPTER 18

The Dirty Room

Whispering now, although not quite sure what they were whispering about, the boys hatched a plan to grab fresh-baked goodies from the oven and get to work in Phillip's room analyzing the mysterious widget.

They just finished the painting when their mothers called them to the kitchen for lunch. Ham and cheese sandwiches on warm kaiser rolls were set out on the long, harvest kitchen table. Signature cinnamon rolls smothered in pure white frosting were set out as dessert.

Phillip and McClure pulled up chairs as Claire struggled, dragging yet another overflowing basket-load to the laundry room. Socks fell out and littered the kitchen floor while she continued to mutter complaints under her breath. McClure noticed that his mother seemed happy here, relaxed, and even more calm than she seemed in their own home.

"Oh, these rolls are the greatest!" Sylvie said as she inhaled deeply, and McClure noticed that she had icing on her lip. She was eating a gooey cinnamon roll dripping with sugary white cream cheese icing. Raisins dotted the top, and Abby had arranged them to look like two eyes and a smile. *In honor of our work crew*, she had said.

"Abby, you sure McClure won't be in the way, it being Saturday and all? He wants to stay here for a bit, that OK?"

"Sylvie, he can stay here as long as he wants. You know that both of you are always welcome. We've got the West Wing all painted now, you know."

What she's really saying is that if my old man goes off the rails we have a place to hide, thought McClure, blushing briefly, embarrassed at the drama his father caused. *That sour look, like he is gonna go ballistic if I even smile, like he's just daring me to be happy, old fart.*

McClure looked down at his worn, broken-down shoes, embarrassed that his father could not stop drinking even though it was destroying their family. None of his friends mentioned his father's drinking, but it was there, silent, like a snake coming out from under a rock. *Everyone probably knows, but no one calls it for what it is,* he thought sadly.

He eyed the sugary cinnamon rolls and reached for one as he finished his sandwich. *So nice to just relax somewhere safe,* he thought. His mother said her goodbyes and hugged him quickly. Soon the boys were locking themselves in Phillip's room.

"This is the biggest mess, you slob!" McClure laughingly chided Phillip.

"How can you live in this wreckage? Go get a trash bag, and I mean a BIG trash bag, com'on man, we can't work in this disaster!" He twirled his phone out of his pocket, and deftly plugged into Phillip's speaker system. *Running Through the Danger Zone* blared as McClure started dancing and snapping his fingers. Simultaneously, he picked clothes up off the floor and tossed them onto the bed.

Phillip complied, sneaking past his mother to the utility room to retrieve a laundry basket and industrial strength trash bags, not sure why he was even sneaking. It just felt fun. Truth be told, he was meticulous about his appearance, but his room was a grand mess. His mother had all but given up the battle. They argued about it to no end. That was the thing about McClure. McClure had not given up on *anything* about him; McClure never would.

Phillip serpentined back to his room out of eyeshot of his mother and Claire. The unexpected ringing of the doorbell forced him to hide behind the clothing rack in the laundry room. He stifled his laughter as Claire, wrapped in her hoodie, toted pillowcases stuffed with dirty laundry and heaved them onto the laundry room floor, narrowly missing Phillip's feet.

"Claire, can you get the door?" their mother called out. Grumbling under her breath, Claire stomped to the foyer, annoyed since she had stayed up late working in her lab and had planned to sleep way past noon.

Opening the front door a crack, it was pushed open by a flighty little French woman named Nesta. Her glasses were perched on the tip of her nose, and most people thought she looked quite like a bird.

"Claire Weathermore, *dahling!*" The woman intoned forcefully.

"Where is your lovely mother and that rascal brother?" Her multicolor striped stockings and her parrot necklace were accessories she always wore. She tossed her head back and cackled loudly, heading right for Freddy's tall, Victorian cage in the front room.

"And just how is that plucky little parrot? Freddy dahling, you look marvelous! Haven't seen you since the last bird fair!" Claire ignored her, walked away and called to her mother.

"Mom, Nesta's here, come talk to her!" Not saying a word, and wrapping her hoodie all the more tightly around herself, Claire headed around the house to collect the trash.

"Nesta!" Abby gave her friend a big bear hug.

"Dahling," Nesta replied excitedly, "how are the Weathermores? And how is that adorable Freddy? I heard the story about how he saved the house from the burning pot of chili, AMAZING! Dahling, can you help with the bird fair in a few weeks? I need help in the booth, and you have learned so much about the African greys, I was hoping you could help rehome several Amazons? No? And maybe those adorable children can help? We always need people to set up the booths."

"Well, I don't know Nesta, can I call you next week?"

"Of course, Dahling! There is ONE thing however, I was wondering of you might bird sit an Amazon that has been put out by his owner, a poor, poor gentleman with a tumor. I told him I was looking for a home, I mean, oh well, a *temporary* home, maybe just for a few weeks? No?"

"Oh Nesta, you know I can't refuse to help, especially after you taught me so much about the African greys. Why, look at how great Freddy is doing!"

With that, the feisty gray parrot with the beautiful scarlett tail feathers proceeded to make explosion and rapid-fire artillery sounds aimed directly at Nesta.

"Oh dear, he never has forgiven me for calling him a Thanksgiving turkey! Well, got to run Weathermores!" With that, she flounced out the front door.

"Bye Nesta. Freddy, manners please!" Abby chided as the little gray bird continued to make explosions and firearm sounds until Nesta was far from sight. As Abby headed back to the kitchen and her baking, Phillip crept stealthily back to his room, clutching several unused black trash bags.

"Waddid ya do, go on a vacay?" asked McClure when Phillip finally returned to their sanctuary. Within thirty minutes they had collected all the dirty laundry and pushed the overflowing basket just outside Phillip's bedroom door. They collected all the trash: empty drink bottles, old school papers, candy wrappers, half-eaten cracker packets, and made room on the desk. They filled two large trash bags with garbage and pushed the trash bags outside Phillip's door. They screamed loudly to alert Claire that there was more laundry, and now also trash. They locked the door and snickered together when they heard her grumbling as she collected it.

"NO MORE you dweebs, no more!!!" she shouted, as she smacked the door with her open hand for emphasis. They covered their faces with their hands and laughed uncontrollably. McClure rolled back on the bed as his ribs shook. They heard her muttering as she dragged the laundry basket and trash bags down the long hall. Laughing, they stripped the sheets and comforter from the bed, shoved it outside into the hallway, and slammed the door shut.

"So, gimme the widget."

McClure fingered the brass widget, noting the gear design, the address, and the inscription.

Najeem's Tailor Shop
1426 Wenderling Way
Norwall

"So weird, that Norwall is all by itself," McClure continued. "You never see just a country, or just a city, and there's no zip code either. Addresses always have a zip code, ya know?"

Phillip had already thought of that. Holding the widget, pushing the gear device with his thumb, he turned it around and around, almost spinning it.

"Come on," he sighed, "let's look one more time." He settled in comfortably in front of his desk-top computer. "We'll look up the street address in the maps program."

The boys entered "Wenderling Way" in the national map search, and could find nothing. They researched Norwall and could find no country, state, or territory anywhere in the world which carried the name. Leaning back in the chair, staring at the ceiling, McClure scratched his head and ran his fingers through his hair, flicking it back.

Phillip threw himself onto the bed, now covered only by a mattress pad. They heard another round of lamentations by Claire as she pulled the dirty linens and bedspread to the laundry room. They shook with laughter, clasping their hands over their mouths to hide the sounds.

"You dweebs think I'm your slave dog?" Claire said, fuming and muttering loud enough for the entire house to hear. Freddy was making dog bark sounds and that infuriated her all the more.

Phillip realized he hadn't told McClure about Pebby yet.

"I saw this dog, this dog with the dry-cleaner guy next to Mom's office. Ya know, I saw this dog, and I went back mostly to see the dog, and the guy gave me the backpack, ya know, the camouflage? And there was this thing in the pocket."

McClure interrupted him.

"What's this thing about a dog now? You never mentioned a dog before, what's with the dog now?"

"I don't know, I don't know. I just saw her, and I don't know. I just saw the vest with the gears, and I just really don't know, there was something about her, the look in her eyes. It's like there's a story in there somewhere, and you know, well, it's like Naji appeared out of nowhere, and he can't really tell me anything, like where they came from. I don't know, there is just something, I don't know, something I just can't figure. I sure would like to get my hands on that dog."

He covered his head with his pillow. McClure sat up, grabbed the widget, and all of a sudden, the conversation got serious.

"OK, so we know there is no Norwall anywhere on the planet. Maybe Naji is an alien, and they took a ship from another planet? "

"What the heck?" His voice drifted off as he stared wide-eyed at his hand. He had been rolling the widget in his hand, and SNAP! All of a sudden, the gears began to click on their own, *click, click, snap,* and they clicked into place. A small curvilinear door on the circumference of the widget slid open, and the pointed end of a key now protruded from the widget.

They stared at each other, locked eyes, and Phillip's eyebrows raised as high as they could possibly go.

"Out...standing!" he muttered, smiling widely. Hearing footsteps coming down the hall, he ran to the door and made sure it was locked.

Still holding the widget, McClure turned it over and over in his hand. The gears did not move now, and there seemed no way to have the key pop back in.

"Tell me more about this dog, Phillip. Tell it to me right from the very beginning. Tell me everything you know."

The Old Pocketwatch

Phillip and McClure were sure of one thing: they had to get back into the dry-cleaning shop to look for clues. All through the week at school they could talk of nothing else but Norwall. They speculated that it was a planet outside the earth's solar system. They opined that there was a tiny rogue country high in the mountains of Nepal from where the man and his little dog had escaped. They constantly invented scenarios to explain everything from Naji's unusual vernacular, to the strange gears on the vest worn by the tiny scruffy dog.

They whispered constantly in class, which did not escape the notice of several teachers and resulted in after-school detention for them both. Detention was a new experience for Phillip, and he embraced it all the more as if the boys were co-conspirators in an adventure that they envisioned outside the realm of teachers and administrators.

McClure sat beside Phillip in most of his classes and he shared his sarcastic sense of humor about the goings-on at the middle school. Not only was McClure a better student than Phillip, but he was an avid reader. He loved mystery stories, magic and mayhem in the form of ridiculous practical jokes. More than once, McClure had been sent to the principal for pranking teachers and other students. There wasn't an insect alive that he wouldn't capture and release later in the vicinity of an unsuspecting and soon-shrieking victim.

This week in fact, he had served detention for not only being late to class, but also for getting caught taking all the toilet paper out of the bathroom stalls and putting it in the recycle bins three days straight. That, following the capture and release of two small lizards into the second floor girls bathroom, led him to serve several more days in after-school detention. For McClure, staying after school meant less time at home. If he was really lucky, he could miss dinner altogether. The hateful old fart would be asleep by the time he trudged home and McClure could dine in his bedroom in peace.

Dinner conversations at his house were littered with his father's acerbic questioning about his schoolwork and his "marks" as his father called his grades. Nothing short of perfect top-of-the-class "marks" was acceptable. His father had an annoying dinnertime habit of slapping the portions of mashed potatoes, a staple of their diet, down on everyone's plate with the admonition, "Eat all you take, and eat all you are given!"

He would sip his beer and sneer, smiling a crooked-toothed smile, and watch McClure choke down every last bit of the mountain of potatoes on his plate. When there was conversation between the three of them, usually his mother left the table crying and McClure was left to face the sarcastic snickering of a man who not only took his family for granted, but delighted in their suffering as well. McClure couldn't remember when he had heard a kind word cross his father's lips, neither to him, nor to Sylvie, his mother.

If only to get him out of the crossfire for a few hours, Sylvie McClure agreed to let him go to the movies with the Weathermores this Friday night, and Phillip was anxious for their contrived plan to unfold. The foundation had been laid earlier in the week when Phillip, with stealth deliberation, had hid his math book in his desk at his mother's office.

As his mother and Claire got ready to leave for the Friday night movie, Phillip texted McClure. The plan was now in motion. When they stopped to pick up his friend, McClure quickly exited his house and hopped into the Weathermore's car without so much as a glance over his shoulder. Phillip gave him a thumb's up and smirked. Claire immediately and perceptively realized that something was afoot.

"What... are you dweebs up to?" she whispered softly, as not to alert her mother, pretending to be interested in the *Smithsonian Magazine*, but sizing up the exchange between the boys. If there was an intrigue in the offing, Claire would not tolerate being left out.

Phillip had spent his free time during the week playing with the widget that McClure had inadvertently switched into a key. No amount of manipulating the little device would turn it back into the widget. *Norwall. Najeem's Tailor Shop, 1426 Wenderling Way, Norwall.* If he could find out where Naji had come from, he could find out where the little scruffy dog had come from, and if she did not have a home, well, maybe there was a chance he could have her for his own. He thought about her almost daily; her mop-top haircut, her long and silky ears, and big brown eyes, too big for her face. The warmth he had felt when he had held her, *outstanding!*

Norwall. He knew that there wasn't a state called Norwall, but it looked like there wasn't a country named Norwall either. In fact, nothing in his research mentioned *anything* named Norwall. He had researched it a million times over, and still, there hadn't been even a trace of a city, state, or country named Norwall. He was brought out of his reverie by a swift kick from McClure. "Oh, Oh, Mom," he cleared his throat and tried to sound both studious and innocent.

"I left my math book at the office, could we get it? We gotta work on math bright and early, right Clure?" Phillip gave McClure a thumbs-up from behind the seat.

Giving a deep sigh, and pulling into a gas station to turn her vehicle around, Abby grumbled. "Phillip, do we really have a choice? We *have* to stop by there now, lucky you told me before I got on the interstate!"

A bit exasperated, she glanced at him in the rear-view mirror. Sliding down out of her view, eyebrows raised, he glanced at Claire, who was trying to make sense of the exchange. The boys kept nudging each other, trying to look sheepishly innocent. Claire was highly suspicious that there were covert activities afoot. She huffed, and crossed her arms in front of her chest.

"I shudda sat in the front, with Mom, not back here with the dweebs," she whispered softly to herself, sighing deeply.

Annoyed, she pulled her hoodie tighter around herself, texting wildly to her friends. As they pulled into the parking lot of the office, Naji and Pebby were just returning from their evening walk. Naji was looking forward to resting upstairs. He was very tired today, and found it hard to breathe deeply. He was becoming short of breath even on the short walk around the complex. It had been a busy day at the cleaners, and the job was pushing him beyond his physical capabilities.

Jumping from the car, Phillip could barely hold his excitement. He could not wait to tell Naji about his spelling test, as well as his invitation to play the national anthem at assembly. His mother waved to Naji and quickly unlocked her office door as she disappeared to retrieve the forgotten book. Claire watched with interest as Phillip scooped up the tiny scruffy dog and hugged her close. She could not resist the temptation to get out of the car and she bounded toward Naji and reached out her hand.

"Hi, I'm Claire, glad to mee'cha, so this is the little pup he's been talking about?"

"Yeah, and this is McClure," Phillip interjected, grabbing McClure by the upper arm and pushing him forward. Phillip held Pebby up so that she could lick Claire's face, and for once, germaphobe Claire didn't mind the licky-lick.

"Look at those silky ears! Good girl, that's a good girl!" She affectionately rubbed the little dog's head as Pebby revelled in the attention. She was just as friendly with McClure. Naji smiled, pleased that Pebby was making friends.

"You are the great engineer?" He opened his arms expansively to welcome Claire.

"Phillip has told me of your achievements. Your mother must be so proud. You have an interest in air filtration, is that right?"

"Actually steam sterilization and neutralization of bacterial and fungal counts in steam purfied industrial air to be exact," Claire boasted proudly.

She was surprised that Naji already knew about her projects. Had Phillip really been paying attention? She didn't think he knew what she was involved in at school. Maybe she had underestimated him; it would not be the first time.

"Well, come in, come in, all of you, please come in," Naji urged. "Rest here until your mother returns! I want to hear all about the backpack and how the week has been at school, and by the way, Phillip, I thoroughly delighted in the nix-lettuce last week! I must remember to thank your benevolent mother for introducing me to a new and highly enjoyable luncheon meal!"

He ushered them into the store lobby, past the threadbare chairs. It was clean, but shabby all the same.

"Nix-lettuce? What did you guys give him? You know how I feel about lettuce!" Claire whispered softly, grinning at Phillip. She took it all in; the faded, framed Florida beach pictures, the old silk plant adorning the corner, the worn, patched chair cushions, the torn and outdated magazines. Claire noticed that the place needed a good dusting. The counters were clean however, and she pulled up a stool and leaned on her elbows. Phillip put Pebby down, and she ran over to grab a drink of water.

"Well," Phillip started, "first, I just nailed my spelling test, no sweat!"

He continued, rolling his eyes, and looking at the ceiling as though he was being forced to recount the successful week at school.

"After that, Mr. Haney picked me to play the anthem at the assembly next week!" Taking a deep breath, he continued. "Claire helped me organize my new backpack with folders so that I can find all my papers now! I tell you Naji, I'm on it now, no doubt!" Phillip slammed his fist down on the counter for added emphasis. Claire tried so hard not to laugh that she was biting the inside of her mouth.

"Well, champion, looks as if you are moving closer to the prize!" Naji reached down and picked up the tiny scruffy dog and rubbed her head. He handed her to Phillip who cuddled her unashamedly.

"Remember our bargain? You improve on your lessons, and you shall have time with our tiny champion. You are becoming a leader!" Smiling broadly at Phillip, he turned his attention quickly to Claire.

"Now tell me all about your steam project. Would you call yourself a scientist? Are you considered, let's say, an in...ventor?"

"More of a design engineer," she replied, flattered at the attention.

"I enjoy inventing new safety ideas for people who have to work every day. I want to design for big companies, so that they don't forget about the little people!"

Naji drew closer, anxious to hear about these so-called "little-people." Were there really miniature people here?

"Think I'll refill her water, Naji, OK?" Phillip wandered back farther in the shop toward the industrial sized sink and he saw a table where Naji had been folding laundry. His eyes were immediately drawn to a pocket watch lying open on the table. The top of the watch was decorated with tiny gears. The gears seemed to be burnished-copper and gold, and they were slowly turning. Phillip thought it was probably an antique, as it looked very old.

On the inside top of the pocketwatch was a sepia picture of a tall, slender woman dressed in Victorian-style clothes. Phillip could barely make out her features. He thought he had seen her somewhere before, but he couldn't remember where. *She kind'a looks like someone I should know?* The background sky was cloudy and her hair was quite windblown. Interestingly enough, there seemed to be some kind of unusual airplane in the sky behind her. Phillip had never seen anything like it before. *What the heck?*

She was holding a tinydog, and the dog seemed to be wearing a black derby. Phillip just could not help himself. He took out his phone and snapped a picture. Raising both eyebrows, he furtively and quickly snapped several pictures in rapid succession. Hearing his mother entering the front of the shop and calling his name, he slid the phone back in his pocket and quickly joined the rest of the group.

CHAPTER 20

Grooming Time

Merry McGuttchen was anything but merry. To everyone who came in contact with her, she was a disgruntled, complaining old nag. Some even called her "Naggy Haggy". But she was tight with Gleena Gleeson, and she had been appointed proprietress of the Groomerly Grooming Salon, a place dedicated to keeping the delivery dogs looking their best. Merry and Gleena together had championed for an inviting environment, so the entire inside of the salon was painted a soft yellow. The workers, mostly teenage girls, wore pinafore aprons over soft gray pants and shirts. The yellow-striped pinafores had ruffles on the shoulders and decorative white piping. These were the most beautiful work uniforms in Norwall. The uniform shoes were a darker gray, and the girls were permitted to wear soft yellow ribbons and other yellow cloth pieces as ornaments in their hair.

This afternoon, one of the uniformed girls was brooming the reception area. Treena Trembly was wiping her eyes on the sleeve of her shirt and trying not to cry as she swept. Despite her best efforts, Merry had been displeased with her efforts grooming a larger working cart dog. The dog had been too rambunctious for Treena to control. When she tried to cut his nails he leapt off of the grooming table, shook loose hair all over the floor, and bolted for the door.

In quite a frenzy, Merry had given chase, wrestled him down, slipped on the wet floor, sprained her already bad back and got covered in dog hair and debris. Treena had received a harsh dressing-down and a formal reprimand for not controlling the dog. She would lose an entire day off, as well as her lunch ration for three days straight. Her eyes were red and her head was down as she swept the front lobby. Her long, dark ponytail was still tied back with a yellow bow, but wisps of long hair had escaped during the morning frenzy. Her usually immaculate appearance was compromised.

Suddenly, she saw the tinydog with the black velvet derby bolt through the dog aperture and come to a screeching halt in front of her. Pebby tilted her head and stared at Treena. She knew something was quite wrong, and that she had arrived just in time to bring some comfort. Sure enough, Treena brightened and broke into a wide smile.

"Pebby! I'm so glad to see ya! Come to Mamma!" She dropped to the floor as the black-coated, silver-eared dog tossed off the derby, shook out her mop top, and rushed into Treena's arms. Giving her face three quick and wet licky-licks, she rolled over in Treena's arms to get a belly rub. Treena laughed, then remembered she was on thin ice with Merry and she clasped her hand over her mouth.

"Oh, always gotta get da' belly rub, don'cha?" she whispered into the ear of the tiny scruffy dog. "What's going on with Deen?" Pebby pushed the grooming token Deen had tied lovingly to her harness toward Treena. Seeing the marking he had scratched on its back, she smiled and dried the last traces of tears from her eyes. He had engraved the word HOPE on the token.

"Hope? Really Deen, hope? That's about all we got left!" She wiped her watery nose with the back of her hand, quickly dropping the token into her apron pocket.

"Well, come'on pretty girl, let's git started! First, you know, into the bath you go!"

Pebby knew the routine and she could hardly wait. First came the warm soapy bath which soothed her tired, overworked muscles. The water was heated by giant rotating steam turbines at the back of the shop; the hissing steam muffled conversations. Treena soaped Pebby as she updated her on the gossip at The Groomerly. She told her how Jack the cart dog bolted off the grooming table, and she detailed how Merry had slipped on the floor, resulting in the loss of Treena's three lunches.

Treena scrubbed Pebby gently but thoroughly, using a soft cloth to clean around her eyes. She cleaned her ears gently, and brushed her teeth. She rinsed the tinydog with crystal clear water and applied coat conditioner, working it in until her coat was soft and silky. She gave special attention to the long and silky ears, lovingly working the treatment into every strand of the hair. After a final rinse, Pebby was wrapped in the softest pale yellow towels and carried to the drying table. Treena cuddled the little dog as she carried her, and Pebby cherished every second of the warmth and love she was given. As Treena did the comb-out, the spinning gears of the dryers gave a soft, warm breeze. Resting comfortably, Pebby started to snooze, but was brought back to the reality of having a nail trim, her least favorite part of the grooming.

Next came the trimming of the coat, and Treena took extra care to give Pebby the perfect cut. As she trimmed her, she hugged her gently, making sure that Merry was busy in the back. Crabby old Merry McGuttchen did not like any groomer to show too much attention to any one dog. After all, they were there only because they were critical to the delivery of foodstuffs. Merry, being a no-nonsense proprietress like Gleena, would broker no foolishness, and no favoritism. She would think nothing of disposing of an animal or a groomer for that matter, who did not follow the rules.

"Pebby, sure would like to just walk down the street with ya, get me out of this shop. Just for a day, all I'm asking for is a day free out in the sunshine, ya know? I'm stuck here day after day, ya know, my bunk is in the back of the shop in the Habitron with the other groomers, and old Merry watches every move we make with that sour face o' hers, never a kind word, never a kindness." She felt her eyes swell as she continued brushing Pebby.

"I ain't seen Deen for ages. How's he doin' now, kin ya tell me?"

Pebby nodded her head, shaking her ears to fluff them out. She gave several short licky-licks to Treena's hand for comfort. Her heart broke for the sadness, but what could anyone do? *It was work, work, go, go and... GO! each and every day.* They were all so tired that nothing else mattered but trying to get some rest.

Treena leaned close brushing her ears, and Pebby perked up to pay attention as Treena whispered.

"Pebby, listen closely. I want you to take this grooming token to Naji. Don't, and I mean don't let anyone else see it! I knows that you spend your nights at Naji's, God knows it's better than the floor at the Habitron! I am going to put some bows on ya, I know you don't like 'em, but just for today, just for today girl, take this to Naji. People set such store by him. You know, he used to be the leader. They say, way long ago, Naji used to be in charge. Take ya' this token from Deen, and I'll tie a yellow grooming ribbon on it, that way he'll know it's from me. I remember Naji's shop, and goin' with me mum to look in the windows. Yep, I think he was the Governor or somethin' like that. Anyway, perfect, ya look perfect!" Replacing the derby and vest on the tinydog, Treena hugged her so long and so tightly she thought she would never let go.

"Remember, we are family, you and I, an' I love ya so, no matter what. I love ya, tinydog, and I'll always look out for ya. Now, go, go, and... GO! before Merry gets on to us, and ya watch for the Automats! Head straight to Naji's cause it'll be gitin' dusk and it won't do for ya to be roaming' streets when the delivery dogs are in for the night! Now go, go,and... GO!"

Setting her down, she straightened the dog's vest, and as Pebby headed for the aperture she gave a last look back over her shoulder and nodded her head to say thank you. She carefully made certain the grooming token was hidden by the bow. The cobblestone streets were deserted now, the curfew in effect, and short of Automatons patrolling and the occasional hiss of the steam cleaning machines, the town was quiet. The Habitrons were on lock-down for evening curfew.

Pebby trotted at a moderate pace, still relaxed from the grooming but troubled by the information from Treena. Everywhere she went, folks were asking about Naji Najeem. Had he really once been a leader of the people? What had happened to change the lives of her friends? Naji had been her friend too, and her protector. He had made a place for her and shared his food with her. And yet, maybe she really did not know him at all. Maybe there was more to Naji than the tailor shop. But as she tried to sort it out she noticed an Automaton following her slowly and steadily, watching her closely, looking for an excuse to hunt her down. Gears spun quietly on his back as puffs of steam wafted up from his head-pipe. She was closing in on 1426 Wenderling Way, third store down on the right. Speeding up, she bolted through the oval aperture at the bottom of the stairs, breathing a deep sigh of relief. Safety. And for now, *home.*

CHAPTER 21

The Scary Walk Home

The boys could talk of nothing else. They had snapped a picture they felt surely would give them the low-down on the mysterious tailor as well as the tiny scruffy dog that increasingly infatuated Phillip. Whether it was the unusual leather vest dotted with burnished gears, or the almost sad look in her eyes, Phillip was clearly besotted with her. Of course, the Victorian style dress of the woman could be only a costume. But, there was no denying the fact that the dog in the photo was a dead ringer for Pebby, and there was a strange-looking flying machine against the background of the clouds. They trudged along in the suffocating moist heat of the afternoon as they headed to McClure's house.

"Hey, Dude, why this dog? Get your mom to take you to the shelter. Plenty of dogs to pick from, why this dog? I mean, she is kinda a girl's dog if ya know what I mean, those long cute ears and those big sad eyes, well, ya know what I mean, don'cha?" McClure stammered, not wanting to demean his friend's choice.

"Hey, Dude," Phillip interjected, "sometimes you pick the dog, sometimes the dog picks you, and anyway, what do you make of the crazy vest she has?"

Phillip started humming and snapping his fingers, ignoring McClure's comments on the scruffy dog. He remembered when they got Moushka. They were travelling in Pennsylvania, near the Amish farms. The Weathermores had ridden old steam engines back into the Pennsylvania countryside and visited the Strausburg Railway Museum. Phillip had climbed all over the old trains and had taken a lesson in running a miniature railroad. For reasons he could not now recall, they had toured a farm and visited its kennel. He remembered seeing all the dogs, mostly Malamutes and Huskies, lying peacefully on the cool concrete floors of the pens.

One dog in particular jumped to greet his family and he wagged his tail uncontrollably when they patted his head. When they left, the dog intensely watched them leave and jumped high on his back legs up and down, trying to leave his enclosure. No longer the quiet pup, he became the whimpering, left-behind pup. They could hear him baying and crying as they unlocked the car and drove away. The next day, they returned to the farm and took him home. They called him Moushka, and he had been their constant companion ever since.

Phillip chuckled to himself. His mother had told him, sometimes you don't pick the dog, sometimes the dog picks you, which certainly seemed to be true. Phillip smiled to think that this tinydog was picking him. *But, what if she already has a home somewhere else? What if she already belonged to someone, and that someone was missing her?* He felt his stomach tumble, and his heart race. He hoped with all his heart that she wanted to belong to him.

He was brought back to the present by the musty, dank smell of the neighborhood. The walk had turned a bit creepy, what with trash littering the sidewalk and overflowing trash cans. Many of the dirty, worn plastic cans were pushed to the curb, forcing the boys to dodge them. Phillip could smell the poorness; it hung in the air like an enveloping fog. He could taste a dirty sour-smell just by breathing the air. The canopy of trees presented a frightening tunnel, and in places the crooked, cracked sidewalk was slippery and slimy with gray-green mildew stains. Phillip's mother had expressly forbidden him from going to McClure's house. It was unspoken between the boys, and the reason was never discussed. Phillip was starting to understand his mother's reasons.

He saw for the first time what his friend endured every day when he went home. He understood now why McClure tried to stay late at school, and why he loved to spend time with the Weathermores. He felt sorry that he had not asked McClure to come over to his house more often. *I didn't go out of my way to help him*, he thought, and he was filled with guilt and remorse. He vowed to do better.

"Remind me why we walked all this way?" Phillip was out of breath, sweating, and regretting that he had forgotten his water bottle. His shoes were getting dirty as well, and that irritated him.

"He used to fly for the government, remember?" added McClure.

"Remind me how grounded I will be if my mom finds out where I am? Remind me please! Why am I risking everything?" Phillip waved his arms expansively.

"Hey, Dude," McClure added, "remember, my dad knows planes. If *anyone* has seen a machine like this, he'll know about it." McClure was getting tired too.

"And why, oh why, do I have to be here for this? Can't *you* just ask him? I mean *show him the picture and ask him*! What's the big deal?"

Sweating, and sorry he had worn his canvas black vest over a long-sleeved gray t-shirt tucked into heavy black jeans, McClure answered hesitantly.

"It's just that he goes bonkers when I ask him anything. He finds a way to down me. Anytime I ask anything, it ends up with him calling me a loser. If I stick up for myself, the yelling starts, gets louder and louder, and then my mom comes in to quiet him down, and well, he gets really mean. I've seen him shove her."

Phillip threw his head back and laughed demonically out loud, to McClure's consternation. "So, I get it, I'm the distraction!!!"

Still laughing, Phillip leaned over, then rose dramatically with the loudest demonic laugh he could muster.

"Woohaaa!!!" Then suddenly, he stopped as he saw what was ahead. They were approaching the front steps now, slimy with a combination of green algae and black mildew. Cracks in the concrete steps made them crooked. Overgrown spindly trees gave the appearance that they were walking into a dark tunnel. Four very wide steps led to a broken sidewalk, and four more wide wooden steps led to the front door which was in need of both a good scrubbing and a coat of paint.

"Welcome to paradise!" McClure laughed as he pulled a key from his backpack and unlocked the front door.

"Hi, boys!" his mom called from the back of the house. They walked past a living room where a lanky, near-bald man with a few tufts of gray hair on each side of his head lay snoring on the brown leather couch. The bottoms of his feet were brown with soot and he had them propped on the pillows. He wiggled his toes as he slept, and Phillip thought he looked like he had just crawled out from underneath the car, grease stains on his clothes, stained old white undershirt harboring a few holes. He smelled stale. He smelled old.

A paper plate of half eaten fried chicken and yellow potato salad lay on the floor by his head, and

Phillip thought he saw a cigarette butt sticking up from the potato salad.

The man heaved another snore, grunted, and turned over and curled up into a fetal position. He smacked his lips and wiggled his toes as Phillip wrinkled his nose and crept silently away. He followed McClure into the kitchen.

"Hey, Honey," McClure's mother gave him a quick kiss on the top of his head. "Just doin' a little work here," she giggled. Newspapers and magazines were spread over the table along with scraps of paper where she had been clipping coupons.

"Now, you let your Dad sleep, his shoulder is bothering him again. Can I make you guys a snack?"

"Sure, Mom. Hey, Mom, is it OK if we work in my room awhile? We got a project."

"Oh sure, just be quiet as mice!" She raised a finger to her mouth, letting out a quiet *shhh*. "Let your father sleep! Now go on, I'll bring a sandwich up in a bit. Hey, Phillip, how's your mom? When is she picking you up? How's the house coming? Painted more walls? We sure could use your painting skills here, ya know?"

Phillip didn't mention that he had coerced Claire into picking him up. She would be outside McClure's house in two hours, but in return he would clean the cat litter for a solid week if she would not breathe a word to their mother. Phillip looked at the cracks in the walls in the tiny kitchen and noticed the dried food hardened onto the stove. The sink was stained and yellow, and the small round table covered with a plastic tablecloth had barely room for three people to sit. Dirty dishes littered the counter and cheap plastic cups of different sizes and colors, some still half filled, were everywhere. He wondered if it was even safe to eat here. *But I'm starving!*

He knew it would take more than an afternoon of painting to clean up this place and he felt sorry for his friend, who did not seem to notice the dank, dark, cluttered place. *Or maybe he did*, thought Phillip, *but what the heck can Clure do about it?* He felt a deep-down sadness, guilt for enjoying so much while his friend had so very little, and yet Phillip had never heard him complain.

McClure led the way as his mother returned to her coupon clipping. Climbing the carpeted stairs slowly, McClure pushed open the door to his room. Phillip saw a long, cylindrical insect scurry across the carpeted hallway and run into the room across the hall. Phillip could not help himself, and he stared intently at the little bug and followed it.

Peeking inside and pushing the door open slightly, Phillip saw an unmade bed topped by a tattered comforter which was rolled into a giant ball. A rocking chair sat mournfully in the corner, covered with folded but worn-out bath towels. Clothes littered the floor, and underneath lacy window curtains on a small, particle board desk sat an outdated console computer monitor. Beside it was a small three-shelf particle board bookshelf, with Robert McClure's collection of aviator textbooks and weathered torn tomes on the history of aviation. *Maybe, just maybe,* Phillip thought, *we can get some answers.*

One thing Phillip had to give to McClure, his room was spotless. Small trophies lined shelves above his desk, attesting to the many academic contests he had won. His presentation of the courtroom soliloquy of Atticus Finch had won him statewide honors in the last Junior Thespian competition. He remained at the top of his class in math as well as science, and this honor had yielded certificates which were neatly framed and displayed.

There were two large posters for *Revolutions of the Ages,* his favorite video game. Both boys plopped down on the bed which was covered by a worn, but clean red, white, and blue quilt. Not one dirty piece of clothing, not one speck of dust, could be found in the room.

"Dude," Phillip whispered, "I just gotta know, does the closet look this good too?"

"Watch, and learn!" McClure said expansively as he pulled open the worn bifold doors to show the clothes organized by color, mostly white, black, and gray, and t-shirts neatly folded and stacked. Four pairs of worn, but clean, shoes sat neatly on the floor. Phillip was amazed.

"Wow! Outstanding! All I can say is wow!" You a freakin' Julia Child or something!"

"You mean Marie Kondo, dude?" McClure laughed. "No, I just would rather stay in my room than deal with downstairs, know what I mean?"

"Got it!" Phillip shook his head up and down affirmatively. He had a new appreciation for his own surroundings and respect for his friend who endured so much, but succeeded where others failed. Even still, he had never once heard McClure complain. Not ever.

"OK, do you know what to do?" McClure queried.

"Tell my Dad that we are working on a project and Suarez gave us this picture and said to write a story, blah, blah, blah, about the picture. Thing is, due Wednesday, and we need help fast!" He paused briefly, heaving a big sigh.

"Then, I will ask him to give us a clue, ya know, tell him he is the best with planes, and give us a clue. Like, has he ever flown one of these? I mean, he was in the military, so if this is a Russian spy plane, well, we thought he might know, I mean, Russia, China, no matter, all the same."

Phillip pulled up the picture which he had carefully saved on his phone, and tried to make out the details in the picture: the wind swirling wildly behind the woman, her clothing, the hat on the dog suggesting another place and time. Whatever was in the smoke clouds behind her had a face like a dragon. Behind the face, where the body should be, was a cylinder with gigantic fan blades attached to its back.

McClure's mother knocked lightly and opened the door.

"Sandwiches, guys!" She smiled broadly as she set a tray on the desk. Two paper plates each held a dark-bread sandwich and Phillip was pleased to see lettuce sticking out the side. She had tossed some chips on the plates and poured two glasses of milk. Store-bought cookies rounded out their dinner.

"Thank you, Ms. McClure." Phillip wondered if they ever all ate dinner together.

"Mom, we wanted to ask Dad a question about an airplane. When will he wake up?"

"Supposed to wake him at five o'clock for supper. You know how he likes to eat right on the dot. How about I call you guys down when I wake him? That okay?"

"Sure, Mom," McClure added, ashamed that his father was always sleeping in the middle of the day. He was also ashamed that his mother cleaned the Weathermore's office on the weekends, which supplemented his father's monthly retirement check from the Air Force. He had once served as a pilot.

Sylvie McClure disappeared down the stairs as quickly as she had come, treading lightly on the steps to avoid waking her husband for another thirty minutes. Meanwhile, the boys devoured the sandwiches and polished off the cookies. They got out their homework, and studied science furiously. Phillip had not forgotten his promise to get his grades up. He was enjoying his new-found status at the upper end of the grading curve. His teachers were treating him with new-found respect, and his mother was pleased as punch at the improvements. He had to admit, most of the improvement was because he stopped turning in assignments late, or stopped merely not turning them in at all.

Nevertheless, when five o'clock had come and gone, Phillip was getting impatient. Claire would be outside at six o'clock, and Robert McClure had yet to stir from his afternoon stupor. Just when Phillip took out his phone and looked at the Victorian picture for the millionth time, Sylvie McClure tapped softly on the door.

"Hey, boys, Dad's up and having dinner. Come down in a few minutes, OK?" she whispered softly. Phillip wondered why everyone in the McClure household seemed to whisper in the middle of the day, as if they would wake sleeping tigers. Phillip was growing increasingly uncomfortable with a queasy feeling in the pit of his stomach. He had a funny feeling this was going to end badly.

CHAPTER 22

The Bad Meatloaf

Tiptoeing so as to not make noise, the boys crept quietly down the stairs. To the left was the living room, which still smelled like old cigarettes. To the right, hunched over the kitchen table, sat Robert McClure.

Strands of greasy dark hair fell over the front of his face, but he was actually almost bald. Phillip tried not to notice the rips in his stained white t-shirt, and the crude way he hunched over his food as if he were a fox getting ready to devour a frightened rabbit. It was obvious that dinner would be quick and brisk. Sylvie set the small plate of meatloaf and lumpy mashed potatoes in front of him immediately after he slurped the soup. Phillip noticed that Mrs. McClure was not eating; she served Mr. McClure, clearing dishes away as he ate. There were no places set for the boys, and Phillip was just as glad; the meatloaf looked gray and unappetizing. *Oh please, oh please, don't set a plate of that in front of me!* he thought. He worried he would be expected to politely eat it.

"Well, boys, come on in, come on in!" Robert McClure gestured expansively, waving the boys into his inner sanctum.

"And you must be Phillip? It is Phillip, right? Isn't your mom a doc? Must be nice, havin' all that dough rollin' in, right Sylvie?" He sneered and gave a short *humph.*

"Not that much, sir, and she has to work really hard," Phillip replied softly, not wanting to let the insult to his mother pass unchallenged.

"Yep, cake-eaters, that's what I call the rich-folk, cake-eaters. Ye'ver heard that?" He laughed demonically, then quickly returned to a pinched, serious facade.

"No, Sir, haven't heard that one," Phillip gave a little chuckle trying to humor the elder McClure, and continued. "I hear you know airplanes, Sir. I hear that you know 'em better than anyone around, Sir," Phillip was nervous now. "Is that right?"

"Guess you could say that," the elder McClure replied, nodding his head and tapping the fork on the plate to a tune only he could hear.

"Guess the Air Force wouldn't keep me on if I didn't know sometin', right Sylvie?"

"Oh yes, Robert, you were the best pilot they ever had, and you've got medals to prove it!"

"Still am, Sylvie, still am, and you don't forget that!" He pointed a fork at her as she looked down, embarrassed at the chiding.

Forgetting his best days were far behind him, Robert McClure puffed up and continued. "Wasn't anyone who could flip a plane like me," he boasted, shoveling in more meatloaf and talking with his mouth full, still pointing with the fork. "Squadron leader I was, with every last one tryin' to git me! But none could! Notta one could git the job done, 'ceptin me!"

Phillip tried to look interested, but his mind was on the picture.

"So, Mr. McClure, have you ever seen a ship like this?"

Pulling out his phone, he pulled up the picture that he had stared at all week. Gingerly getting up from his chair, he stood beside Robert McClure. A sour, acrid smell almost made him wrinkle his nose, but he dared not flinch.

"Let's see it, com'ere. Sylvie, gimme my glasses. Where's the damm glasses?"

"Robert, your language. The boys." Sophie nodded her head toward Phillip and she admonished Robert McClure cautiously and quietly.

Perching his cracked, dirty, wire-rimmed frames on the edge of his nose, Mr. McClure focused on the picture. Whether it was the tinydog wearing a derby in the foreground, or the tall woman in Victorian dress, or the clouds of smoke half-covering a gear-driven steamship, whatever the reason, he furrowed his brow, shook his head back and forth, and pushed the glasses back up his nose frowning severely.

"What teacher did this to you? Just who is pranking you? This thing is out of a fantasy book!" Shaking his head slowly back and forth, he continued.

"Who ever gave you this assignment is messin' wiff yous. This is some fantasy machine. Ain't nothing like it in this world!"

He laughed, throwing his head back. Phillip noticed that a piece of meatloaf was still on his lip. He was laughing almost hysterically, wiping his mouth with the back of his hand. Phillip watched the tiny piece of meatloaf drift downward and land unnoticed on the stained, yellowed t-shirt.

In the blink of an eye, Robert McClure stopped laughing. He became dead serious, ripping off his glasses and tossing them recklessly onto the table. He took a deep breath in, bit his bottom lip, and rotated his head to make full, intense focus on the boys, who were both wide-eyed and terrified.

Sylvie McClure had her back turned, quietly washing dishes at the sink, pretending that there was nothing to be concerned about.

"You boys wouldn't be tricking me, would'ja?" He stared at them intently, his upper lip curling into a snarl. "You boys think I'd fall for some trick, did youse? Wha'd ya take me for, some fool? This ain't no flying machine of this entire universe, got that? I don't know what ya'll are thinkin' except that I'm some *fool*? Is that what this is about?"

Phillip slid the phone back into his pocket. McClure grabbed Phillip's jacket sleeve under the table, trying to pull him away as Robert McClure continued his tirade.

"You boys makin' fun o'me? Is that what this is?"

"No, Dad, no way, we just never seen a ship like that before, and the teacher wanted us to figure it out."

Rising from the table, the elder McClure pushed his plate away, sending it spinning across the table.

"I've a mind to go to that school tomorrow and check it out. How would that be?" Raising his eyebrows, he smiled sardonically.

The younger McClure dropped his head. His father had never even been to his school. He doubted his old man even knew where the school was.

"Oh, I know, better'n that, I have a good mind to ground you for a week, that's right, no movies, no nothin'. Sit in your room for a week, meals and all, and read a book on da' history of flying machines. Seems like you shoulda' done youse' homework fore you try to pull one over on me, now off wich' ya!!" Robert McClure, forgetting that Phillip was there, staggered pompously back to the couch in the adjoining room, muttering all the while.

Sylvie McClure, unfazed, continued to hum to herself as she washed dishes in the small, stained sink.

Phillip grabbed McClure's forearm tightly and whispered, "Sorry, man... sorry, sorry, I'm so sorry!"

Phillip looked down and wrinkled his brow. He bit his curled lip and clenched his teeth. McClure looked down too. Both boys were frozen, afraid to move lest the monster begin another ranting tirade.

Then, unexpectedly, loudly, thankfully, pounding on the front door with the flat of her hand when she discovered the doorbell was broken, was Claire.

CHAPTER 23

The Pitter Patter Rescue

I t took not even one minute for Claire to see that something was terribly wrong with Phillip. He leaned back in the car seat, held his stomach, and exhaled a big breath.

"He's grounded, freakin' grounded! For what? I was the one who took the picture out, not him, it was me!" He made a big circle with his arm and pointed his thumb at his chest. "ME, *me!*"

Rubbing his hands on his face, he covered his eyes with his open hands as if the nightmare of what he had just seen was too much for him to bear. His chest heaved a few more times, then he was silent.

Claire concentrated on driving safely. It was dark and the streets were narrow. Trash cans were pushed out into the street and she had to keep turning on the high beams to avoid smacking into one of them.

"What in the name of heaven came down in there?" She looked at him with pity as she spoke. "What kind of place is that anyway?"

"Hell on earth, if you ask for my opinion," Phillip answered solomnly while he stared straight ahead. Then, he continued, "His mother just stands there doin' dishes like nothing's happening, while the old fart freaks out, raises his lip like some animal, and grounds him flat for nothing, I mean *for nothing*. He thought we were pranking him!"

"What were you even doing in that house? Mom would freak out if she knew. Why'd you even go there?"

"It's all about a picture." Phillip was almost in tears, but he was holding back, sniffing his runny nose. "We just showed him a picture. See, there was this picture, and we were not sure if it was a spy machine. It was surrounded by a smokey sky, so it was hard to make it out. It was some crazy flying machine that we are trying to figure out, and we thought that since he used to be a pilot, he would be able to tell us where the ship came from, ya' know?"

"Whoa, whoa, whoa!" Claire raised her hand off the steering wheel motioning him to stop. "Picture? Where did this picture come from? Is this something from school? What the devil is this all about?"

Phillip cradled his head in his hands and sniffed, taking in big, deep sighs. He felt so alone. In desperation, he began. "You have to swear on your life not to tell Mom. Swear Claire, swear. You can never tell her how I got the picture. I mean it, you have to swear."

"Have you done something you shouldn't?" she raised her eyebrows quizzically.

"No, no, no, nothin' like that. I just saw this picture on someone's watch, and I thought it was weird, so I took a picture with my phone. That's all. I mean it, that's all!"

"If it's no big deal, then why the secret?"

"Because, Claire, this is my deal, all mine this time."

"Whadda ya mean, 'all mine this time' Whadda' ya mean, what the heck is all yours?"

She pulled the car off the road into a gas station.

"I am not moving till you tell me what the heck is coming down. I mean, I gotta know! What is causing all the drama, the arm waving, all the grounding, I mean, all this drama? What's it about?"

"Claire, every time you get into something, you take over. This is my thing. This is my mess, and that's gonna' be my dog!"

"What? What mess, and what dog? Something about Moushka? He belongs to everyone, it's just that Mom mostly walks him. What's wrong with Moushka?"

"You've got it wrong. I mean the tinydog, Naji's Pebby. Did you know she's not really his dog? Did ya? He's just keeping her till he figures out who she really belongs to. I mean, since she really doesn't belong to him, I mean to have her for *me*. Just me. Something that is *only mine*. I mean, Claire you've got them cats, Mom's got Moushka and Freddy, so I need something that belongs to me. I gotta have *something* that I figure out all by myself!"

He looked at her pleadingly, dolefully, and she realized for the first time how she tended to take over. She saw clearly now, by trying to help, she had really not let him succeed on his own. Although she never had done it with even a hint of malice, she could see how her brash, easy self confidence could intimidate *anyone*.

He was not like her. Things did not come easy for him. But, he had something she did not. He had determination, and a steadfast resolve that she admired. She had done wrong by not encouraging his independence; she wished that more times, especially of late, she had encouraged him to take the lead. Still, all her efforts had been from her kind, good heart. She had seen how proud he was now that he was succeeding in school. His growing self esteem helped him rise even more; she wanted to be there to applaud him in whatever he did. His sincerity and honesty almost took her breath away. She inhaled deeply, then thoughtfully replied. "OK, I get it. How about I just help you figure out this picture, and you don't even have to tell me where you got it? I'll just look and tell you what I think, no questions, no telling Mom, nothing more unless you ask me to. OK?"

Phillip exhaled deeply and was quiet. He had no reason not to not trust the deal Claire was offering. Whatever faults he found in Claire, he had to admit, she was a keeper of her word. If she promised not to tell their mother, she wouldn't. But, whether she would try to jump in and figure out the mystery of fourteen-twenty-six Wenderling Way, he didn't want to know. He could not take that risk. He decided then and there that he wouldn't let her know about the clockwork key, and he wouldn't let her know about sneaking around Naji's shop either.

Gingerly, he pulled his phone from his pocket. First, he texted McClure a short "Hey" just to see if the elder McClure had confiscated his son's phone. Getting no reply, he quickly pulled up the photograph of the watch and carefully handed it off to Claire. He took off his glasses and rubbed his eyes with both fists. He was tired; the trauma of the long school day followed by the drama at the McClure household had exhausted him. Claire squinted, enlarged the picture, and squinted again.

"OK, OK, first," and she cleared her throat, trying to be analytical, her keen powers clicking into action. "First, it looks like this is an old-timey photo, you know, the lady's dress is Victorian, probably late 18th-century England. Those must be the ancestors of that scruffy dog. Sure looks just like her, but why is she wearing a hat? Looks like a derby, and weird, the vest has little designs, looks like maybe gears? Didn't Pebby have a vest with gears? Maybe it really *is* Pebby and they were in costume? Have you thought of that? You know, like when we went to the old timey place and you got a picture in that cowboy gear?"

Phillip thought, *she is jumping all over the place in a million different directions, but that's Claire. Darn smart, but all over the place in a New York minute.*

"Yeah, Yeah, I remember that. Maybe it is a costume. It sure looks like Pebby though, and what do you make of the smoke? Does it look like something on fire?"

"No, it does *not* look like anything on fire, it looks more like steam than smoke. I think it is dirty air, like steam, but terribly dirty. Looks like steam, sure does. See, you don't see flames, or anything burning, and the buildings aren't on fire. What buildings I *can* see look like they are dirty and covered in soot."

"Yeah, I see what you mean. What about that airship? Recognize anything?" Phillip queried, starting to breathe easier.

"Ya know?" Claire scratched the top of her head, snapping an elastic hair tie as she pulled her long hair into a ponytail, "Ya know, have you ever read Jules Verne? H.G. Wells? Kinda looks like the flying machines in their books. It certainly doesn't look like something from this century. I mean, the Hindenburg and all the dirigibles weren't until the

1920's or so, and that does *not* match with the Victorian dress.

Phillip could not contain his disappointment. This was no help at all. All Claire was doing was confusing him. "Look, Claire, I'll tell you. The photo was in Naji's pocketwatch. He left it out by the sink. When I was getting Pebby her water, I saw it, and I thought it could help me figure where she came from. I really wasn't trying to spy on him. Mom would have a fit!"

"Yeah, you're right. Sneaking around taking photos of people's photos, she won't be a happy camper on that one."

"Wait. He said I could have Pebby for a day. What if we ask him to come over, and while I am playing with her, you scope him out? Ask what time it is, and see if he gets out the watch, and ask him who's in the picture?"

"Could work, could work. That's assuming he brings the watch, and the picture is still in the watch, and we keep Mom out of the way too."

Relieved, Phillip relaxed back in the seat. For the first time in hours, he could let his shoulders relax. He had a new respect for Miss Pitter-Patter-Perfect, and maybe, just maybe he had been a little too mean to her two smellicats. He smiled as he thought of misting their faces with the plant sprayer. He took deep breaths and started to almost doze, but the ringing of Claire's cell phone brought him back to reality. It was their mother, wondering where in the heck they were. They looked at each other, and froze.

CHAPTER 24

The Workroom

The aperture behind her snapped shut. The whirring, puffing, angry Automaton did a three-hundred-and-sixty-degree spin in front of Najeem's Tailor Shop. Pebby had made it just in time; there was a strict curfew in Norwall, even for the delivery dogs. Movement after nightfall was *expressly* forbidden.

She had spent more time than usual at each of her delivery sites and she definitely had spent more time than usual at The Groomerly. But Treena kept watch on the schedule for the more important deliveries, and she knew that Pebby had an upcoming delivery to the Council Breakfast during their quarterly meeting at the Norwall City Center.

Treena had taken care to make her cut just perfect so that no criticism could come to Pebby. Some of the Council wanted to do away with the delivery dog system and switch to a specialized Delivery Automaton that was in the process of being perfected. Delivi-bots they were called, and the Council had entertained the idea of these steam powered units replacing the dogs, who required food, shelter, and maintenance.

Well, she had made it in time. The three-foot clock high on the wall read five minutes past seven. Even the Chief Delivery Dog was not above the rules, and the Automats would like nothing more than to catch a high profile dog in violation. She would have been required to appear before the Council Tribunal and risk being sent to the Steampod for destruction. No matter, now she was safe. To the right of the clock, the stairs to the cramped apartment led her straight to Naji, who was clattering around the tiny room preparing meager rations for their evening meal.

"Well, well, well! How nice you look! I see we had a Groomerly visit?" Naji laughed as he rubbed the top of her head. "I don't think I have *ever* seen ears so silky, and how is Treena?" Naji had known Treena since she was a baby. Her mother had died in the same garment factory explosion that had taken Hannah, his wife.

Sliding off her gear-vest and laying it on Hannah's rocker, Febby nudged again up to Naji, who was sitting on the floor. She shook several times to loosen the ribbon that Treena had hidden under the vest. The yellow ribbon coarsed through the grooming token, and Naji gently untied it.

"Well, what have we here?" Holding the wooden token, turning it over several times in his hand, he rubbed his eyes. It had been a long day, what with fitting several Council members for new suits, and cutting fabric. His eyes were itchy, but now they were tearing as well. Perhaps it was the long day, or perhaps it was the rough wooden token that he clasped now to his chest. Under the word Deen Diggins had scratched, *Hope*, Treena had scratched the word *Faith*.

The old man coughed a few times and let the tinydog climb in his lap. She flipped over and let him rub her belly. As she happily flipped, her derby came loose.

"And what is this? A new feather?" Naji laughed. "I don't remember this being part of the hat! You have been busy today, I bet you've been to the Falconry, no? So tell me how are Jeeson and Norra?"

Naji touched the feather and hatband ever-so-carefully. A tiny, folded white paper, hidden under the hatband, had micro-sized writing too small for him to read.

"Oh, and did you meet Noah, their son? The Council wanted to send him to the shoe factory, but I argued his case. He's one of the brightest minds in this town! They consented to let him help his mother design the mechanical bird and Norra got to keep her son. I think he would have died in the shoe factory, it's rough there with the chemicals and all. I don't know what the Council will do if they are not successful with the bird project, but come, let's not think of the worst, let's enjoy our biscuits!"

He stood and moved to the counter, where he divided the day-old rolls and cooked up a treasure. "Look! One of the Council, an old friend, brought me some butter, and look! He shared one of the best apples from the hydrolab!" Slicing the apple, and judiciously buttering the rolls, he grinned.

"How was Lee Anna Loo? Does she still want to keep you? You know, Pebby, she has a lot more to offer than this old tailor. If you went with her, why, all you would have to do is mind the hydroponics lab, and there is plenty of food there!" He set her plate down in front of her.

"You know, all you have here is day old bread, but you have as much freedom as any dog I know." He scratched the top of her head affectionately and hung up her vest and derby. Hungry, he ate quickly. He had not forgotten the small piece of paper Pebby had unknowingly brought from the falconry.

"Come, quiet as you can, follow me!" Ever so slowly, breathing heavily, the old man and the dog crept down the stairs in the dark. On the landing, which was barely five feet across, a worn mat muffled their steps. Straight ahead was the dog aperture, which was tightly closed. To the right was the locked door to the tailor shop. Behind them, high on the wall, was the clock, which now read eight o'clock. Leaning far over the railing, Naji reached for the hands of the clock and moved them both together, straight up to the twelve.

Ever so softly, Pebby could hear gears turning, grinding, and spinning, and Naji hurried down to the landing.

"Come, quickly now, hurry!" He dropped to the floor, and amazingly, Pebby watched as a panel at the bottom of the wall slid upwards. An opening barely three feet high by two feet wide could be seen, and through it another set of stairs was visible. Crouching and sliding feet first, the chubby old tailor crammed his body through the tight space. Half-sliding down the rickety steps, he grabbed a precious match from his pocket and lit a candle sitting at the bottom of the stairs.

"Quickly, now, quickly!" He motioned the tinydog down into the cellar, and she scurried. Turning a rusty crank on the wall above, he closed the trap door. Breathing a long sigh of relief, he hugged the tinydog close. As he stood, Pebby could see that the ceiling was only a few feet above his head. But as he swept the candle around, she could see a short tunnel ahead. She could hear the sound of water dripping in the distance, and when they emerged from the short tunnel, a cavernous opening welcomed them. Illuminated by the small candle, long tables, like she had seen in the falconry lab, held various contraptions. Wires, gears, tools, and glass containers and tubing were scattered everywhere.

"I don't know how to use much of this stuff, but I do know how to bargain, no?" Naji laughed as he led her to a small anteroom filled with used furniture, pictures, and books. Walls lined with bookshelves stretched to the ceiling. Pebby sneezed from the dust. The stones under her feet were dry, despite the water sounds that she heard deep in the catacombs.

"Pebby," Naji sighed, "the tunnels go on for quite a ways under Norwall. There is a small reservoir where run-off collects. Here the water is clean and safe, and sometimes I catch a fish in my trap. So, I survive a bit, you know, it is all about surviving, you know?" He moved to one of the lab tables and seated himself at a tall stool.

"My breathing has betrayed me. I am no longer the strong man I was. I can barely make it up the stairs to my bed. The fog and the dust have scarred my lungs, but still I survive. I know the others look to me, but I am old, and I cannot lead the fight. I just cannot." Tears formed in his eyes and blurred his vision.

"The others look to me to lead them, but I've grown weaker and can barely keep the shop open. I have not the strength. I have the will, but not the strength. You see, Pebby, it is not just about wanting to do something, it is about having the tools to do it. My body is wearing down now."

Sniffing back tears, he looked through a huge magnifier and adjusted it to the correct height. Drawing the scrap of paper from his shirt pocket, he carefully unfolded it and placed it on a small platform. Adjusting the magnifier, holding the candle close, he read the inscription aloud:

Naji
You must help us
Please
You must help us
Our time is running out.

Weary, the old tailor shoved the magnifier out of his way so hard that it slammed onto the heavy granite lab table. Pebby rubbed against his leg and he picked her up. Clutching her close, he sobbed, burying his face in her soft coat, wishing for all the world that he could get his strength back. Licking the tears as they fell, Pebby believed that her heart would break. Her friends were in danger, grave danger. She was the link between them, and she would not let them down.

CHAPTER 25

The Plan

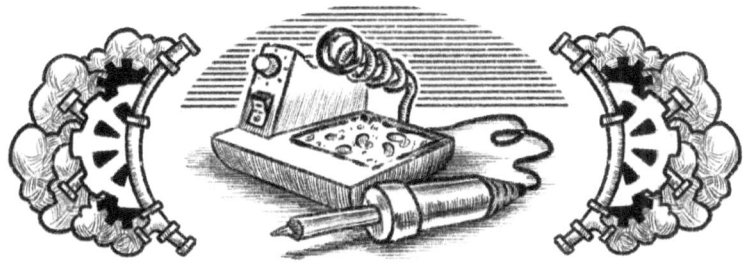

Abby Weathermore dropped onto the couch in the front living room. The feisty African gray parrot perched in the ornate Victorian cage had a sour and skeptical look. Freddy had not been out of his cage much this week, as Abby had been working overtime every day, some days not arriving home until after dark. *So lucky, Claire has been able to fill in and pick up Phillip,* she mused as she stared, lost in her thoughts, at the irascible bird. Freddy stared down his beak at her, imploring her to get him out onto his perch.

"OK, com'on, step up!" She extended her hand into the cage and gladly, he stepped up.

What he really longed for were the tasty Bio Berry treats he was usually given when she took him out. She carefully set him on the wooden tree perch next to the cage and scratched his head a few times. He cooed softly, mewing like the smellicats. As she stood up and stretched, Abby Weathermore called out loudly to her missing children.

"Hey, guys! Freaky Friday meeting now called to order! OK, Freddy," she added now softly, "you win. I can't stand that sour look for another minute!"

She opened the plastic tub of treats. Before he would accept it, he lowered his beak sharply giving the signal for her to again scratch his head. Only after a few more minutes of scratching would he consent to take a Bio Berry. As he munched happily, Abby dropped back onto the sofa, ready for a nap. If she had her way she would cancel the Friday Festivities and pull a cover over her head and sleep. Her eyes were fluttering closed when Phillip sauntered into the room, clarinet case in hand.

"Ready Mom? I've gotta' warm up a minute and I'm good. Just give me a minute." He hurriedly unpacked his instrument as his mother tried to hide a deep sigh.

"Wonderful, really, just what I've been waiting for all week." She continued, "Maybe I'll get *extra* lucky and Claire will screech out a few notes on her violin! Think that can happen? Wherever is your sister?"

"I think she's holed up in the lab. Want me to get her?"

"Yep, let's bring this meeting to order before you start serenading me, or I might just fall asleep! I wouldn't want Claire to miss all your news, right?"

Phillip was already half-way down the hallway, looking through the arches of windows that looked out on the yard. Rapping on the lab door gently, he called out. "Claire? Claire, Mom's ready to get started, are you in there?"

"Sure, Bud, coming now. Give me a sec." He heard several clicks and turns of the locks and the lab door swung open. "Here, come'on in."

Slowly, with trepidation at first, he entered her private sanctum. The sun was just starting to set through the curved conservatory windows, painting the entire room in a soft pink light. Claire was perched on a high wooden stool in front of the wooden work table that stretched across the back of the room.

"Com'on, take a seat." She nodded her head to an empty stool next to hers. Smiling, she winked, and pushed her safety glasses farther up on her nose with a hand that was shrouded in a thick, black cotton glove. She was holding a soldering pen and using it to connect several wires onto a three-inch by five-inch prototype of her design.

Phillip stared in amazement. He had never been invited into the inner sanctum before. He watched as she carefully connected the wires, scraped the excess, and soldered again, sparks from the pencil illuminating her face. Phillip pushed some of the scattered cords, metal pieces, and switches back and rested his elbows on the counter as he stared at her.

"Know what I'm doin?"

"No clue. No freakin' clue!"

"I'm connecting the circuits on the motor. This switch's gonna run the blower, which is gonna cool the motor, which is gonna run the pumps, which is gonna push the water through the filter, which is gonna heat the water and clean the air! Got that?" She laughed, and continued. "You see, it's nothing but a series of steps, one step after the other, to clean the air!"

Phillip nodded. "OK, I get it. But air purifiers have been around for years, right, what's the deal? What's different? Sounds like stuff that's already been invented?"

"Wrong Phills, wrong." She set her soldering pen down and flipped her glasses to the top of her head. Swiveling the stool to look at him directly, she peeled off her protective gloves.

"That's where this is different. We've had air conditioners for houses, we've had air filters for rooms, but this Phills, this could be leveraged to clean the air coming out of pipes in a factory. It's what I call 'nanofiltration,' which can clean all the nasties out of the waste air from an entire factory!" She leaned even closer to him.

"See, the secret is in using water to cool and clean the filter, and a separate system which sterilizes the water, but doesn't heat it. Cool cleaning. Here. Wanna try to solder?"

Phillip lit up with a smile that stretched across his face, but he tried not to look too eager. He raised his eyebrows and put on thick, black, protective gloves and safety goggles.

"Here, sit here." Claire stood and let him take her place on the stool. Standing behind him, she placed the delicate pen in his hands. "Now, you're going to melt the metal together, hold it like you're writing, that's it, finger on the control, now slowly, slowly, give it a try."

"OK, OK, I got it, I got it!" Phillip bit the inside of his cheek and watched intently as the sparks flew and the metal bonded together.

"OK, now attach the wires to this little plate. Can ya do it?" Claire stood back and watched in amazement as Phillip perfectly, cleanly, and crisply connected the project together.

"Can I do more?" Phillip asked quietly, not wanting to end the moment.

"Do you know what this is called, Phills?"

"Not really, tell me, please!"

"Soldering is joining some electronic parts together by melting stuff called solder around the connection. It's using a metal alloy that melts, but when it cools, it makes a strong bond between the parts. Got it?"

"OK, looks like the tip of this pen is really small."

"Yep, there are bigger chisel tips, but for my tiny wires we use a tiny tip to get the heat to the smallest target, and not heat up other stuff. By the way, the tip gets up to about... ummm nine hundred degrees? So, you'll cook your butt off. Gotta be careful. Think you can do it?"

"OK. Yeah, I got this." Phillip focused all his attention on the tiny pen tip as he held a small piece of copper solder wire with the other hand.

"Excellent, excellent!" Claire said as he perfectly joined the two wires.

"Where's more? I want to do more, com'on Claire, this is great!" he exclaimed, as he pushed the stool back from the counter. He set the safety goggles down gently on the lab counter.

"Whoa, Buddy," Claire laughed, "you gotta start at the bottom. I mean, I can start you on some simple stuff, like, well, ya'know, bein' my lab assistant?"

"Yeah, Yeah, whatever. I'll do whatever you need, Claire. Need the trash emptied, I'm in. Need a soda? I'm your guy. I wanna learn. Wadda ya think?"

Remembering Naji's words, a perfect trade is where both parties get what they want... Phillip looked at Claire imploringly.

"I mean it, Claire, I'll start at the bottom. I'll wheel your stuff into the trade shows. Come on, make me a deal. All I'm asking for is to start at the bottom. Whatever it takes."

Claire tilted her head thoughtfully.

"OK. Laundry help?"

"You got it!"

"Lay off the cats?"

"Got it!"

"Walk Moushka?"

"Got it!"

"Help with dinner clean-up?"

"OK, I guess, for one month?"

"OK. Litter pans?"

"NO WAY!"

Taking off her goggles, Claire tossed them carelessly on the counter.

"OK, guess I can't expect that. So, we start tomorrow. You get lessons, I get help. Deal?" Ushering him out of the lab, she pushed the buttons to set the keyless lock.

"Just don't expect to mess with my stuff until I'm sure you can handle it, OK? Don't want a fire in the lab, and I don't want you to get hurt. Mom wouldn't be happy if you got a big jolt of electric current, ya' know?"

"Yeah, OK, but can we start tomorrow?"

"Yep. I have the project to finish, and I can use some help. Meantime, I'll show you how to run the Saturday laundry! You'll have a full schedule tomorrow, say, why did you come get me in the first place? Oh crap!!! MOM! She probably was waiting this whole time? Why didn't you say? Com'on let's hurry!"

Phillip just smiled. Nothing would have distracted him from getting a piece of Claire's lab. For years, she had been so secretive she would not even let him through the door. Now, he would be her apprentice! He could not contain his excitement as he hurriedly followed her up the hallway. Hearing a loud "SHHH" coming from the little gray bird still perched, thoughtfully watching over his owner, they found their mother snoring loudly, arm flung over her face as she slept soundly on the living room couch.

"Well," whispered Phillip, "there goes the concert!" Raising his eyebrows, he chuckled quietly.

"I know we were all anxious for the violin solo, even Freddy," who was now looking at them menacingly, head down and black beak pointed as though he was planning an attack should they dare to disturb his mistress.

"That bird is a mess!" giggled Claire. "Hey Phills, let's pop in pizzas, whadda ya say?"

Phillip nodded, as he headed for the refrigerator to retrieve pizza dough and two large pans.

"I'll do mine, you do yours," Claire offered as she collected toppings from the refrigerator and laid them on the counter, deftly setting the oven at the same time.

"Yep, dueling pizzas!" Phillip added, as they laid out pepperoni, chopped an onion, diced a green pepper, and placed their personal choices on the crusts. Sprinkling hers with three different cheeses, Claire changed the subject.

"So, why do ya care so much about that picture? I mean the pocket watch? Is this all about getting another dog? You never asked Mom for a dog before, what's the deal Phills, can't you just level?"

"It's not just the dog. Oh sure, I want her, and sure, I think there's something special about her, but the picture?" Dropping into one of the ladder back chairs, Phillip rested his head on his hands.

"Yep, Phills, the picture." Taking the seat at the head of the table, Claire continued, "Why this fascination with the picture? I don't get it?"

Reaching into his pocket, wrapping his fingers around the widget which he always kept with him, he cleared his throat.

"Claire, it's this. This thing. I found this in the backpack he gave me, and, well, look at it and give me your take on it." Opening his palm, he produced the key, and was almost shaking as he handed it to her.

"I've been trying to figure it out, but no luck. Clure looked at it too."

Taking it from his hand, she thoughtfully turned it over and over, inspecting every crevice. Pulling out her phone, without even looking up, she quietly asked, "May I?" She scrolled and thumbed her way to one of her research sites and snapped a picture. Rising slowly from the chair, she leaned over her brother and whispered, "This is really weird. I don't even recognize some of the metal in a few of the gears. Where is Norwall anyway? Please, Phills, we gotta' be careful. Other than McClure, who knows about this?"

"No one, Claire, no one. I wanted to figure it out on my own, but I think I need help. Your help. You'n Clure are the only ones I can trust."

"I know. We gotta be careful. I don't know what you think about this, but I got a friend I can trust, had a summer internship at the Smithsonian in the metallurgy department. He got to do some tests on the space rocks. I'm starting to think that maybe this came from another planet? Wadda' you say we ask him to help? Confidentially of course?"

"No, Claire, not yet. I say we get Naji *here*. I couldn't get any information from him, but maybe you can. I can walk the dog and you two can be alone. Maybe you can ask him about his pocket watch and get some talk going and find out something. Anything. Anything would be better than what we have now, which is nothing."

"I got'cha." Taking the pizzas out of the oven and deftly slicing each pie, Claire threw several pieces onto paper plates. "We'll see what I can find out. Meanwhile, say nothing to Mom, OK?"

"Well, I haven't yet. Let's try to get them over to the house real soon, real soon Claire, OK?"

"I agree. This could be the discovery of our lifetimes, and might be your only chance to get an out-of-this-world-pup." Claire was smiling widely now. Hearing explosion sounds coming from the parrot in the front room, they heard their mother stir.

"Hey! What happened, guys, I guess I fell asleep?" Abby Weathermore came into the kitchen, limping slightly on her stiff ankle, sore after the brutal workload of the past week.

"Well, my little chefs working together, I love it!" Setting herself down gingerly onto a chair, she propped up her foot.

"Any pizza left for me? You guys gonna clean up this kitchen, right?"

Phillip grinned, noticing for the first time that the entire counter was covered with pieces of the shredded cheeses Claire had rained on her dough. He headed to the freezer and brought his mother an ice pack for her ankle, even before she asked for one.

"Sure, Mom, we got this. Sure, you just take the night off!" Claire reassured her as she winked at her brother, who echoed her.

"We got this! We got this!" answered Phillip, as he winked back.

CHAPTER 26

The Walk in the Park

The little scruffy dog opened her eyes and stretched. It was a good stretch. She raised her rump high in the air and lowered her chin to the red-and-black plaid blanket, stretching every muscle that ran down her spine. She bobbed her head from side to side, stretching her neck muscles.

Then, she remembered the most serendipitous, silly, stupendous something. In an amazing throw of the lottery, which enabled the middle managers of the Norwall stores to take one day off from work each month, Naji Najeem had today off. In an unbelievable twist of fabulous fortune, Gleena Glisson had given Pebby the day off as well.

Oh, Pebby had no illusion that Gleena had done this so that Naji and Pebby could enjoy time together. Rather, Gleena had sprung for grooming yesterday because Pebby had a delivery scheduled to the Council breakfast meeting tomorrow. It wouldn't do to have her coat messy or her ears matted with road soot. She had to be in top form or it would reflect poorly on Gleena and the Octagon Enterprise. One thing about Gleena, it was all about presentation. She wouldn't let the council catch her unaware, no sir... eeee.

Naji was already awake and puttering around in the kitchen, or rather a two-foot length of counter that he called a kitchen; a simple worn cabinet with a hard stone top where he prepared their morning meal. This morning in particular began with the heating of a cup of water over a candle burner, and soaking a tea pod in his favorite blue, chipped cup. Hannah had made his tea every morning before she went to work at the garment factory, but now tea was rationed too; he stretched the pod to last for at least three mornings. By the last day, he was only sipping hot water, but he sipped it just the same.

"Good stretch Pebby, good stretch," he yawned, "good stretch, and get those muscles out! You know, we haven't been to the park in ages, and why not, I say? Let's have our meal and head to the park while the air is fresh, what say?" He placed a piece of moistened bread in her bowl, along with a few spoonfuls of kibble that Deen Diggins had dropped off on his last free-day.

Pebby gobbled it down hungrily. If she was going to go out, she was going to dress for the day, even if she wasn't making deliveries. It was a matter of pride. Quickly finishing her grub, she slipped on her vest. Her derby sat at the exact proper angle on her head and she shook out her ears to fluff them.

Just let everyone know, The Chief Delivery Dog is out and about, ain't no one else that sits this derby, and I'm the best in this ol' clockwork town. Don't let anyone forget it! she thought smugly, following Naji down the stairs.

Glancing behind her, she looked at the giant red clock hanging on the wall. She remembered that Naji had moved both the hands up to the twelve and the trap-door had opened. But now, the clock was working just fine, little hand on the seven, big hand on the twelve. No matter, Naji was opening the real door, and stepping out into the crisp morning air of the three suns. The day was early and the gray mist that settled in the town each day was still high in the sky. It was their moment to enjoy the clear sky, and Naji breathed deeply to clear his lungs of the soot from the day before.

He coughed a few times. He felt in his jacket for the tailor shop key and his prized pocket watch. He never was without it. While he would sometimes take it out to look at it, he kept it close. The watch itself was contraband, but the daguerreotype photo of Hannah on the underside of the top was his link to the past, and to her beloved memory. Squeezing it tightly then dropping it back in his pocket, he strolled quickly past the Automatons at the corner, standing guard as usual. Pebby trotted along at his side, a bouncy little high-tail trot. She looked smugly at the menacing robot, who raised his blaster and sneered a menacing, vicious sneer.

Stinking Automat! She bounced along and shook her rump at the vicious metal man. *Not today loser, I'm off, and you can't get me now! It's official!* She turned her nose up in the air and shook her ears as if to shake off the menacing look. They were at the old Favingsham Park now; a four-block area of half-dead trees and a wrecked pavilion which had been neglected and left to rot. The place had seen better days. Families used to come and listen to concerts under the stars. Families with dogs walking by their sides, majestic birds flocking high in the trees, all would gather to listen to the strains of beautiful rhapsodies. Rainbow colored flocks of majestic birds would perch in the trees and feast on the crumbs left by the snacking children. Those were years before the dogs were banished to work details, and the birds sickened to death by the gray-sky air.

It was all different now, and as Naji looked around, he spotted his favorite stone bench. He became teary-eyed as he remembered sitting with Hannah as they watched the children. They had hoped one day to have their own family, but it had never happened. The years had passed, the Council had taken over the city, and then, so quickly and so cruelly, she was gone.

He heaved a sigh and dropped down on the bench. He remembered the cool weather and the circular stone firepit where they had warmed their hands and watched flames dance as the musicians played on the stage.

"It was all a lifetime ago, Pebby, long before your time, a lifetime ago."

He watched the tinydog sniff for squirrels and tunnel her nose in the brush, hoping to jump them. She loved watching them fly out of the brush in surprise and run for their lives. She never actually caught one, and Naji wondered what she would do with it if she actually got it. The thought made him chuckle.

He watched her intently, as if to distract himself. He saw, from far away, a figure approaching them; a ghost-like apparition in a long white dress. The glare from the sun was blinding him and he raised his hand to shield his eyes as he tried to focus. His eyesight had deteriorated lately and he was quite relieved to see his old friend Gleena Glisson coming into focus.

"Naji, you rascal, didn't realize you had today off too, and Pebby! You had the day off, but you were supposed to keep tidy after Treena done your groomin'! Now, I find ye' runnin' around in your work clothes getting your coat all dusty chasing squirrels?" Gleena huffed and rested her hands on her hips.

"Whatever am I to do with the two of you, Ye'ere a sight for sore eyes!" She laughed, and cuffed Naji on the arm, stomping the dust off her shoes. She reached down and affectionately rubbed the tinydog's ears.

"Why ever are you in your derby and wagon-vest on your day off?" Pebby gave an innocent little growl, and shook her head side to side.

"Oh, I see, mind me own business ye say, right?" She laughed. 'Well, I been overlookin' the fact that ye not been sleeping at the Habitron like the other dogs, but ye've been campin' out with a friend here, right?"

Laughing all the more, she plopped her sizable frame onto the concrete bench. Pebby ignored her, and proceeded to sniff out more squirrels.

"Come, old man, come on an' tell Gleena your worries." She pushed her long white sleeves up to her elbows. Her forearms were scarred from the burns she earned fair and square reaching into the bakery ovens.

"Come on, humor an old woman who wants nothin' more than a little company of a handsome gent, huh?"

Naji laughed too.

"Handsome? Those days are long gone for me. Gleena, remember when we had Hannah, and we came here at night to watch the stars? The place looked better then, the grass green, and the boys playin' songs from the stand there? I can almost hear them now. Or maybe it's just the ghost of them, ya know?"

Lovingly, he placed his arm around her shoulders and gave her a quick squeeze.

"Better watch Naji, you'll get us both vaporized. Remember my Carl? After they took him, things were never the same. I am afraid Naji, so afraid." Her voice quieted to a whisper.

"The Council keeps puttin' pressure on me to produce, produce, and more producin' but the peoples is worn out, and dying from lack of a good meal. They lackin' sleep, and too many hearts broken. Know what I mean Naji? Too many hearts broken when lives lost to the gray-skies and peoples are taken by the lung sickness like Carl was." Her gray eyes began to mist with tears.

"Here, here, now Gleena, you done a good job now, and you got the respect o' the Council, just like I got the tailor shop. We should be able to survive right?"

"But Naji, things is so much worse since you lost the Governor's seat! They spared ye life, and they gave ye the shop. I know ye took it to save you an' Hannah, but Naji, the people are dyin' as their lungs give out. There's no hope for them, no hope at all for the people, just like there wasn't no hope for Carl!"

Gleena sobbed into her handkerchief. Naji worried that her crying would attract the attention of the Automats. He tried to comfort her, but it was no use. Her face was streaked with tears.

At that very moment, Pebby jumped a squirrel who flew two feet in the air. Pebby, unable to control herself, bounced once and gave pursuit. Cornered, the frantic squirrel headed for an overgrown shell of a tree covered in vines. He grabbed a foothold and raced up the tree away from the vicious teeth of the barking tinydog.

Naji and Gleena both laughed at the chase. Gleena bent forward, as now tears of laughter stung her eyes.

"Oh Naji, don't let her ever lose her bounce! She just can't!" Laughing hysterically now, Gleena heaved deep breaths and wiped her eyes again. "She just can't lose that bounce!"

"Gleena, I know, she's the bounciest, is she not?" Addressing the tinydog now, Naji continued.

"Pebby, promise your old friends here that you will never, I mean never, ever, lose your bounce!"

Laughing himself, he threw his head back, and crossed his arms in front of his chest. "You know

Gleena, I think that's what happened to us, we really just lost our bounce."

"You think so Naji? You think that's all it is? Is that why we gave up so easily?"

"Yes, I think I just got too tired to fight anymore, too tired. Just way too tired." He leaned back on the bench.

Gleena stood up to leave. She looked around her, as though she was looking for invisible ears that might hear her, and she leaned over and whispered softly in his ear. "Well, think about it, Naji, there are people who still look up to ye, and they would follow ye if you should so choose, ya know. I gotta get back, gotta get back, but think about what I said will ya? Just promise me ye will think on it?"

She leaned down to rub the ears of the tinydog, who had come over to say goodbye.

"'Just think about it, my friend, please?"

And with that, she gave him a loving pat on the shoulder, turned in the dust, and was gone, her voluminous white clothing giving her a ghastly, ghostly appearance. They could see the Automatons turning and following her to make sure she didn't take any unauthorized detours.

"Well, that was a good laugh Pebby. Don't lose your bounce!"

He began to laugh again as he stood and stretched. Unfazed, Pebby focused again on tormenting the squirrel, who dropped from the tree and teased her again, begging her to give chase. So, furiously, the little dog gave pursuit and circled the old stone fireplace, raising a cloud of dust.

"Stop that now, you'll get filthy! Your hat and coat! Pebby, STOP!"

He made his way to her, trying to intervene but the little dog would not listen. She ran faster and faster in pursuit, her precious derby launching off of her head and landing in the dirt. The dust cloud, irritating Naji's lungs, surrounded him in a smokey cloud covering his eyes and forced him to cough. Not seeing the uneven terrain, he tripped.

In a flash of an instant the dust cloud rose higher and higher, until he realized that the shadowy haze was arising from inside the fireplace and was quickly enveloping him. The dust was copper-gold colored and produced a shimmering, glittering haze. He saw the black derby on the ground and he was aware that he was being consumed. He was fighting it, but he started to cough, and cough uncontrollably.

He felt himself falling and sinking deeper into the mist. In the last moment of his consciousness, he felt the tinydog jump into his arms as he fell. It happened so fast that there were not even seconds for him to realize that four Automatons had quickly surrounded the fireplace. Blasters drawn, the squirrel, who only minutes ago had tormented the tinydog with a silly chase game, narrowly escaped vaporization as he leapt from harm's way back into the dead tree as the man and the tinydog disappeared from sight.

The vapor from the blasters of the Automatons turned the ground inside the fireplace to a dark charcoal, and blasted the fireplace so hard that part of it crumbled to dust. Believing that they had reduced the old man and his tinydog to rubble, they circled around, headed back to position, and returned to guarding the park as if nothing had happened.

Far away, in another dimension, the man and the tinydog were falling out of control, spinning wildly, falling as though someone had rudely shoved them over the edge of a cliff. They fell into hot summer weather, and, as if they had ridden on the top of a cloud, touched down into hotter than hot weather in a dried-up grassy field.

They walked a long way after that. Naji carried Pebby much of the way as the pavement was burning her tiny feet. They were shocked at how different this modern city was, but always the survivor, Naji didn't lose sight of the fact that night was approaching and they would need food and shelter. It was hard for both of them to catch their breath in the suffocating heat. Both of them craved water.

They came upon The Adventura Shopping Center, a poorly maintained, low-budget place. Naji, resourceful as ever, saw a "Help Wanted" sign in the window of The Imperial Dry Cleaners, a small corner storefront. In an instant, not only did the relieved business owner take them in, but he also settled them in the tiny upstairs apartment. He gave them a key and a money card for groceries, and bought them a sandwich at the deli next door. He disappeared into the steamy humid evening, relieved to have someone to take over his business. He was free to catch his long flight home to see his mother in India. He was in no hurry to return to Florida.

Exhausted, dusty, dirty, and unsure of where they were, the tired tailor and the little scruffy dog washed up quickly and ate the sandwiches the man had left them. Thankful for their safety, the pair who survived with so little for so long felt lucky to have a soft mattress and a roof overhead. No matter that the journey had transported them to another place and time, they had each other, and for that, they were most grateful.

The Invitation

True to her word, Claire invited Phillip to her lab every day after school. Their mother got used to the idea that they were working together on a project, and after making sure Phillip was staying safe and following Claire's guidance, she relaxed a bit.

Phillip perched on the high lab stool as he turned on the soldering gun. Under Claire's tutelage he opened the container of flux, and alligator-clamped the wires in the vise Claire had fastened to the table. He frayed the ends of the wires until they were splayed, and twisted them together.

"Looks clean, Phills, looks neat. Clamp it and get ready!"

Claire watched approvingly. Seeing him carefully untangle the cord on the soldering iron, she watched him touch the flux to the twisted wires, careful not to touch the solder to the iron.

"Hey, not too much, keep it clean!"

She handed him the silicone paste to waterproof the wires. Handing him a shrink wrap tape, she watched him carefully put the soldering gun down and use a heat gun to shrink wrap the wire connection.

"Whatcha' think Claire? Why bother with the shrink wrap?" Phillip pushed his goggles to the top of his head and pushed his stool back from the bench.

"Well, think about the water we have in the project. The shrink wrap will protect the electrical connection and make sure the system does not either short out or fail!"

Smiling widely, Claire let her goggles drop. Hung from a cord around her neck, they were her favorite fashion accessory.

"So, how are we going to work this?" she whispered, as if their mother cooking dinner in the kitchen could hear their plans. "How are we going to get Naji here to the house? Why don't we just go over to his shop and I can talk to him there? Why are you so set on bringing him here?"

"Cause, for one thing," Phillip responded very matter-of-factly, "I want to take him up on the deal that I get to spend the day with Pebby. I want to see how she acts with Moushka and the other pets. Besides, I brought all my grades up and he promised me a day with her," he said quite nonchalantly.

"OK, I know, and maybe he will spill the info if we have him in our territory?" Claire replied.

"Claire, he's not our prisoner, we can't really interrogate him, we just gotta find out where they come from, whatever is Norwall, and what's going on with the key to the tailor shop, right?"

"Phills, what about the picture in the watch? I thought the deal was you wanted me to try and get him to show me his pocket watch, no?"

"Yeah, that too. That too. But also, don't forget, I want to spend time with the tinydog. If she doesn't really belong to him, I mean to have her for my own, really my own, ya know?"

"OK, OK, I get it. Just don't forget the airship and the Victorian lady, I can't imagine that dog was really wearing a derby, ya know? Now come on, let's fold laundry, enough inventing for today!" They headed up to the laundry room, where, true to his word, Phillip folded clothes, fed the cats, and even petted the nasty tuxedo cat who hissed at him just for good measure.

The next day, Phillip walked to his mother's office after school. He got right to work, finishing his homework in record time. He straightened his office, giving the globe a spin.

Oh, where do they come from, where on this earth are you, Norwall? he whispered, priding himself that the desk was clean and organized, and the trash can was no longer overflowing. There was no sign of the used candy wrappers and empty snack bags that previously littered his small office. Leaning back in his chair, which he had mended with new tape, he grinned. He heard his mother greeting Claire, as she came through the inner door of the office.

Right on time, right on time! He glanced at his watch. Their plan was unfolding with military precision. Unpacking his latest grade report from his organized backpack, he looked once more at Naji Najeem's tailor shop key which always stayed safe in his pocket. Once, he almost had an anxiety attack when he had left it in the pocket of a pair of pants headed for the washing machine. Claire had rescued it, and slid it back into his hand without their mother seeing it.

Opening his door, he took a deep breath, turned off his light, slung the pack over his shoulder and hurriedly marched up the hall.

"Claire! Hey, Claire! How was traffic?" He tried to sound as adult as possible.

"Oh, hey, Phills, not bad, not bad. Got your homework done?" she asked, smiling as her mother looked on with interest.

"Are you two up to something?" Abby inquired, sensing that her children were acting a bit formal, as well as a bit strange. Laughing, but sounding a bit phony, Phillip jumped into the conversation.

"Up to something? Mom, you know I'm getting to the end of the school year, so I guess I'm supposed to get a little crazy. Mom, I was wondering, could McClure come over Saturday?"

"Sure, but I thought he was grounded. I haven't spoken to Sylvie lately, but I thought you said he got grounded over some argument with his Dad? I heard you talking to Claire about it."

"Oh yeah, but I think that's all over now, and he got his phone back this week. He's really wanting to come over and play some *Revolutions* again, ya know?"

"OK, OK, you know I can never say no to Mc-Clure," Abby Weathermore said looking far off into the distance, as though she was seeing something the rest of them could not see.

"Fine! We're all set!" Phillip quipped, only to be interrupted by Claire.

"Were you not supposed to take a paper over to Naji? I mean, he gave you that backpack hoping that you would pay attention in school. Although, I believe it was *my* help more than that old dirty backpack, wouldn't you say so, Mom?"

"Well, Claire, let's not get adversarial over how it happened. Let's just be glad your brother was able to pull his grades up, focus, and get on track to make the Honor Roll! Phillip, I am so, so proud! If you want to go over to see Naji Najeem, of course we will go. I still have work to do, so after that, you and Claire head home and start on supper. Walk Moushka and finish chores. I'll head home in a few hours, OK?"

Turning his nose up in the air, and furrowing his eyebrows, Phillip feigned indignation.

"Yeh, Claire, let's not get adversarial!"

"Oh HUSH!!!" Claire replied, not falling for the bait. "Come'on, let's see what's going on next door!"

They made their way through the office. Passing quickly, they exited, with Claire and Phillip leading the way. They gave each other thumbs-up behind their mother's back, which was seen, and met with a disapproving shaking of her head by Jaceena, who was watching their every move.

"Doc, you got only about thirty minutes till the next appointment, and you need a bit of a break, so don't stay long!" The short, elegant office manager who would protect Abby Weathermore with her very life, looked skeptically and sternly at the children who appeared to be hiding *something*.

Entering the Imperial Dry Cleaners, they found Naji Najeem leaning on the counter with the broom in his hand. His lips were blue and he was obviously short of breath.

"Naji!" Abby exclaimed. "Whatever is wrong? Why are you breathing so hard?"

"Madam," he replied, "just tried to do a little more work than I should have. I be getting very poor on breathin' lately. Oh, it's nothing, I'll be better in a bit. What brings my favorite family here to visit this old tailor?"

Phillip ran to pick up Pebby, who was excited to see her friends and was wagging her tail wildly. But truth be told, today she was sadly missing Deen Diggins, Treena Trembly, and grumbly Gleena Glisson.

"Hey, girl," Phillip whispered," how'd you like to come and spend a day at the house? Got lots of room for you to run, and two cats you can chase, wadda' ya say?"

Turning next to Naji Najeem, but not letting go of the tinydog, Phillip presented his case, pulling the crumpled supporting evidence from his pants pocket.

"Ya' see, Naji, I organized my stuff, and sailed, *I mean sailed*, to the top of the class! Claire's my witness, aren't you Claire? And, I played the opening of the assembly, and this time, finally made honors! Look, I brought the proof! Wadda you think Naji, can you and Pebby come visit Saturday? I'm dying to have her come to the house! What'cha say, can we do it? Please, please?"

His mother interrupted, not wanting to pressure the old man.

"Phillip, let's give Mr. Najeem a chance to answer." She gently put her hand on Phillip's shoulder,

"Maybe he has plans for Saturday?"

"No, no," Najeem offered up. "There is nothing I would like better than to see this young student play his songs, and I would like nothing better than to see your fine home! Maybe you would be so kind, fine doctor, to comment on my breathing? Maybe some potions you have that would ease me a bit?"

"Yes, perhaps I can listen to your lungs and hear what is wrong? We can stop over at the office first, and the girls can help you fill out papers, then I can examine you. Maybe I can help make your breathing a little better. We have a new x-ray machine, and we can take a picture of your lungs so I can see what might be wrong. No charge to you, of course!"

Naji bowed his head in appreciation.

"Yes, Madam, Saturday will be fine, I will be most grateful for some help, any help, so that I can feel better. I am wearing out so fast, so fast I can hardly walk this little girl around the plaza any longer! I will be glad to see her play and walk with a young lad with so much energy and so much enthusiasm!"

Seeing Claire smiling in the background, he was determined not to leave her out.

"And Miss, I would like to hear more about your grand inventions! Perhaps I can see the laboratory where you work? Hmm?"

"Sure, Naji," replied Claire, "Sure!" We just gotta haul you over to Mom's office first to see about your breathing, yes? Then you can come see our house, and the tinydog can meet our particular, peculiar, persnickety pets!"

Phillip hugged the tinydog, squeezing her tight. He gave a thumbs-up sign that only Claire could see.

CHAPTER 28

Swirls and Secrets

By seven o'clock that morning, Phillip had set his alarm, showered and dressed, texted Mc-Clure, and woke up Claire, who promptly buried her head under her pillow and muttered *five more minutes, five more minutes.* He met his mother in the kitchen. She was dressed in comfortable black leggings and a long black top, her long hair tied back. On her feet were comfortable, worn, athletic shoes. They were her favorite pair, speckled black and gray.

"Mom, can you show me how to make the coffee? I'd like to do it this morning? Please?" Phillip begged, surprising his mother.

"Sure, but why today? You never wanted to make the coffee before, why so interested now?" Abby asked.

"Oh, nothing Mom, just wanting to help, ya know? Whatever I can do to help?" he smiled as he raised his eyebrows, filling up the water receptacle at the kitchen sink.

"Wouldn't be because you're hoping to soften me about that dog, now would it?" she smiled widely, yawning, still waking up. Phillip didn't answer her question, he just continued.

"So, let's see. Coffee filled to the line, and wadda ya know, *morning joe!*" he exclaimed. Dropping into a chair, Abby tied her sneakers and smiled tenderly at her son.

"Phillip, it's not that I don't want you to get that dog. In the first place, we don't know who the dog's real owner is. Second, Mr. Najeem seems to love the dog a lot, and it might not be so nice to take the dog away from him. You know, he is not really well. Remember the trouble he had breathing? Well, maybe the dog is his only friend. I don't think he has been in Florida too long, know what I mean?"

"Yeah, I know, I guess I'm a little selfish, I bet Mr. Najeem would be sad if she wasn't there at the shop with him every day." Phillip started to frown. "But, I really like her, Mom, I really do. I just feel something special about her, and I can't stop thinking about her."

"Phillip, I know you think about her a lot, but having a dog is a lot like having a little child. Their needs have to come first. When you want to play *Revolutions*, what if the dog wants to go for a walk? When you want to go to the movies with Clure, the dog will be sitting at home. You know, sometimes love is doing what is best for the other person, even if they cannot see it." She touched his face lovingly.

"Phillip," she sighed, staring right into his eyes, "sometimes love is very hard work. Sometimes it's doing the right thing, even when it would be easier to do something else, you understand?"

"Yeah, Mom, I know what'cha mean. But I can bring them here and show them the house, right?"

"'Course you can," she hugged him tight.

"Let's just see what happens after that, OK?"

"Sure, Mom, maybe I better get Claire up?"

"Yeah, I'll warm up a croissant for you. How about some cream cheese?"

"Awesome!" Phillip headed back to shake Claire awake a little harder than before.

"Claire! Come on, we're headed to get Naji! Come on, coffee's on, today we try and find out what the heck is going on with that guy!"

"Oh," she yawned sleepily, whispering. "Right Phills, you guys go pick them up and I'll shower. Now I remember, I'm on widget and pocket watch, right? You're on the tinydog, right?" she laughed.

"Maybe by the end of the day, we will know what the heck is going on. Now get outta here, I got to wake up my brain!"

So, Phillip and Abby headed to the Imperial. True to his word, Naji Najeem was eagerly awaiting them.

"Welcome, friends!" he exclaimed loudly as he unlocked the door to the small shop, taking care to keep the 'Closed' sign visible from the outside. Motioning them in and pulling down the front window shade, he directed them to the waiting room chairs.

"Well, here is the champion, come to claim his prize, and here is the tinydog, come to spend the day with her new friends! I am glad she can have friends to run and play with her, I am getting so out of breath!"

"Oh, yes!" Abby interrupted, "Naji, don't forget we are going to stop over at my office and snap a quick x-ray, right? I can listen to your lungs for a minute and try to help you, no?"

Phillip hurriedly chimed in.

"Mom, yes, take him over there, I'll stay here with Pebby till you guys are done. Go ahead, Naji, just go and let Mom help you out, go on!" Phillip shooed them away as he picked up the tiny scruffy dog, who licky-licked his face. "We'll be OK here, no worries!"

Naji shyly accepted their offers.

"If you could Ma'am, this old tailor would be ever so grateful! My breath is getting so short, some days it is troubling to go up the stairs to my room."

He looked down and shook his head, hating to admit that he was growing weaker day by day.

"Come, come on friend," Abby took him by the arm. "Let's give you a quick check up and take a picture. Might be something we can fix, no worries, just come on now," as she turned to her son.

"Phillip, keep the door locked, let no one in, and just give us a few minutes, OK honey?"

"Sure Mom, take as long as you need guys, I'll be talking to Pebby, right girl?" Pebby licked his face again affectionately.

By the time his mother and Naji returned to pick him up, Phillip had looked over every inch of the dry cleaning shop. He had not found one bit of information to shed light on the widget. Nothing. No pictures, no watches, nothing but a closet full of collected discards from the Adventura Mall garbage. Nothing. Disappointed, Phillip climbed into the back seat, cradling the tinydog in his lap.

When they arrived at home, Claire greeted them at the front door. "Naji! Great to see you! Come on in, I've been waiting to show you my lab, come, let's show you around!"

Her mother looked puzzled.

"Why the rush? Let him get settled, Claire. Let's show him the kitchen, how about getting him a glass of iced tea? Mr. Najeem, would you care for tea?" Abby asked.

Naji nodded. "Such hospitality, such friendship! I am unaccustomed to such kindness. This house is magnificent!"

"Oh yeah, shoulda' seen it when we started!" Phillip added, "disaster-zone!" shaking his head side to side, and making a grimace.

Setting a tall glass of tea down in front of Naji, Claire placed a small plate beside him with packets of sweetener, sugar, and a spoon. He looked at it, trying not to betray the fact that he had no idea what it was. Sipping the tea gingerly, he smiled and addressed the group.

"Excellent, excellent, and what is that tinydog doing? Why is she barking?"

Pebby had seen her reflection in the mirrored wall of the dining room and was barking furiously at her reflection. She ran around the circle between the dining room and the kitchen, chasing an imaginary predator. She stopped directly in front of Moushka's crate where he was snoring soundly.

That dog is gigantic! Bet he knows I'm the chief delivery dog, so watch out buster, I can outrun you, but, ... She had to stop and remind herself that they were no longer in Norwall, and she was no longer chief delivery dog. She was no better than this old dog lying in his crate waiting for his people to take him for a walk. She dropped flat into a t-bone position and heaved a big sigh. How did dogs stand this boring life?

"Phillip," Abby intervened. "Why don't we take the dogs down to the park? It will give them a chance to get to know each other, and Claire and Naji can talk about her inventions, right Claire?"

"Oh, Mom, you bet. I can't wait to show him my lab. Naji, do you know what time it is?"

"Claire, there is a clock straight ahead of you on the wall," Abby remarked as she laughed.

"Oops, sorry Mom, yeah, you two walk the pups, Naji and I will just relax in the kitchen for a few minutes and then I'll take him to my lab, OK?" She winked quickly at Phillip.

"OK," Abby replied, hooking up the tinydog to her leash.

"Come'on girl, let's walk!"

"Mom," Phillip added, "McClure is only a few minutes away. You go ahead and we'll bring Moushka in a minute, OK?"

"Sure!" Abby headed out the front door with Pebby in tow. The little dog marveled at how easy it was to walk alongside this woman, mother to the boy. Pebby had not had much of a mother, and didn't know much about mothers, but she liked this mother. She liked the way she looked at the boy and the way she looked after Naji. She liked the kindness of the woman, and other than Hannah, Naji's wife, Pebby hadn't had much information about what a mother was supposed to do. But if this was it, she was all for it.

As she trotted along, she imagined that perhaps this could be an easier life; easier than the Council, the parcels of food, and the endless work-days. But there was Treena, and Deen, and Gleena, all those she had left behind, and her thoughts were a million miles away.

The little scruffy dog just could not help herself. The weather was warm and beautiful. A soft breeze fluttered her ears as the tinydog trotted by the side of the tall, chestnut-haired woman. Immense old trees shaded the park and bare flecks of sunlight filtered through the overhead canopy. The sight of a squirrel taunting her was just too much. The shrill *cha cha chee, cha cha chee*, was more than the little dog could bear. Not thinking, she dug her hind legs into the soft dirt, leaped up, gave a snarl and two short barks, and forgot that the woman on the other end of the leash could be thrown wildly off balance.

Nothing could ever take back that second, that instant, when Pebby forgot that there was a person attached to the other end of the leash, a person who couldn't scoot as fast; a person who couldn't get out of the way quick enough. Then, the scream came, a loud, shrieking, painful, revealing scream. With that scream came the coppery-gold haze, and in that quick moment, the woman teetered for a second as she tried to right herself. The soft, uneven ground held onto her shoe however, and try as she might, she could not stop herself from falling. Leaning, trying to catch herself on the edge of the stone fireplace, she heard a sickening CRACK as the ankle held fast in the stuck shoe and the weight of her body toppled her over the ring of stones. She gasped and felt herself let loose of the leash as she toppled head-first into the fire pit. Her head struck a log.

Her eyes fluttered closed and then opened again, just as she caught sight of her youngest child running toward her. The glittery, copper-gold haze swirled around her and obliterated her view of her boy and his friend approaching from the distance. She did not see the bewildered stare of the tinydog whose wild running had pulled her off balance.

Frantic, the tinydog could do nothing. She froze, too upset to even bark, as she saw the boy running toward her from a distance, followed by another boy and the galloping husky she had met earlier that morning. *Oh, it was my fault, NO, no, and... NO!* she thought, as the fog encircled the woman. The tinydog was filled with a terrible sense of dread. This was so terrible, and so unexpected, that all she could do was drop flat to the ground and cover her eyes with her paws. Nothing, absolutely nothing, would ever be the same now.

CHAPTER 29

The Elastic Band

It was all happening in slow motion. At first, Phillip thought that it was just dust swirling up around the fireplace. Pebby was running in circles chasing the squirrel, and the dust was rising higher and higher. Then he realized, horribly understood, that the shadowy haze was arising from inside the fireplace and enveloping his mother. The dust was copper-gold colored and produced a glittery haze. His mother was, however, aware that she was being consumed and she was fighting it. He saw her cover her mouth for a moment, and then start to cough, and cough, and cough uncontrollably.

It looked as though the swirls might be dying down, but in that instant, he watched her slip and lose her balance on the sand. He heard the loudest crack he had ever heard in his life, as her leg twisted in a bizarre angle and slowly slipped out from under her. Her face contorted in agony, and he felt deep pain himself as he realized her ankle had broken. *Stupid leg*, which had bothered and hurt for years, *stupid leg*, which had been broken and fixed before. The slow, clumsy leg found the sand and the weight of her off-balance body too much and it cracked and splintered into a million shards.

The crack of her bone breaking pierced him like a knife and he saw her falling, sinking deeper into the mist. Her arm rose toward him as she sank to the ground, as if she was reaching for him. Their eyes met, and in that instant, he felt as if his heart would break. At that moment, that instant, he regretted everytime he had made fun of her. He had laughed at her nixing the lettuce, laughed and snickered at the spelling words, the stupid cupcakes with the weird face decorations and her dumb board games. The look on her face, the agony, was not so much for the pain of her broken leg, but was for the knowing that she was being taken from him, and she could not fight the enveloping cloud.

The sheer, unmitigated horror at the thought of leaving her youngest child so contorted her features, that for a moment he almost did not recognize her. He had never seen her so scared. It was at that moment, for the first time, that he realized, stupidly late, that to her, he was the most important person in her world. He was more important than the patients, more important than the old house, and more important than even herself. She saw the worst sides of him, and supported and cherished him just the same. He saw for the first time, at that moment, that she loved him and Claire equally; she just loved them in very, very different ways

"*Help... me,*" he heard her softly whisper, as if there was no strength left to force the words out. The words carried on the gentle breeze were almost too soft for him to hear.

It was at that moment that he felt his throat close, and he took a step toward her. It all happened so fast that there were not even seconds for his tears to fall, nor seconds for her to realize that her head hit the edge of the brick. As she lost consciousness, swirls of dust and fog overtook her and she was gone from his sight.

Pebby whimpered pitifully. She raised her little snout to the sky and bayed the most sorrowful wail he had ever heard. Phillip felt himself trying to scream, but he could not. He started to hyperventilate as he ran to the stone fireplace, running his hands over it, as if by wishing, he could will her back. He ran his hands through the sand, looking not so much for clues, but for any trace of her, any small bit of her that had been left behind. His eyes were so wide open that they consumed his face.

Crawling in the sand, holding back tears, blinking hard, he saw a black piece of elastic; it was the band with which she had tied her ponytail back that morning. Clutching it, he put it on his right wrist as if it were a bracelet. He saw Pebby watching him, tears welling in her eyes too. The tiny scruffy dog slowly made her way to Phillip with her head down, as if accepting blame. He reached down and picked her up. He held her up on his shoulder, and they both breathed in and out slowly.

Phillip pushed his face into her silky ears, and for a moment, he remembered his mother laughing, and hooking up the tinydog's harness just minutes ago. Everything was changed now, she had been taken by some unknown force to an unknown place, and she was taken there hurt; her leg shattered, her skull bleeding, her consciousness gone. She had left his world like a broken toy the world had discarded. He breathed in deeply several times, as the realization hit him square in the chest.

Out of the corner of his eye he could see McClure stumbling along trying to reign in Moushka, who was pulling as if he were the lead in the Iditarod Sled Dog Race. McClure was trying to keep from tripping on the uneven ground as he labored to keep up with the big dog. They were just approaching the park, when he heard McClure screech.

"Hey! Come back here, Mutton Chops!"

Phillip saw that Moushka had struggled loose from his harness and was bounding toward the stone fireplace. It had always been only Abby Weathermore who could control the big, strong dog. Moushka himself stirred up the sand as he came to a quick halt. As if on a mission, he dropped his head and sniffed the ground following her trail. Then, spontaneously, planting his front feet, tilting his nose high in the air, he bayed the loudest, most doleful sound that Phillip had ever heard. McClure, out of breath now, raced to his side.

"What the..?"

"She's gone. My mom is gone!!!"

Phillip waved his arms wildly up and down, now agitated.

"Something happened when Pebby went racing around her in a circle, around those stones, and the dust flew. Then, Mom tripped. I heard her ankle snap, and before I could grab her, she fell and hit her head!"

"No way, man, no freakin' way! Are you sure? Sounds unbelievable man. Sounds like a bad movie."

"I'm sure, man, I'm sure." Phillip dropped his head. "I wish I wasn't." Then he covered his face with his hands.

"Ohhh, wadda' we do?" Wadda' we do?" Phillip continued.

"Nothing to do but hook up the pups and head back to the house, I guess?" McClure didn't know what else to offer.

Phillip rubbed his face with his hands, which were soiled from crawling in the sand. His face was dirty with a combination of sand, sweat, and a few isolated tears. He tried hard to hold back tears in front of McClure.

"Com'on, help me out here Clure," he paced back and forth, kicking the dirt hard with his favorite shoes.

They sat on a bench watching the fireplace, with the dogs lying leashed in front of them. It was as though they believed watching long enough would bring her back. Phillip covered his eyes with his right hand while his left hand held the dog leash. His shoulders heaved, and he sniffed several times.

"Too bad it weren't my old man, ya know?" McClure added, sniffing too. He had such good memories of Abby. She had fussed over him, taken him to movies, baked for him, and treated him better than his own parents. She always had jokes to tell him, and she made sure that he had his special candy at the movie. In fact the only time he got to taste the semi-sweet chocolate rounds dotted with white decorations was when he went to movies with the Weathermores.

"You know, dude," McClure sniffed as well," I can't remember the last time one of my folks took me to a movie. Your Mom took me to more movies this year than they ever did in their whole life. And ya know? She always made sure that I had that damn candy, always remembered to grab it, I didn't even have to ask."

McClure gave a few blubbery heaves of his chest and rubbed his eyes with his free hand.

"She sure loved this ol' mutt. Come on, let's take them home and give 'em water. I'm gettin' real tired. Maybe I can call my mom and see if I can spend the night? We can rest and then try to figure this out, huh?"

Phillip nodded his assent silently. He had no words to say. His head was spinning, his eyes felt like they were swelling shut, not just from the dust, but from holding back tears. He wanted nothing more than to be in his room alone. But, he still had to face Claire. He was sure she would somehow blame him, that is, if she even believed him.

He couldn't just walk through the door and say "Hey, Claire, Mom went down in a cloud of copper smoke, what's for supper?" He wished now he had told her his suspicions about Naji.

Wait a minute, Claire is still at the house with Naji Najeem! What if she was in danger? Who knew who he really was?

"C'mon, Clure, let's go!" They broke into a trot as the dogs pulled ahead and led the way. Phillip urged on the tinydog, who was now in a speedy run, ears flying straight back. Moushka, despite his arthritis and stiff joints, was literally dragging McClure up the asphalt drive leading to the house. Phillip had not a minute to feel sorry for himself. Somewhere, his mother could be lying hurt and bleeding. Claire, nebulous, stubborn Claire, could be in danger too. He had to take charge, whether he wanted to or not.

Pulling himself up taller, he walked up the front walk past the herb garden, remembering how they had learned the names of the plants, and tended them so carefully. Actually, they looked wilted. His mother would be telling him to water them, and he made a mental note to take care of it. The black bracelet on his wrist comforted him, as if part of her was still with him. She would want him to be strong. She would need him to be a leader, and he would not, under any circumstances, let her down. He wasn't going to let anyone down, not him, not now.

CHAPTER 30

The Parallax Contingency

Phillip's mind raced in a million directions. He was biting his liping as he pushed open the front door. He tried not to look at McClure, who kept pulling at the front of his hair. He was forced to organize his thoughts quickly, knowing that he had to face Claire and Naji, both waiting for his mother in the kitchen.

First, his mother was gone, for sure, gone. Second, he had no idea whatsoever, of what had just happened. She was hurt, definitely hurt. He knew that at the very least, her ankle was broken and she had hit her head, which was bleeding the last moment he had seen her. So, wherever she was, she was badly injured and would be unable to help herself.

How did she disappear? It had to have something to do with the tinydog stirring up the dust at the fireplace, which had seemed to start the chain of events. He had slipped his mother's hair elastic over his wrist like a bracelet when McClure wasn't looking, and he snapped at it nervously as he felt himself starting to shake. The bracelet was all he had left; the last thing she had touched, and perhaps the last of her he would ever see. He blinked hard, trying to hold back so many mixed and confused emotions.

His anger started to rise. He could feel his temper boiling and getting out of control. Stomping into the galley kitchen, at the table where he had sat and worked on school work so many times with his mother, he saw the heavy, worn-out tailor eating the cherry pie his mother had baked a few hours ago.

Phillip grabbed Naji's arm, and pulled him to his feet so hard that Naji cried out.

"AHHH! WAIT!!! Hurting!!!" Naji was trying to shake free from Phillip.

"Where is she? Where is my mother? What is going on, you old fool, what is this dog about anyway?

Why did you even come to our house?" He squeezed the old man's arm so tightly that Claire jumped up and pulled him off the elderly tailor.

"BUD!!! Hey, Bud, what the heck's goin' on with you anyway? What's wrong? What's wrong? We invited him here, remember?"

She saw the mixture of terror and anger in her brother's eyes. It was an intense look she had never seen before. She didn't know what to make of the melee.

Softly now, putting her hand on his back gently, she queried. "What's wrong, Bud?"

"Mom's gone. Period. I think this dude knows what's happened, Claire. She really is gone, and I think this freak-show has something he needs to tell us. Something about where Mom is, or if she is even OK."

"Whoa, Whoa, WHOA!!! Whadda ya mean Mom's gone? I thought she was walking the little dog, you mean she's taken off to the store? Seems odd, her backpack is sitting here on the bench. Ya' know, she never goes anywhere without her stuff. Maybe the office called and a patient had an emergency?"

He wanted to shake her, and it was becoming increasingly hard for him to resist the temptation.

"She's gone, Claire, gone, gone, GONE, you hear me, not to the store, not to the office, not to the million, zillion other places she USUALLY goes! She is G... O... N... E... GONE!!!"

Claire grabbed him by the shoulders, and put her face directly in front of him, looking straight into his eyes. "An accident, she's been in an accident? What the heck is happening, tell me NOW exactly what's happened to her!"

Suddenly, he felt much older, and he rubbed his eyes. They burned, as the dust and the sweat and the tears stung them. Claire thought for a minute he might break down and cry, but he only gave a huge sigh, exhaling every last bit of breath that was in him. She felt his shoulders drop, and he raised his arms and gently pushed her hand off of his shoulders.

"Claire, I know you're all logic, all science, and all one-hundred-percent black-and-white facts. But, what happened just now to Mom now, well," he paused, turned away from her, and spun around to face Naji.

"THIS guy, this guy right here knows *something* about what happened to Mom!"

He looked at Naji, who was breathing heavily and had dropped his massive frame into one of the kitchen chairs. Naji did not have the heart to look at either one of them, and he kept his head bowed so low it was almost resting on the kitchen table. His arms hung loosely in front of him. They could hear him wheezing with each long, slow, breath. Phillip started to worry that the old tailor might collapse and need medical attention.

"Sit down, Claire, sit down," Phillip ordered, in a surprisingly calm voice. "Sit down, Claire. For once, I'm taking charge. Sit down and I'll tell you everything I know."

Claire slowly, frozen in amazement, pulled out one of the ladder-back chairs and dropped into it. She was holding onto the seat of the chair with both hands, as if a strong wind was coming to blow her away. She straightened up and looked at him quizzically, nodded her head toward Naji, who was still slumped over, and nodding her head back and forth several times as she met Phillip's gaze, she signaled her readiness to hear him.

McClure had dropped to the floor, his head propped up and resting, as both hands clasped the edges of his chin. He was shaking his head rapidly back and forth as if out of control, and was tapping his outstretched foot in the same rhythm to a tune playing in his own private world.

Pebby lay in a t-bone position, her face flat on the floor. The only things that moved were her eyes and the shaggy bangs of her haircut, her glance darting quickly from one person to the next. She was taking it all in. Moushka has retreated to the safety of his crate, soft padding cushioning his fragile, arthritic body. He circled twice, dropped, and heaved a sigh as he settled in. A few torn cloth toys in bright primary colors littered the cage. He picked up an old Raggedy Rag doll and chewed the red yarn hair.

Phillip was sitting straight up, shoulders pulled back and frozen to the back of his chair. His left eyebrow was arched, his cheeks were puffed, and his bottom lip stretched over the top one. He kept glancing at his mother's chipped coffee mug. It sat on the table, her lipstick stain visible on the outside of the cup. He bit the inside of his mouth.

They all froze for what seemed an eternity, and it was Pebby who broke the silence. Her tiny nails clicked on the floor as she slowly stood, stretched out, and made her way to Phillip. She sat solemnly beside him. He dropped his hand down, and rested it on her head. His shoulders dropped; rose and dropped as he exhaled a deep breath. It was almost too sad to talk about. Claire was the first to break the silence as she turned to look at McClure, who was still tuned into his own world while he sat on the kitchen floor.

"OK, give. What the hell is going on? Where is Mom? Tell me all you know RIGHT NOW!" Glancing at McClure, she directed rapid-fire questions at him.

"How did you show up this morning, I thought you were grounded. Did Mom go to pick you up? When in the world did you get here?"

He sniffed, and gave very measured, staccato answers. "My mom was going to get groceries, and I told her I had an end-of-the-year project we had to finish. She brought me over and dropped me off. I saw Moushka sitting by the front door still on his leash. I grabbed the end of it and he dragged me to the park, so hard I couldn't keep up. Then I saw Phills crawling on his knees around the fireplace, so I thought he lost something. The dogs started baying something awful."

Claire nodded, turning back to Phillip.

"So, you guys dropped off Naji here at the house, and Mom took Pebby for a walk while you were waiting for McClure?"

"Yeah. She just took Pebby real quick, to see how she walked on the leash. I hooked Moush' up out front. When she took too long, I walked down the park to see if maybe the dog was loose, or she was talkin' to someone."

"OK, I get that," she continued, "then what?"

"Well, when I got to the park, Pebby was off the leash running crazy circles. Mom was standing by the fireplace and I saw the dust swirl around her, which turned to smoke, which real fast turned to a glittery smoke, kind'a copperish. Mom started to cough, and cough hard, and the next thing I knew, she tripped. I saw her fall down and the bad leg kind'a fold under her. She fell and her head was bleeding. I tried to get to her, but the smoke pulled her in, and next thing I knew, it was like she got sucked down into the middle of the fireplace. The smoke was gone, and so was she." He sniffed loudly. Claire got up and silently handed him a box of tissues.

Refusing to give in to tears, he exhaled deeply and continued. Naji turned his head and finally looked up. Trying to hold back his anger, Phillip turned and directly and forcefully addressed Naji.

"So, Naji, remember the new backpack? Well, I found a widget from a tailor shop, someplace called Norwall. Looked it up. Place doesn't exist. At least not in this world. Then, the day we did the painting,

Clure was playing with the widget, and the gears started moving, and it flipped into a key."

Claire was intently listening, as she pulled out her phone and was wildly researching Norwall. She hunched over her small screen, searching uselessly for a town that she already knew probably did not exist.

Naji was now sitting straighter, looking at both of them, and sadly shaking his head from side to side.

"I never wanted you to find out. I never meant harm. I never, never..."

He started to cry big wet sobs, and his shoulders shook uncontrollably.

"I can't go back there, my lungs are too bad. I am very ill, as your most kind mother has told me just this morning. She said I am breathing with only part of my lungs, so I cannot go back there, the air is so bad, just so bad, oh, so BAD!" He slammed his fist down weakly for emphasis. "But, they need me there!"

Sobbing now, his heart broke for the people he had left behind. Tears streamed and dropped on his white shirt, tears raining like raindrops, making gray spots on the clean, pressed white linen. The crying was making his breathing even more labored and the wheezing was getting worse.

"Go WHERE???" shouted Claire, now reaching up and pulling both sides of her hair straight out. She shook her head back and forth. Phillip could feel the heat from her anger from across the kitchen, and for a moment he worried she was spinning out of control.

"Norwall, she's gone to Norwall," Naji whispered in between each wheeze. "Norwall, and the Parallax Contingency. The three suns align in the exact middle of our year, and the portal to your world can open. I wasn't thinking about it, I had forgotten about it, but one day I stopped to sit at Favingsham Park on the edge of town."

Claire rolled her eyes and huffed, but did not say a word. Phillip sat, motionless and speechless.

"Pebby ran around, as fast as she could, chasing something, I dunn'no, I felt everything in front of me move, then BOOM, as if someone pushed me on the back, I fell, and I felt everything spin."

He raised his hands on each side of his head and covered his ears.

"Then, I felt the hot hot sun of your sky, and the grass sticking on my skin, and it was hot, very hot, and I was here. I was lying in a dirty, grassy field, burning up with the sun... so hot... so very hot!"

All at once, Phillip jumped up fast, landing on both feet.

"So! Probably Mom went through this port, or warp, or whatever you wanna' call it, right? And, she probably went the other direction to Norwall, right? I mean, how many ports are there?"

"No one knows. The Automatons don't allow us to use them. But people have figured out that they can escape Norwall and come to this world, but it only makes passage for a few times a year while the moons and suns are aligned and the Parallax Contingency opens. Once it closes, it can be centuries until the moons align in that way again. We never know when the Parallax will open, and we never know if it will open again."

"Wait, wait, wait...' Phillip insisted. "Why do they want to leave Norwall? And what's an Automaton?"

"The air is bad. The steam machines of the factories make the air bad, and people die from Graysky Lung Disease. The Automatons are machine men who are not bothered by the thickness of the air, and they own us,"

"Own you, like slaves?" Phillip pressed on with the questioning, "Whaddaya mean?"

"They oversee the humans of the territory for the ruling class, the Council."

"But, OWN you? Whaddaya mean, own you?" Phillip was incredulous.

"We are slaves to them. They work for the Council, and we work and live in the factories until we cannot work anymore, then we die or they kill us. Those of us who are skilled," he puffed up a bit, "like myself, can be shop owners. But, we are all slaves to the Automatons, life-long slaves, even the little dogs! The Council parcels out our food rations, which are never enough."

Weeping openly, Naji lowered his head to the table. Claire stood up slowly, as if taking it all in, and she handed him tissues. She rubbed Moushka's head as he whimpered pitifully. She stood face to face with Phillip, rubbing his shoulder, trying her best to comfort him.

"Well, at least we think we know where she is now," she smiled tenderly.

Looking for the first time a few inches taller than Claire, Phillip turned away from her. He took a few steps away and took a deep breath and turned back around to face her directly. Holding up his left arm, and tapping lightly on his watch, his most prized possession, he clicked the button which started the timer.

Lowering his eyes, he met Claire's gaze dead-on. Authoritatively, definitively, wasting no words, he stated directly."If we don't find her by the time the Parallax closes, Claire, we will never see her again. Clock's ticking Claire, clock's ticking."

CHAPTER 31

The Grassy Field

Sunshine was bright in her face, but Abby thought she could feel a breeze blowing, cool enough to give her a little chill. She was so thirsty, so very thirsty. What had happened? Then the pain grabbed her, the pain in her ankle. So many times before it had hurt, but *nothing* like this. If she moved her hips, the pain would rack her and bring tears to her eyes. She gasped; the pain was so bad it hurt just to breathe.

Then as if out of nowhere, soft, white fluffy fur was next to her neck, and a small pink tongue licked the side of her face. It tickled, and she reached up to scratch her face, surprised to find blood on her fingers.

A dog tag glittered in the sun. Seeing the name, she softly called out.

"Linus? You are so tiny, are you really a dog? You're so little! Where am I, Linus? Why am I hurt?" A white kerchief around his neck was dotted with red circles of gears. He was friendly enough, and more than sweet. He was sniffing her ankle, then jumping up to her face, licking to make sure she was awake.

"Go get help," she whispered. "Get someone! You hear me? Wait, come here you rascal!" She wiped some blood from her face with her index finger, and put spots of blood on the kerchief.

She faded in and out of consciousness. She lost all track of time, but then slowly, almost as in a dream, she saw people approach her. They were dressed in white, which gave her assurance that they were a medical team. The people approaching her were speaking in soft, muted voices, and she felt as though her hearing was lost on her right side. She did not know the people, and they spoke to her softly, asking her name. She was unable to answer; couldn't think of what to answer.

They lifted her carefully onto a gurney, but not until they wrapped her ankle tightly. She felt them wrapping cloths around her head too, and for a moment, she thought she would pass out. They seemed to be taking good care of her. They had white caps on their heads, and kind, but pale faces. They spoke gently to each other, and gently to her. They kept asking her her name, which right now, for the life of her, seemed far down in her memory bank, buried deep under the layers of pain, and pitifully out of reach.

They asked her where she came from. She *had* to know, should know, but for now, did not know. What she was doing to end up flat on her back in a field, with not a possession to her name? They were hurrying, and telling each other to hurry, as if they were hiding her. She felt them lift her up onto a gurney, and waves of pain too terrible to acknowledge, washed over her again.

"Quickly now, quickly before they see us!" she heard them say.

"Move faster!!!" She felt whoever was carrying her bump, bump, bumpity-bump as she was carried along. Each bump aggravated the pain, which came in waves of torture. She was fighting to stay conscious.

Head still swimming, she felt them turn her head to the side and offer her a cup to drink. The sweet taste was unfamiliar, but soothing. She felt her head spinning, and her body floating out of control. She grabbed the jacket of the woman holding the cup to her parched lips. She read the name on the jacket; perfectly embroidered red letters, "Octagon Bakery." She felt them lay her head down, and was pleased to find the softest pillow under her loose hair. Closing her eyes, she stopped fighting.

Fluttering her eyes, she saw the sky was a muted shade of gray, and some contraption buzzed overhead. The white-clothed people were running now, carrying her carefully toward a woods where they loaded her onto the back of a flat wagon. She thought she heard whooshing puffs of steam as she felt the wagon lurch, and the pain grabbed her, overwhelmingly grabbing her, intolerably grabbing her, as she felt the little dog sitting now by her head, giving her face a few licky-licks.

"Stay with me, Linus, *please stay with me*," she pleaded, as she felt unknown hands holding her ankle steady. She stopped fighting the pain, stopped fighting to stay conscious, and slipped into the deepest sleep she had ever known.

CHAPTER 32

The Toy Robot

Naji Najeem had taken quite a liking to the tiny, hardworking canine vagabond he had met two years ago, and he had fashioned her hat and vest himself back in Norwall after a busy day at his tailor shop. Now, Claire and Phillip led him to a massive brown leather armchair in their front living room. The tinydog followed along and watched as he dropped into the chair. Freddy, the parrot, gave a few explosion sounds, which made the nervous tailor jump. The African gray laughed at his startled reaction and rocked furiously on his swing.

Naji sunk into the comfortable chair as Phillip and Claire lowered him down and raised the leg support. Claire threw an afghan over him and Phillip placed a soft couch pillow under his head. Naji sighed and remembered the tattered and patched armchair in his tiny apartment back in Norwall. Seeing that he was having trouble breathing, and was exhaling against pursed lips, Claire ran to the utility closet. She set up a nebulizer machine that their mother had used when they had childhood respiratory problems. Thankfully, she remembered all the details of its operation.

Naji heaved a deep sigh as he breathed in the vapor. He coughed once or twice, and let his mind relax. His breathing became easier, and Claire and Phillip relaxed and headed back to the kitchen table where McClure, who had regrouped and gotten a hold of his emotions, had found a tablet. He was furiously writing notes on everything they knew so far.

Pebby heard the discussion in the kitchen getting louder and louder. Quietly, she crept into the kitchen and edged herself under the long harvest table out of view of the three friends who were now confronting one another. Claire was bordering on the fringe of anxiety laced hysteria.

"You can't be the one to go!" she fumed, throwing her pen down onto the white narrow-ruled tablet in front of her, as her voice got louder and louder. In the background, the perceptive bird in the front room started making explosion sounds again.

"I have Mom missing, and if something happens to you as well, and then Mom comes back, and I was the one who let something happen to you? Are you kidding? She would kill me. I mean, she would never forget that I was the one who let you go. Nope, you still have to listen to me when Mom is not around! There is no way I'm sending you off into the Parallax whatever, or some kind of contingency, not knowing where you are. Suppose you go to another dimension, like prehistoric dino-land, somewhere Mom is not? You could be trapped there. This is not some *Back to the Future* movie where everything is neat and scripted. This is, well, this is just,... catastrophic!" She threw her head back and shook it wildly, pulling out her ponytail holder. She shook out her hair, rubbed her face roughly with both hands, leaned back, and crossed her arms.

"Hey, Clure, did you call your folks? It's better if you stay here tonight. I'm in no mood to drive, and it's going to take us most of the night to figure this out."

McClure kept his head down, but directed his gaze upwards to stare at Claire. Although he liked her, at times he was glad she was Phillip's sister, and not his. She was a bit too flighty for him, and bossy. Claire was *real* bossy all right.

Still, at least, she had the foresight to have him check in with his family. The last thing he needed was his old man suspecting something was amiss at the Weathermore's.

"Hi, Mom," McClure's voice was shaky. He tried to sound serious but casual at the same time.

"Mom, Ms. Weathermore wants Phillip and me to paint some walls in her study tomorrow. OK if I stay so we can get started early? They can bring me home tomorrow. OK? Please? Please, Mom?"

"OK, sure," Sylvie replied, not at all displeased that she would have time to lie in bed and watch movies. "But make sure you are helping her, and be polite, please, ask her if she has some old clothes you can wear, so you don't get your clothes all painted, OK?"

"Sure, Mom, sure, I'll call you tomorrow. Bye now," he sighed. The world could be falling down around her, and she would be worried about his manners and the cleanliness of his socks. He didn't understand her most of the time. How she could make a career out of clipping coupons for things they didn't need was beyond him.

He smiled and clicked the phone off. *Done.* He was at least rid of them for the next twenty-four hours. He was free for the time being, and he turned his attention to the two Weathermores who were arguing passionately in front of him. Each of them was standing at different ends of the long oak harvest table shaking their index fingers at the other.

McClure huffed. This dispute was not going away any time soon. The Weathermores were strong-willed, and both Phillip and Claire were determined to have their own way.

"Claire!" Phillip was adamant.

"I'm the one who got the backpack. I'm the one who found the widget. I'm the one who wants the dog, and I'm the one who was trying to solve the problem, long before you ever got involved!"

He could see that this argument was getting him nowhere, as she dropped into her chair, shaking her head, not even letting her gaze meet his.

He continued, getting louder, raising the volume of the discussion.

"Shhh!" interrupted McClure, trying to moderate. "You'll wake Naji! He's worn out, let him sleep. Come on you two, let's figure this out, let's all calm down and think about the best moves here, right?"

Heeding his friend and quieting his voice to a whisper, Phillip continued. "Look, I know school is almost out this term, but think of this. If you go, and I stay here, I can't drive. I can't take care of all these pets without being able to drive. Plus, people will get suspicious if I am at the house alone. If you are here, no one will ask questions. You just say me and Mom went out of town for a few days."

He turned and squarely faced his friend.

"McClure. You cover me in school. There are only two weeks left 'till summer vacation. We'll say something like, oh, had to go out of town for a few days, something like, Mom had a conference, something decent like that. I can finish the finals in the next few days, and we'll forge a note from Mom saying I have a family emergency."

He stood, pulling his frame up to showcase his height.

"Think about it Claire, it's the only way it will work. You don't want me to go, I know, but you can't leave me here alone. Next thing, we'll have people suspicious. You can handle that, I can't."

McClure chose his words carefully, and he delivered them softly and kindly. "You have to admit Claire, he's right. Leaving him here alone, even if I would stay here too, would cause everyone to be suspicious. Plus, we couldn't drive to get stuff we would need."

Frustrated, Claire hung her head and sighed deeply, then threw her head back and yawned.

"You guys, I can't take it anymore, I need sleep. Clure, you set up in the West Wing, you know, the room behind the bookcase in Mom's study. Bed's all made, should be towels and soap in there. Bud, give him a pair of pajamas, and Clure, you hand out your clothes, I'll throw them in the washer tonight and dry them in the morning, OK?" Claire continued, yawning all the while.

"Guess we have a plan now, maybe things will be easier when we get some sleep," McClure offered, "wadda'ya say we all sleep on it?"

"OK, I'm gonna let this little girl outside for a minute, I think I'll let her sleep with me, OK, Claire?" And before she could answer, he picked the tinydog up and held her like a baby over his shoulder as he headed out the front door.

"I'll take out Moushka, Claire, you get some rest," McClure offered kindly.

"Good idea Clure, I'll clean up and set out clean water for all the guys. We've got particular, peculiar, persnickety pets," Claire said in a sing-song fashion.

"Particular, peculiar, per... snick... ity pets!"

Par... tic... ular... peculiar... per... snick... ity... pets!" *She's losing her mind*, thought McClure, as Claire continued to chant, dancing around the kitchen while she refreshed all the animals' water bowls.

Phillip headed to his room, still carrying the tiny scruffy dog. Throwing himself down on his bed, his mind drifted to the figurines adorning his room. His Mom had hired Ravinni to mount the shelves high on the wall, and he had placed his collectibles there. He focused on a small rock from a school field trip to the Museum of Natural History in Washington, D.C. He remembered the trip, where his mother had served as a chaperone. The school did not permit the students any soft drinks, only milk. He remembered his mother had spirited him away to a quiet, secluded section of the museum, where she produced a cup of icy cold, raspberry-grape soda, his favorite, while she sipped her diet cola. They laughed and furtively sipped, and he smiled to think of her pirating him away from the group to sneak him his favorite soda.

She had broken another rule when he asked for the quartz crystal he had spotted in the gift shop. The school had prohibited the purchase of souvenirs, and after he had pleaded for it, she winked, and told him to return to his group. She slipped away for a matter of seconds, and the coppery-gold quartz crystal found its way to the store checkout. Now, it sat in a place of honor in his room. It looked like a giant glittering glacier, and it reminded him again of the sparkly haze into which his mother had fallen that very afternoon.

He held it, gripping it, noticing for the first time how heavy it was. Funny, it had just never crossed his mind that his mother had carried this weight around the museum in her backpack all day. Now that he thought about it, many of the collectibles on his shelves reminded him of places he had gone with his family.

There was the whistle from the train trip in Philadelphia, and the Monarch butterfly encased in lucite from the Butterfly Gardens in Key West. One had landed on his shoulder, and his mother said that it would bring him good luck. Then, the robot, silly baby-toy, sitting on his shelf, a square face, eyes aquamarine, hands clenched as if they might have previously been holding something.

His mother had given that to him several years ago at Christmas, and he could not find the door to put the batteries in and make it work. It looked sort of used anyway. She had laughed and said it had been given to her when she was little, and she was passing it on to him. He thought it was a joke, but she had been dead serious.

They had been short of money the year they bought the house, so he hadn't said anything. He thought it was sort of ugly anyway, and that the face looked mean. His mother seemed to like it. *Could there really be a city where mechanical men patrolled the streets?*

It seemed almost too unbelievable. He reached for the robot. Pebby growled softly, and looked as thought she might lunge. He laughed.

"Easy girl, it's not real, just a crappy old toy." Taking it down from the shelf, he found it heavier than he expected.

"Guess it's just to look at, not really a toy, huh?" He held it down next to her face, and Pebby started to growl again. Gears of many colors of metal, from copper to tin, to stainless, decorated the back of the robot. The dome-shaped cap ended in a point on top, and a pipe extended off of the top of the head. The eyes were turquoise, and although they were not lit, they looked as though it could be lit, if only he could find the battery compartment! Pebby continued to take biting snaps at the little robot.

"Shhh! Quiet, girl!" But she continued a low growl. "

"Wow, you really don't like this old thing, do ya?"

He looked again for a door or opening to insert batteries. There was none to be found. But, on the bottom of the robot's boot, unnoticed by him before, was a small white strip. The print on this label was tiny. Phillip didn't even think that the labelmaker would make something so small, and he reached into his desk and took out his magnifying goggles, which he used for model building.

Turning the robot upside down, shining his phone flashlight on the bottom of the boot, he could barely make out the letters.

Your Story Begins Here

Puzzled, he stood the robot back up on his desk. He guessed he could show Claire and McClure in the morning, no sense bothering them tonight.

"Come on, girl, settle down." He lifted Pebby up onto his bed and she settled herself on the blanket near his feet. Phillip fell into a deep sleep almost instantly. His breathing was regular and quiet. He never heard Pebby continue to softly growl, almost under her breath. And certainly, he never saw the little robot, face frowning, blink his turquoise eyes not once, not twice, but three times in rapid succession.

CHAPTER 33

The Vanilla Coffee

So, it was decided that Phillip would be the one to make the trip. Claire was beside herself with worry. She was still heavily conflicted about standing by while her brother risked everything. Even if he could locate their mother, Claire knew that he faced a monumental ordeal in trying to bring her home. In the first place, from what Phillip had described, her mother had, at a minimum, a fractured leg and a head injury as well. Claire had said nothing to Phillip, but deep in her heart, she wondered if her mother had even survived the transport after such serious injuries.

Nor would she dare mention that possibility to Phillip. She had to prepare him for the possibility that, if alive, their mother may not even be able to walk. Phillip could not delay getting her home, but he needed to make sure she was stable enough to make the trip. He would need to be tutored in first aid and able to assess her injuries.

Phillip might be anxious to leave, but there were many things to be done. Although it was the end of the school year, their mother, if she did come home, would never forgive them if Phillip missed the end of the year exams, and worse, if he tanked them. There was prep work, projects, and final exams to be dealt with.

It was Saturday, and Claire showered and dressed quickly. She stood at the bathroom mirror for a few seconds and searched the front of her hair for gray ones, as she had seen her mother do. Not finding any, she yanked out a few pieces just for the heck of it.

The boys were still sleeping, but Naji had, a few minutes ago, hoisted himself out of the recliner, straightened his clothes, and made his way to the kitchen. His gait was wide-based and somewhat unsteady. He was not fully awake and he held onto the wall to steady himself. He took a deep breath and inhaled the sweet aroma of the vanilla coffee Claire was brewing.

"You've just got to help us Naji," Claire pleaded as she set out a small pitcher of milk, sugar, and sugar substitute, as well as four mugs. Her mother's mug, the rim stained with her favorite pomegranate lipstick, still sat in the middle of the table where she had left it yesterday, just before she took Pebby to the park. Claire could not bring herself to move the cup. It was as if the cup was not moved, her mother would walk through the front door with Moushka pulling her, fresh from the early morning walk in the park. Moushka however, was sound asleep in his crate. Occasionally he would look up at Claire, his eyes sad.

"OK, Moush, give me a few minutes to wake up. I'll take you to the park, just give me a minute to wake up." Claire hated mornings, but absent her mother, the big dog would rely on Claire to carry out the household routines, and Claire was not about to disappoint.

Pebby, hearing movement in the kitchen, started to stir. She had slept at the foot of Phillip's bed, nose pressed to the crack under the door, eyes closed, but her protective senses heightened. The little robot, tossed on the desk late last night, had made her restless and kept her from letting her guard down. She was perplexed as to how the robot, so similar to those in Norwall, could be here in Phillip's room. *Looks like a baby Automat to me!* she worried. No way she would let any harm come to this boy now.

Pebby jumped up, putting both paws on the side of the bed, and whimpered until she woke Phillip. Stretching and yawning, he suddenly remembered what had happened yesterday. He remembered too, that McClure was sleeping in the West Wing and they had left Naji snoring loudly in the living room recliner. Suddenly, he realized that he was starving. He couldn't remember when he had eaten his last meal.

"Come on, girl," he flipped back the covers and slid his feet to the floor. "Let's get us some grub, huh?" Changing quickly into athletic shorts and a soft, comfy t-shirt, he scooped up the scruffy dog and headed for the kitchen. He was glad to see that Naji was already awake.

"Mornin', Naji," he sighed, is Clure up yet?" Pouring himself a cup of coffee he mixed in half a cup of milk and several teaspoons of sugar. He inhaled the sweet, vanilla aroma, then gulped it.

"Ahhh, sweet indeed! Hey Naji, le'me fix you a cup of sunshine. I take mine with milk and five sugars, I call it the 'high fiver'! That is, until Mom catches me and pours it in the sink, sayin' I'll rot my teeth!"

Suddenly he was silent, realizing she wasn't there to stop him from his silliness. The cinnamon rolls she had made yesterday were still on the counter, and he sighed deeply as he unsnapped the plastic cover. The kitchen was dead silent until Claire spoke up.

"Phillip. I know you are anxious to go, I know that there is a time crunch here, I just want you to go prepared."

"Claire, I am as prepared as I will ever be!" He brazenly poured another coffee for himself and also prepared one for Naji. Spilling sugar over the counter, he brushed it thoughtlessly onto the floor.

"Phillip!" Claire ran over with a dish towel. Why don't you just invite the ants in! Think for a minute! Phillip, think, think, think!" She stared deeply in his face for emphasis and she frowned deeply.

"We've got to get you ready. You are NOT ready to go. Think, think, think! She rattled the words off like a train, chugging along up a hill, like a little engine that wanted to, but couldn't.

"What's all this thinkin'?" McClure sauntered into the kitchen, pulling at his front lock of hair which was standing straight up. Yawning, he scratched himself and headed also for the day-old cinnis, decorated with cream-cheese icing dotted with raisins.

"Phills, wadda' ya' got for java?" He dropped into a chair as he bit into a roll and dropped crumbs on the floor.

"I give up on you guys, I can't figure out who's worse!" Claire rushed over to him with a paper plate, shoving it under his roll and catching the crumbs. "By the way, your clothes are in the dryer, they only got a few minutes more."

Until now, Naji had not said a word. He cleared his throat and sipped the coffee concoction Phillip set in front of him as he tried to rise from his chair. The effort was too much for him, and sadly, he sat back down. When he spoke, he directed his gaze and his words at Phillip.

"You cannot take this trip lightly. Even if you can make it through the Parallax, you are going into a place that many would hope to escape from. The Automatons are everywhere, they see everything, and they send every observation to the Council. There is no place you can go where you are out of their sight."

Coughing for at least twenty seconds and giving a few short wheezes, he tried valiantly to continue.

"You will probably be noticed at some point. Any traveler across the Parallax is marked. There will be a price on your head and reward for your capture, and no one will be your friend. *You must trust no one!*"

By this time, Claire had retrieved the nebulizer machine and started blowing bubbling, moist, medicated air into his face. She held it six inches from his face and his breathing improved considerably. Wheezing still, he tried to continue.

"The machines and the industries have soiled the air and breathing can be difficult. You see what it did to me. If I went back, I would not be alive for very long." He coughed again several times and heaved some deep breaths.

"I will tell you how to find my tailor shop, and if you keep the lights off, no one will know you are there. It will be a safe place for you to stay. Above the shop is my most humble abode, use it to sleep and to be safe. So long as the lights are kept off, the Automatons will not suspect any activity. It can be your refuge or homebase, so to speak. You will find clothing there and cans of food. Use whatever you need. If you can, there is a picture on the mantel, my Hannah." He dropped his head, knowing he would never get back there to retrieve it. "Please bring it to me if you can. Anything else, I must leave behind."

Tears were welling in his eyes. Claire hugged him tightly and handed him several tissues as her mother had taught her when she helped in the office. Claire really didn't know what else to do.

"We don't know where your mother might be, She may have already fallen into the hands of the Automatons.

"And," he hesitated, covering his face with his hands, "we don't know if she can walk. Things are different, very different there..." His voice drifted off. He was tired.

Claire did not want to stress him further, but she needed information if her brother was to survive. Their mother's life might depend on how well Phillip could think quickly and decisively, which had never been his strong point. Claire scratched her head and pulled on her ponytail, still disheveled from her restless night's sleep.

"Naji, can you sketch a bare outline of Norwall? It will help Phills know his way around if we can help him visualize the key areas in the city so he can be oriented. Can you do it?"

"I must go back to the Imperial today, I must keep the shop open. If I don't, I will have nowhere to go. I have a place there, and I can rest tomorrow. You can be getting ready, and in a few days, I will come back. I will bring a drawing of Norwall, the best that I can remember. You know, you will have Pebby with you. You have to take her. She knows every nook and cranny in that town, and she knows the people who will be of help to you."

He rubbed her head affectionately.

"She will help you. You will have the knowledge of the map, but she is better than any map. She knows Norwall, and knows how to take you to my Wenderling Way shop very quickly. There will be clothes there so you can dress like you belong in Norwall. There will be food, and a safe place for you to rest. If you can find your mother, you can bring her there and she can rest too, until it is safe for her to make the return trip to this land. You can use my wife's clothes for her, as they are no good to anyone now." He wiped his teary eyes and continued.

"You must find out how long the Parallax will stay open, or you run the risk of being trapped forever in Norwall. It might not open again for many years. Pebby is the best chance that you will not be seen, or worse, stopped by the Automatons." He picked up the tiny scruffy dog, and held her close. "She is the finest dog in Norwall. She, you know, is Chief Delivery Dog for the Octagon Bakery, one of the largest industries there." His voice quieted. "They keep the people like slaves. You cannot get free once you are taken there. There is no escape, only death. And my friend, depending on the mood of the Council, it can be very quick, or it can be very, very slow. It can be public, or you can be left alone to die unattended."

Claire shivered. It seemed like an insurmountable job for her younger brother. It seemed totally horrific that he could get trapped in a perilous city, and not return until he was middle-aged. How would she live with herself if she was sending him into danger? They had bickered incessantly. He had tortured her cats. But, she loved him deeply, and the thought that he could be walking into a trap was too much for her.

She knew his strengths, but also his weaknesses. She must, even if he resisted, prepare him for the journey. She doubted he appreciated the dangers. She couldn't dwell on them. She needed to focus her efforts on leading him to believe that he needed to prepare in order to keep their mother safe. He would buy that. Making him feel inadequate, or careless with his own safety, would get her nowhere and would make him defensive. She had to be smart, real smart, to get him prepared.

Claire sighed. She looked around the kitchen table at the overweight, gasping dry cleaner, struggling with each breath. Shifting her gaze to McClure, who was dropping sweet-roll crumbs as he giggled at a funny meme on his cellphone, to Phillip, who stirred yet another sugar packet thoughtfully into his coffee as he stared at his mother's abandoned coffee mug.

"Heaven help me!" she muttered under her breath. "How about pancakes for everyone?"

CHAPTER 34

The Final Exams

Much to Claire's suprise, Phillip buckled down on his schoolwork. She saw a ferocity in him that she had never seen before. She saw that he had no intention of skipping out of the final exams. Not only did he intend to take them, he intended to rise to the top of his class.

After they took Naji home, they dropped off McClure. They promised to pick him up on Saturday, which they designated "T-Day," for the travel day. No one could bring themselves to even say the words *Parallax Contingency*; it seemed too surreal to even acknowledge the words by saying them outloud.

Phillip cleared the kitchen table of everything but the flower arrangement and his mother's mug. The pomegranate lipstick stain on the rim reminded them that her return to them was highly dependent on the strength of their preparation. They would not let her down. He spread his schoolwork out, carefully organizing each class, placing the notes onto separate piles.

There were five exams he had to complete this week and he was determined to ace them. He spent the entire day working, as Pebby lay on the cool tile beside his feet. His study time was only interrupted several times during the day when he and Claire walked the dogs. They did not get closer than twenty-five feet to the fireplace, but they watched it from the street, as they both, separately, wondered if it really was the Parallax to another dimension, or rather a bad nightmare trip to the unknown.

Claire didn't interrupt Phillip's studies, but spent the day doing the work usually performed by their mother. She washed clothes, cleaned out Freddy's cage, enduring a sizable nip on the finger when she did not provide the expected allotment of almonds that her mother gave the bird each morning. *Where was Abby Weathermore?* He sat quietly on his perch. She had never left him before. He watched Claire with interest as she swept around his cage and mopped the floor. He imitated the sound of falling water as she mopped, making her laugh. Anxious for the return of his owner, he rocked furiously on his swing.

By Saturday evening, Phillip was ready, at least in Science, Geography, and English. Claire quizzed him without mercy. Phillip paced around the kitchen answering her questions, which she peppered with her comments.

"Think, Phillip, think! You know this! Now, give me the three steps of cellular respiration!"

She unlocked her lab and carried a four-foot-tall whiteboard to the kitchen. Hanging it carefully on the wall, she opened her new pack of markers and offered the green one to Phillip. He was taken aback at how quickly Claire shared her office supplies. She usually and fastidiously kept her supplies closely monitored.

"Now! Quick! Draw me the Krebs cycle! Don't forget to show the ATP in red. Come on now! Quick!"

Phillip didn't argue. He stuck to the business of getting the information implanted in his brain. For the first time in his life, he actually appreciated Claire. He was amazed at her facility in helping him with his assignments. She already knew everything. He wondered how her brain could even store all that knowledge. They studied until late into the night, calling it quits just after midnight.

Coffee cups, used paper plates, and empty plastic vita-water bottles littered the oak table. Papers, markers, pens, and crumpled pages of graph papers were strewn everywhere, including the floor.

"Disaster zone," Claire sighed resolutely, *so what, she's not here to see it, and it can all wait until morning.* She pushed the ladder-back chairs in.

Phillip suddenly and unexpectedly stepped over to Claire, wrapped his arms around her, and squeezed her in a tight hug, something he hadn't done for years.

"Ya got my back on this, don't cha, Claire. Ya got my back."

She hugged him back as tears came to her eyes and she blinked fast to hide them.

"Always have, dude, always have." She gave him one last squeeze and hurried to the solitude of her bathroom. Turning on the bath water full force, hot as it would go, she sprinkled her favorite mineral soak into the water. Watching it foam, she rubbed her eyes. The desperation of the situation was all too clear. She was sending her brother, who had always had a devil-may-care attitude, into danger where his carelessness could cost him his life. Wasn't there any way they could communicate? As she slid into the scalding water, and added just enough cold so that her skin would not burn, she wracked her brain. There just had to be a way to keep in contact with him, just had to be!

Back in the kitchen, Pebby, who had not left Phillip's side the entire day, got a cool drink of the ice water they had set down for her. Slowly, she trudged back to Phillip's room. After a shower, he threw himself on his bed and pulled the covers over his face. He tried to ignore the low growls of the tinydog, but it became impossible. Then she started a series of shrill barks, which were even more annoying.

"What the heck?" Flinging the covers down, he saw that she was poised in attack mode, the object of her fury being the two foot tall robot still standing on his desk. Now Claire was knocking on the door.

"What's wrong with her? Does she have water? Phills, I gotta' sleep!" Opening the door, she saw the tiny scruffy dog snarling her lips and displaying a vicious line of canine teeth. Claire gingerly reached down to quiet the upset canine, who allowed her to pet her head.

"She's spooked out by that robot, dusty old piece of crap," Phillip yawned, as he pulled the covers even tighter around his head. "It doesn't even work. No place to put batteries, I looked already."

"Well, I'll put it in the kitchen and we'll deal with it tomorrow, get some sleep Buddy, you too Pebby, quiet now!"

She carried the robot to the kitchen, softly closing the door. Phillip came out from under the covers just long enough to lift up the tinydog and set her on the foot of his bed. In less than five minutes, they were both asleep. They didn't hear the ruckus in the kitchen as Claire set the robot on the kitchen table, which was still covered with the litter of the study session.

Moushka, who had been soundly snoring, as his toes wiggled and he dreamed of bounding through a field covered in pristine snow, bolted upright the minute Claire set the robot on the cluttered table. He began a low menacing growl. He shook his head to get the sleep out of his eyes, and pawed at the door of his crate to get out. Claire, who had opened the fridge to get a water bottle, shook her head, exasperated.

"Come on, you guys, let us sleep!" she groaned pleadingly, tossing him one-half of a Biscuit-Bone snack. Exasperated, she picked up the robot, and carried him back to her lab, which she had left unlocked. Setting the robot carefully on her workbench, she turned to leave.

"Good night, you pain in the butt!" she laughed. "Where did Mom ever find you? Must'a been at a flea sale or something, maybe Thrifty-Shoppes? You're an outta time, piece of old junk. Now, robots can do voice commands and everything. You don't do anything but collect dust. What was Mom thinking?"

Muttering to herself, she turned and hurried off to bed, leaving the lab door with its series of complicated locks standing ajar. She trudged down the hall toward her room. Moushka had settled down and was dreaming again, and Phillip's room was quiet. Pulling her pink quilt over her face, she imagined that she heard a hiss coming from the front room.

"Silly bird. Oh Freddy, I'll feed you in the morning. Go to sleep!" she murmured to herself, drifting off to a deep sleep, never realizing that back in her lab, the turquoise eyes had flashed at least three times and the lips had parted slightly. The corners of the mouth downturned into a frightful sneer and the hissing sounds continued through clenched, menacing teeth.

Sunday morning arrived too soon, but Claire and Phillip eschewed their habit of sleeping until ten or eleven o'clock. They were awake, showered, and sipping hazelnut coffee by eight o'clock. Phillip cleaned the kitchen table, tossing refuse into a large industrial sized trash bag as Claire cooked eggs-over-easy and thick, country bacon. She popped English muffins into the fire-engine red toaster and cut up fruit and vegetables for Freddy, who was rocking and singing in the front room.

First on the agenda after they devoured the bacon and egg muffin sandwiches, was an online first-aid course. Claire had insisted that Phillip be trained, as they had no idea of how badly their mother was injured. If he could even find her at all. He needed to know how to care for her, and he needed to be able to take care of any minor injuries he himself might suffer during the transport.

They both hoped that he would transport without major injury. Naji had briefed them on the conditions in Norwall, which were primitive, with medical care dominated by herbs and plants, similar to that found in eighteenth-century Victorian England. According to Naji Najeem, herbs and roots were administered by physicians who often wore elaborate masks shaped like bird beaks. Their long noses were stuffed with flowers and fragrant leaves to prohibit the spread of deadly disease. The working classes had little or no access to medical care, while those who ruled, namely the Council Members, enjoyed more advanced treatments which were still very inferior to modern technology.

First, was an online first-aid course. Claire sat with him as he watched the video and completed the online test with ease.

"Congrats, Buddy!" she shrieked as she gave him a high-five. "You did it! Now, come-on, it's back to the books for you!"

"Outstanding!" Phillip shrieked, and Freddy from the front room gave a loud *SHHH!*

Now boasting certification in First Aid, Cardiopulmonary Resuscitation, and thoroughly worn-out, Phillip hauled a large store-bought pumpkin pie out of the refrigerator.

"Wanna slice? Got whipped cream too!" he rattled the plastic lid.

"Oh gosh, all you ever think of is sweets, how can you be hungry after that breakfast?" He ignored her and expertly changed the subject.

"Hey, Claire! How about I take my camo backpack? I can load it with stuff I might need, and take some medicines for Mom, bandages, stuff that they might not have? Yeah?"

"Well, I don't know if you can make it through the warp. I was thinking the same thing last night. What if you take your cell? I mean, it's worth a shot. Anything to try and keep me in the loop. I was thinking even of a small radio? Who knows what will work. Anything light enough for you to carry, anything that might let me know where you are, and that you found her, yeah?"

Phillip nodded his agreement. Next on the agenda was more study time. Both Phillip and Claire were committed to what they knew their mother would want: Phillip completing the school year with an improved grade report. Phillip studied furiously until dinner, reviewing the material Claire had quizzed him on the night before, and utilizing the whiteboard to imprint the biochemistry cycles in his brain. He drew the cycles, checked them for accuracy, then erased them and drew them again, and again, and yet again. Claire busied herself with the laundry, stacking piles of neatly folded laundry on the now-spotless kitchen counter. Phillip's head was drooping, and he was too tired to continue.

"Come'on Claire, we gotta walk the pups. I gotta get some fresh air, huh?"

Pebby jumped into his lap, and he buttoned her leather vest.

"You really think Norwall is real, Claire? That there could be a city of gears, and robots? Do you really think it could exist? Or maybe Naji is just some demented old guy babbling about some imaginary stuff?"

"Phills, I don't know. All I know is that Mom is gone. I know she never would have left on her own, and you SAW her get sucked into the Parallax, didn't you? We are too far into this to question it now. If you got doubts, then you gotta be the one to stay, and I'll go in your place."

"Not a chance Claire, not a chance! I got this Claire, I got this!" He ran ahead with Pebby, who now was used to walking on a lead.

"Come on, girl, you gotta follow now, but in a few days, you'll take the lead, right?"

Pebby looked at him knowingly. She was used to him now, used to sleeping on his bed, used to lying under the table while he studied, used to following his lead on long walks through the neighborhood. It seemed like she belonged there, as if the other world had never existed. It seemed as if all her life, she had been looking for this family, these people to love. Still, she could not help thinking of Norwall, and Gleena, and Deen, and Treena. Radon too, had always expertly fixed her wagon. How were they all surviving?

The next morning, it was Claire and Pebby who dropped Phillip off at school. Taking a deep breath, petting her as she sat on his lap in the front seat, he grabbed his handful of freshly sharpened pencils. He wasn't permitted to take his backpack on these testing days, and it was just as well, for he was filling it with supplies for Norwall.

"Do good, Buddy, just do good, you know this stuff!" Claire told him lovingly, settling Pebby into the seat as Phillip nodded his assent and closed the door. She watched him walk away with a confidence she hadn't seen before. *You got this, Bud, you got this,* she whispered.

CHAPTER 35

Saving McClure

As she stared at the swollen, bloodshot eyes in the bathroom mirror, Claire did not even recognize her own face. At seven o'clock Saturday morning, she caught herself once again picking through the front of her hair looking for gray hairs. She had aged years in one week. She had taken over the household responsibilities usually done by her mother: She had ferried Phillip to school, packed his lunches, washed his clothes, and tutored him as he prepared for his tests. She had taken care of the cats and Moushka, and walked Pebby while Phillip was at school. She had endured little bites from Freddy, who was still angry that Abby was not around.

The week had raced by, but last night had seemed to last forever, as Claire alternatively slept in fitful wakefulness and sobbed occasionally. As she stared at her reflection, she wondered really if she would ever see her mother again. She was so afraid, so very afraid, to be sending her brother off to an unknown fate. The thought of never seeing either one of them again was more than she could bear.

She hoped she was making the right decision. Tying her long hair back with a worn elastic, she quickly dressed in comfortable leggings and a long, loose shirt. It was time to wake up Phillip. Tonight, she would be the only family member left in the house. She shivered. Despite all her bravado, she was terrified, and she chewed her nails down as she walked past her mother's empty bedroom.

Carelessly thrown over the arm of the rocking chair where her mother read stories to her when she was a toddler, was a beige-colored sweater. Her mother called it a *Fisherman's Knit*. Claire hadn't heard the term before, but she slipped into the soft, loosely-crocheted eggshell-beige sweater, rolling up the sleeves and wrapping it tightly around her body, as if it were her mother hugging her. Burying her nose in the shoulder, she inhaled smells which reminded her of sugar cookies, cinni-rolls, and jasmine, her mother's favorite climbing plant.

"Oh, I hope I'm doin' the right thing! Mom, wherever you are, please be OK! Please!" She wiped moisture from the corners of her eyes as she headed for Phillip's room.

"Wake-up time Dweeb!" she called out, forcing a cheerfulness, thinking that this time tomorrow his room would be empty.

"Come on, we've gotta' pick up McClure and Naji too, so come on and get breakfast!" As she started the coffee and threw bagels into the toaster, one word was all she heard Phillip call back in a monotone.

"SHOWER!" he barked hoarsely as Pebby bounded into the kitchen hoping for breakfast as well.

"OK, OK," she whispered to herself, trying to avoid looking at the camouflage backpack sitting on the chair. Hooking up both dogs, she headed outside. By the time she returned, Phillip sat at the harvest table, immaculately groomed in a black turtleneck shirt, black jeans, black wool socks, and black tennis shoes.

"You look like a spy from some creepy movie!"

He laughed and actually used a napkin to wipe the cream cheese off of his mouth, instead of the sleeve of his shirt which was his habit.

"Yeah, my impossible mission, right?"

"Yeah, sure," Claire replied with a half-hearted chuckle, and continued." Let's get these guys breakfast."

As Claire set out the dog bowls, she was surprised when Phillip jumped up from the table, bagel held by his teeth, and retrieved the dog kibble from the closet.

"Here, I got this," and he set the bagel down on a clean paper plate on the counter.

He looked taller, more confident than Claire had ever seen before, as if he had also aged during the night. She wouldn't let herself break down now and interfere with the calm, dignified reserve he portrayed.

"Come on, let's go pick up the team, Claire. Nice sweater!" he added, winking, as if he realized part of their mother was coming along.

The ride to the Imperial Dry Cleaners was quiet. Phillip loaded music from his phone, and the two, who usually never stopped chattering, fell silent. As they arrived at the small shop next door to their mother's office, they saw Naji Najeem peeking out through the blinds. Naji nodded to Phillip, looking for all the world as if he was part of a vast conspiracy. He unlocked a series of complicated deadbolts, clattering them loudly. He pulled hard to open the door.

"Come in friend, I am almost ready." He was wheezing as he walked, with a wide-based gait, twisting his portly frame back and forth, and huffing like a steam machine.

"It looks like you have a clear day for your travels, does it not? Come. I have prepared a map, which will help you find your way to my shop."

He produced a single sheet of paper with a sketched map of Norwall, depicting the main industries and roads. Phillip was impressed.

"OK, we'll go over it, let's show Claire too, come on. Anything else you need to bring?"

Naji shook his head, and locked the door behind him.

"The picture on the fireplace at my home, if you can see your way to remember it? Hannah, you know?" as he sighed mournfully.

Phillip placed his hand on the sick old man's back. "Come on, I got you covered Naji, got'cha covered. Come on now." Leading him to the car and opening the door, he settled him in the back seat and pulled the seatbelt over him, helping him adjust the fit.

Claire, still silent in the driver's seat, gave a little wave to Naji as she started the engine and backed out of the lot. Seeing her mother's business sign had suddenly reminded her that there would most definitely be a lack of money coming in with Abby suddenly gone. She had forgotten about the business interests, and now, for the first time, she realized she would have to protect the business that her mother had worked so hard to build. That was a whole project for the next week, and she willingly wiped it from her mind. *Not today, just not today, OK Mom?*

Trying to be upbeat, turning up the music and nodding her head to the beat, she headed to McClure's neighborhood.

As she expertly parallel parked the car in front of McClure's house, she sighed. Depressing, this place is depressing and so trashy. Couldn't they clean it up just a bit? The steps and sidewalk looked slimy and black, the concrete side walls chipped and pitted.

"OK, here I go!" Phillip jumped out and slammed the door behind him.

"Easy! Slow down, Bud, sheesh!" Claire said to no one in particular as she clicked open her seatbelt and turned around to talk to Naji.

"So, is it a good day for travel, Naji? Whadda ya' think?"

He nodded. "I have faith in him that he can make the trip. But, I am worried for his safety with the Automatons. They are a brutal bunch, unlike anything I have seen here in your world."

He was still finishing his words when the front door slammed open and Phillip and McClure burst out, hair and clothing flying every which way. McClure's jacket was loose and his untied shoelaces threatened to trip him. Both of them were red faced. Phillips eyebrows arched up as high as they could go. Claire had never seen his eyes open so wide.

Next, bounding through the door, slamming the screen door open with a loud crack, greasy tufts of hair standing straight up, face contorted, staggered the elder McClure. He waved his raised fist at the boys.

"You'unz are pitiful! You don't know what you are talking 'bout. Neither of you could get a job if youse even tried! Wasted losers, that's what youse are!! I'll get 'cha, you just wait and see!" He shook his fist at them, spitting as he spoke. "I'll bust you, you wait till I get me hands on ya!!! Go to Hell!"

Shaking, McClure answered loud enough for Claire, Naji, and Phillip to hear. Softly, calmly, he spoke.

"I can't, I already live there." And he got into the car, visibly shaking.

"Well, that's it for me," Claire exclaimed, half to herself, half to the rest of her crew. She jumped out of the car, stomped up the front steps and slipped on the slimy sidewalk, catching herself as she skated wildly. She pushed her way past the fuming, steamy drunk. Finding Sylvie McClure head-down on the kitchen table sobbing, she put her hand on her back.

"Sylvie, we're taking Clure with us for a week or so until things cool down, it's not safe for him here, and you know that."

Sylvie cried even harder, never once looking up.

"You're right, Claire, take him, gwan' up to his room and get some of his things, he can't keep taking this, I almost can't myself anymore. He can't keep taking it, he just can't!" she sniffed, and wiped her eyes on her worn cardigan sleeve.

Claire rubbed the woman's back kindly. It made Sylvie wail all the louder. The slam of the door told Claire that she better get out of harm's way. Much as she wanted to comfort Sylvie, she knew she better get out of the line of fire. If Robert McClure was like this so early in the morning, it would not take anything to set him off even more.

Worming her way past him, running up the stairs, she quickly found McClure's room. She glanced at the awards on the shelves. She opened drawers and pulled clothes out. She grabbed several pairs of jeans and a black hoodie, which she had seen him wear quite often. She stuffed the backpack with pajamas, underwear, and socks. Grabbing another pair of his high-top black sneakers, she inhaled deeply. Shutting her eyes for a minute, it was as if she felt her mother watching her approvingly. It now made perfect sense to her that her mother always seemed to look out for McClure.

She closed the door silently behind her and crept down the stairs. The cheap, worn wood creaked under her feet. The sounds of chaos in the kitchen, with the elder McClure berating Sylvie, moved to the foyer.

"Who'd you think you are, girl?" He spat out the words as he scratched under his arm. His stance was one of attack and he grabbed a large black golf umbrella from the stand beside the front door. His knees were shaking, and they both froze. He wiped saliva from his face with the other arm. His eyes pinned on her, his bushy eyebrows furrowed. He drew the closed umbrella back as if daring her to move.

SLAM! The cheap, cracked front door was jerked open, and the bright morning sun flooded the entranceway. Dust webs hung from the rusted, cheap chandelier. The tall man dressed in all black stepped one foot into the foyer.

"Shut your piehole, McClure, shut... your... piehole!!!" Phillip stood so tall his sister barely recognized him.

"You've bullied all of us long enough." Speaking softly and calmly, Phillip clearly addressed the frightened man. "Now, go crawl back under the rock you came out from, we'll look after Clure until you can act right. You should be ashamed of yourself. Com'on Claire, come on," motioning to her to move toward him.

She serpentined around the elder McClure, frozen with the umbrella pulled back as if it was a bow ready to let an arrow loose. She could hear his heavy breathing, smell his sour skin, and see the saliva running from the corner of his mouth. She tried not to look as she made her way out the door. Taking the stuffed-full backpack from her, Phillip put his arm around her and helped her down the pitted concrete steps.

"What about Sylvie? How can we leave her there?" Opening the back car door and handing the backpack to the shaking McClure, who was huddled in the back seat, Phillip took the shoes from her and held her door while she slid into the driver's seat.

"Ya' know, it's like Mom said, you set up the dominoes to fall. You set 'em up by what you do. Sylvie made this mess by letting him get away with his garbage. She's let it go on for so long. Mom tried to help her, but I knew she wouldn't listen. I spied on lots of talks they had. Sylvie's made a real mess. Best thing we can do is get McClure out of it. He hasn't had a chance with those two. Sylvie has to figure out how to take care of Sylvie before she can even start to look after Clure."

Shutting her door gently, he walked around the car and gave one last glance at the decrepit, dirty facade of the house. The door was shut now, and he didn't hear any screaming. As he slid into his seat, he didn't even glance back at McClure, who was sitting quietly, head down. Phillip couldn't wait to tell his mother what had happened; he was sure she would be proud.

CHAPTER 36

The Last Minutes

Gathered solemnly around the kitchen table, the group made last-minute preparations. All were seated, with Naji at the head of the table, puffing on the nebulizer treatment Claire had set up for him. She sat beside him, holding the puff-pipe as he took deep breaths. Phillip stood at the other end, fists resting on the table, studying the map Naji had hastily sketched last night. He was trying to commit it to memory in case the paper got lost in transit.

Pebby was perched in a chair, her front paws resting on the table. She was wearing her leather vest dotted with gears, and looked for all the world like she was chairing a world-changing conference. McClure, still shaking from the turmoil at his house, was sipping a coffee. Tablets, pens, pencils, and colored markers were still littered over the table. Retrieving a mason jar from the cupboard and appropriating it for a pencil cup, Phillip collected the writing implements and tidied the tablets into a neat stack.

"OK, we all know what we have to do, but let's hit it one more time. Claire, you gotta' maintain the house. Take care of the pets, Mom would want that. Anyone asks about me and Mom, you say we went to visit Uncle Harry; something like he got sick and needed help, I don't know, something like that. Remember, you have to go talk to Jaceena. You gotta talk to Jaceena. She'll know what to do to keep the business going. She can hire a part-timer to see the patients, and we'll still make enough to stay afloat."

Claire scrunched her hands through her hair and gave a deep, exasperated sigh. "She's gonna want to talk to Mom, and why would Mom go off and leave her patients? That's not like her, no way."

"Tell her Mom was really burned out, needed a break, and her brother Harry needed her fast. That's all, the less you say the better! Anyway, if things go as planned, we'll be back, few days to a week at most, and nobody will be the wiser."

Phillip poured himself a cup of coffee, added five sugar packets, and continued.

"Besides, you can't let the business collapse. I thought about this, Claire, Mom has built this for years, we can't let it fall apart now. If something happens, and we don't come home in about a week, you're going to have to take charge. That business keeps this roof over our heads, and you can't let it sink. Mom always paid the bills, paid the taxes, so now, you gotta run the show. Don't, and I mean don't, let Jaceena take over. Let her HELP you, Claire, but you gotta' step up to the plate. Do it for me, and do it for Mom. Do it for the family. We've got to survive this!"

At this point McClure spoke up. "Look, it's not so bad. I'll help you Claire, we'll call a temp service, get some *Doc-in-the-Box* to fill in, pay him by the hour, and still take home profit. You know the password to her bank account?"

"Yeah, she trusted me, I guess."

Phillip admonished her softly, careful not to embarrass her.

"Claire, she tried to get you interested in business, and finance, and umm... I mean, even shopping, but you always just blew her off. Now's the time to bail her out. Bail us all out. You gotta do it, and you gotta do it smart, so no one knows. Don't waste time, Claire. Saturday. Today is Saturday. When you take Naji back, go into the office, collect the mail and pick up all the papers lying on her desk. You can set up shop here in her office. Ravinni finished the floors and the painting, so make that your headquarters. Clure, you can help her figure this out, right?"

McClure nodded, rocking back and forth on two legs of the harvest chair, and offered his opinion. "Oh yeah, we gotta collect the mail from the mailbox. The key is to carry on as if she's still here, and I mean carry on, so carry on we will!" he stated determinedly as he tapped drum beats on the harvest table. "Gotta hand it to your mom, she had it all together. I guess the thing is, that we can't let it fall apart, no, not now."

Claire nodded, pulling herself together.

"You guys are right. We get a fill-in, keep the patients covered, and no one is the wiser. Jaceena will think Mom set it up, right?"

"Exactly Claire, exactly. Just do the things you watched her do that last couple of years. You got this, Claire, I know you got this."

What could she say to a brother who was facing an unknown fate, an army of killer robots, and a search for the mother they had lost? Pebby barked some sharp barks in assent, and Naji was shaking his head too, all the while puffing out the steam from the nebulizer.

Pebby jumped off her chair, and ran to the front door, barking furiously, even before the doorbell rang. Phillip and Claire jumped up, and McClure dashed away to the bathroom, still fearing that the old man would have tracked him down for another round of abusive screaming.

"Nesta!" Claire exclaimed as she pulled the door open. "Nesta! How great to see you! Look Phillip, it's Nesta!" Just out of sight, Phillip rolled his eyes and shook his head, mouthing the words, *Get rid of her!*

"Hello, Weathermores! Darling, how are you, and how is your handsome brother? Is your mother here? I have something for her!" She cackled, and tossed her head back.

"And where is that little plucky parrot? Darlings, he really did save the house when the chili caught on fire, remember?"

Scooping up Pebby, who was in a protective stance, Phillip greeted his mother's friend as if he had known her for years. Truth be told, he found the owner of Nesta's Bird Sanctuary to be more than a little annoying.

"Oh, hey, Nesta, love to have you come in, but we were just getting ready to leave! You here to visit Freddy? How's business at the shop?"

"Oh, business is great, my darlings, but that's why I'm here! Where is your mother?" Pushing herself past Phillip and Claire, she hurried through the foyer right to Freddy's cage, as she looked around the front rooms. Freddy looked down his beak at her. *Nutcase if I ever saw one,* he thought, noting her necklace adorned with plastic parrots, and hoping beyond hope that she would put her finger in the cage. He opened his wings in an aggressive stance, forgetting that it was at her shop where he first met Abby Weathermore, and became part of her menagerie of particular, peculiar, persnickety pets.

Phillip noticed that Nesta had set a tall, but narrow cloth-covered box in the foyer.

"Nesta, what's in the box?"

"Oh, yes, yes," bending over to peer at Freddy, her glasses perched on the tip of her nose, her long beak-like nose nearly sticking into the cage itself.

"Your mother, where is your mother? She said she would foster this majestic, more than majestic Amazon, who had the misfortune to fly off from it's owners. Tsk, Tsk, naughty bird! We have looked high and low, and we can't find the owners! Your mother is going to foster care until we can re-home her, it's as easy as that! Here, let me introduce the Weathermores to Gasparilla! Come, Phillip, quick, quick, help me bring her in, I'm not as young as I used to be!"

Making his way out the front door, he whispered to Claire. "We gotta get her out'a here before she sees Naji! She'll ask too many questions!"

Phillip quickly grabbed the cage from just outside the front door and gingerly lifted the cloth. He feasted his eyes on the greenest, most majestic, most solemn Amazon parrot he had ever seen. She held her head regally, as if she was a queen of bird society. She also had the most severe look Phillip had ever seen on a bird, and looked for all the world that she would rip his face off without a second thought. She was pinning her eyes and looking down her beak at him fearlessly.

"Claire, com'ere a second?" Pushing his glasses up on his nose, he whispered again, "We gotta get rid of that chick. Tell her Mom is coming back in a few days and you'll bird-sit till then?"

Claire whispered back in amazement, now getting aggravated.

"What? Another pet? Bad enough I have to clean up after Freddy! Now this?" Claire huffed, puffed, and threw her hands up in the air in exasperation.

"Look, just agree and get rid of her. Besides, you'll have McClure to help. He's outta school and he's staying here till we get back. I wanna talk to Mom about him spending the summer with us anyway. This is his chance to get to know you, you guys can take care of stuff together, no? Just GET RID OF HER, CLAIRE!"

Phillip motioned to Claire, nodding his head back toward the door. Picking up on his urgency to get Nesta on her way, Claire spoke up, drawing on her most authoritative reserves.

"Oh, yes, Amazons. I have heard my mother speak about them extensively. They are flock birds, and can be trained to speak, and even cry like a baby. Nesta, I will give this bird my full attention until Mother returns, which should be in a matter of days, OK? Gasparilla will be fine here, now we gotta get Phillip to the dentist. OK?"

"Dentist, on a Saturday? Such a devoted sister, no less! I know your mother is proud of how her little Weathermores have turned out!"

Sauntering her way past Claire, she patted her face lovingly, and the moment Nesta tuned away,

Claire wiped her face with her sleeve, as if to disinfect herself.

"So long, Weathermores!" Then noticing McClure for the first time, Nesta giggled as she threw her head back. "Oh, a new Weathermore maybe? My my, this house is filling up fast!"

Phillip prayed that Naji would stay in the bathroom a bit longer so as to prevent explaining the portly gentleman's presence.

"So long, Nesta, I'll have Mom call ya' when she's free. Gassy will be fine, don't worry. Claire's an expert!" he shouted after the flamboyant pet-shop owner as she drove away.

"Com'on, let's go! No more delays!" Phillip took one last look around the kitchen as Naji slowly made his way from the back of the house. "What is all the disturbance? Are you ready, my friend?"

Phillip was folding the map and securing it in his back pocket. "Ready as ever," he replied assuredly. Scooping up Pebby, he rubbed her head. "Come-on girl, let's go find Mom!"

He grabbed the backpack, tossed it over one shoulder, gave one last look at his home, heaved a deep sigh, and called out. "Bye, Freddy, Bye, Gassy, nobody put the bites on Claire while I'm gone, OK?"

As he headed out into the hot afternoon sun, he started to sweat immediately, the black turtleneck itchy on his neck. But, from Naji's briefing, he expected the weather to be much cooler in Norwall.

"Hey buddy, wait up!" McClure was close behind. Trying to make light of the situation, "you really leaving me with Claire and all these guys? Naji too?" Laughing now, "You owe me big time, when ya get back, OK?"

"Sure Clure, sure," Phillip watched as Claire led Naji down the front walk, his breathing heavy. He exhaled long breaths through pursed lips. Phillip wondered if he could even make it to the park.

"Claire, better put him in the car and drive him down. He's too weak. Clure and me will walk."

So, obligingly, Claire did. As the group gathered by the circular stone fireplace, Naji leaned on Claire. His footing was unsteady on the uneven terrain.

Tilting his head backwards and looking at the sky between the canopy of trees, Phillip took a deep breath in, and exhaled very slowly, savoring his last moments in Florida. He was ready to find his mother. He was ready to get on with his life. He was ready to help McClure, if that meant bringing him into the family, then so be it.

He was ready to get along with Claire. His dislike of her had been stupid. Far from being the Miss Pitter-Patter-Perfect he had imagined, her frailties and fears had become more obvious with the absence of their mother. She had strengths too, and now he could learn from her. She had so much to teach, and so much spunk and spirit. He admired her resolve, and vowed to carve a better relationship with her when he returned.

The tiny scruffy dog was squirming to get down. He obliged, retracing his mother's steps around the fireplace. Pebby ran, chased squirrels, and Phillip walked and jogged in circles. He threw his hands in the air, even stood inside the firepit and jumped up and down, getting ashes on his black pants. Nothing happened. The Parallax would not open. After several hours of attempts in the afternoon heat, they were ready to call it quits.

Almost at the point of tears, Phillip and Claire piled everyone in the car and headed home. It was early evening now, and they were tired. Pebby, who for all the world looked as if she had let everyone down, curled up next to Moushka in the kitchen.

Claire and McClure were slumped in chairs at the kitchen table, while Naji leaned on the door frame and gazed out into the courtyard.

"Anything we did wrong, Naji?" Phillip leaned back in the chair stretching out.

"No, I can't believe, although there has to be proper alignment between the planets and stars. The Parallax only opens on certain days, at certain times, and all the citizens of Norwall have not been able to determine the schedule. If they could, many of them would have already left Norwall. I know that the port will not open if there is electromagnetic interference. You didn't take anything with magnets? Anything that could have de-magnetized the ions of the port?

"DUH, yeah, I had my cell phone in my pocket." Phillip was exasperated. "The cell phone. That's probably what kept the port closed. How stupid can I be?"

Reaching deep into his pocket, he threw the phone out on the table.

Claire snatched it up.

"OK, everyone is hungry, we all had a long day, what say I put pizza in, and we try first thing in the morning? Naji, are you cool with sleeping in the recliner one more night? I'll give you some large scrubs Mom keeps in the bottom of her closet while I wash your clothes. Clure, you cool setting up shop in the West Wing? Looks like you are stayin' there for awhile anyway, right?"

"Yeah, good call, Claire." McClure was starting to like Claire. He guessed that he better get along, as they would be helping each other take care of Abby Weathermore's interests once Phillip was gone. She had stuck up for him in front of his old man, and he gave her credit for that.

"I am ready to rest in that reclining bed, but I will take sustenance when it is ready," Naji added. "Yes, we will try again first thing in the morning, when the electromagnetic fields are fresh. But for now, I will rest. May I have a drink?"

Handing him bottled water, Phillip loosened the cap for him.

"Naji, you don't think it was the widget in my pocket?" Phillip fingered the key to the tailor shop that had started the adventure for what seemed eons ago.

"No. No, not at all." Naji puffed, as Claire led him to the chair in the front room. Freddy started making explosion sounds, which startled the fragile old tailor.

"It will happen, just have faith my friend, faith." He dropped heavily into the padded chair. Phillip reached down and pulled the lever to elevate his feet.

The tailor, tired beyond belief, closed his eyes, and he heard rattling in the kitchen as McClure set out the pizza pans and turned on the oven. The clattering and the smell of the baking reminded the tinydog of her long-lost friends at the Octagon Bakery, and the life she had left behind.

She stood on her two back legs and placed her paws on the chair as she watched Naji drift off to sleep. She trotted to the kitchen behind Phillip. She was devoted to him now, in a way she had never been devoted to any other human, even Naji. But still, there were times when she missed the smells and sounds of the kitchens, the harsh, booming orders of Gleena Glisson, and the hot pastries carefully loaded into her wagon for her morning route. It was a trade-off, this life, a trade-off. Still, if she could only find her black derby, load her wagon, and pull off a delivery maybe one more time, all would be right with her world. Then, and only then, would she be ready to make a new life with this boy.

Giving short little yaps in her sleep, her feet moved while she slept, as if she were running, running, free again, running the cobblestone streets of Norwall, her ears were flying straight back, straight back in a speedy run, hot baked goods loaded carefully in her wagon. Running under the watchful eyes of the Automatons, she was proud to be Chief Delivery Dog of the Octagon Bakery. Her derby poised, slightly tilted on her head, she would be pulling her red wooden wagon miraculously on schedule. Her grunts and twitches were watched by Claire, Mc-Clure, and Phillip, who laughed uproariously, as they imagined her dreams, watching her while they devoured every last bit of the pizza.

CHAPTER 37

The Quick Goodbye

He slept fitfully if he slept at all. His black clothes had been tossed on the bench at the bottom of his bed. He had borrowed it from his mother's bedroom, so Pebby could get up and down with ease whenever she wanted. She slept fitfully too, as if sensing that a change was coming. She laid her head on his chest, and he petted her for quite some time.

Neither of them could fall asleep. He looked at his phone, and groaned at the early hour. He was wasting time. Worse, and what he had not had the heart to mention to Claire, was that he worried that his mother was lying in a field, hurt, unable to move, unable to signal for help, and that she would die there from lack of food, water, and basic care. She had been gone a week, and even though Naji assured him several times over that the Automatons closely guarded the port, he worried that they were more concerned that none of the slave residents would leave, rather than who came into Norwall through the port. That would leave Abby Weathermore defenseless and at the mercy of an army of martial robots, the Automatons. Throwing back the covers, he stretched.

"Come on girl, no sense waking Claire, she had a rough day. Let'er sleep, OK?"

Pebby soundlessly jumped from the bed. She gave a little whine, putting her nose into her leather vest, which had been thrown carelessly on the floor.

"Yeah, yeah, I know, yesterday we forgot it. Come here, let's get you buckled up for the ride!"

Dressing himself quickly in the same black clothes, he carried his boots out. Sneaking past Naji, he motioned for Freddy to keep quiet. The perceptive bird shook his head up and down, as if he understood. As Phillip passed the cage, he whispered,

I know, I miss her too, I'm gonna bring her back, Fred, I'm gonna bring her back.

Naji was sleeping soundly. Occasionally, his breathing would pause for several seconds, then he would give a deep gasp. *Mom'll know what to do, I just gotta bring her back*, he thought to himself.

Not wanting to wake Claire or McClure by running the coffee maker, he grabbed a can of soda and his backpack, and then snapped the leash onto the tiny scruffy dog, who was nosing at Moushka's crate.

"Sshhh, let him be!" Leaving his cell phone on the table, he scrawled a note on one of the tablets.

Follow the plan guys,
taking the wild ride.
Watch my back.
Love, P

He softly closed the front door behind himself. The moon was full, and it lit his way to the heavily-canopied park. Pebby trotted quietly behind him, vest in place.

Her ears perked up as they approached the stone fireplace. Phillip took his place, exactly where he had last seen his mother stand. He hooked the backpack over his shoulders, looked straight up to the sky, and heard simply the rustle of leaves as a squirrel darted in front of her.

In a whiz, Pebby was on it, circling the stone edifice, stirring up the dirt, swirling, twisting, higher, as the sparkling mist rose, encircling Phillip and making it hard for him to breathe. He could not see through the fog now, as it grew thicker. He could hear the yaps of the tinydog as she struggled to find him in the mist.

Then, suddenly, he felt something like a push from behind, as if someone, or some force, had walloped him on his back. He felt himself become so dizzy that he swallowed hard to keep from vomiting. Spinning, he could not open his eyes. He felt himself turn vertical, and at the last second before he lost conscious awareness, something slid under him, and he felt something fierce clamp down on his arm.

He let his consciousness leave, and he fell back asleep. When he awoke, he felt the dizziness again, making him sick to his stomach. The feeling of someone pushing into his back hard was gone. He was lying flat on his back. His hands could feel sticky grass, bristly weeds, and he was afraid to open his eyes. He remembered what he had been trying to do, and it all started to come back to him. The transport, the tinydog, his missing mother, all came back to him now, and he was, for the first time, truly afraid. He was afraid that he had failed, that he was still at home, and that somewhere, his mother was lying hurt, injured, and lost to him forever. He felt a cold tongue on his face, and opened his eyes to Pebby licking his face.

"Where are we?" he whispered as he opened his eyes and saw a gray sky full of clouds. Not the big cotton cumulus clouds he was used to, but clouds of dusty, dirty gray clouds. He felt his eyes burn a little, and he rubbed them

"Where are we?" he asked Pebby again as he pulled himself up. His head felt heavy and he shook it gently to clear it. He slowly looked around him, but then quickly startled when he heard the sound of puffing and popping coming from overhead. He remembered Naji had said that the Automatons monitored the warp, and could well be looking for the intruder. Intruder. Now I am an intruder. So this was Norwall. Better hurry now! Then he spotted a dark clump of clothes to the right of him in the field, only about ten feet away. Crawling to stay out of sight, he got close, when suddenly the dark pile had a face, and also a name.

"What? I mean WHAT THE HECK, CLURE, what the heck? What happened to the plan? You were supposed to stay with Claire. How are you here?!"

Phillip was whispering loudly now, and Pebby had her feet firmly planted and her head tilted sideways looking up at him. She had never seen him so angry, and it frightened her. He was shaking McClure, who was waking up, and trying to sit up on his own.

"Talk to me, man, why are you here? What about the plan, man, the plan!?"

Through his own foggy reality, McClure stammered. "There was always only one plan, that was me watching your back. That was always the only plan for me. I just played along. Claire is smart, she can figure out how to handle things. No way you were going off on this thing without me. Just no way Phills, no way! Did'ja like that baseball slide? Remember eighth-grade baseball? I was the best slider in the class. I knew you would try to sneak off, so I just waited, and here we are. Right? So let's go find Abby, hunh?" McClure shook his head, trying to chase the dusty cobwebs away. It had indeed been a rough ride through the Parallax.

The machine now coming into view over their heads was not a friendly sight. The basket hanging from the dirigible had guns mounted on the side. It was flying dangerously low to the ground. The loud rumbling of the machine filled them with dread.

Pebby, sensing disaster, shook her head, kicked up her heels, and broke into a speedy run, straight for the woods. *Go, go, a... n... d... GO!* Her ears flew out behind her, and she was but a blur in the dusty twilight.

"Com'on, we can't lose her, com'on Clure, follow that tinydog!"

Both of them ran, just out of sight of the flying machine, which puffed dirty gray smoke. Pebby, low in the woods and flat to the ground, thought out her next move. She headed quickly and stealthily for Wymore's stone cottage at the edge of the wheat fields. She could trust him, and he would help them, she just knew it. The two friends, dressed in black, crouching as low as they could, followed silently behind.

Crouching, backs breaking, they scuttled through the underbrush, following the tiny scruffy dog, who appeared to know exactly where she was going. They came to a half-door, a wooden door on the back of a small stone cottage. Pushing the door with her nose, it sprung slightly open, enough for Pebby to get her head in and open it for the boys to squeeze through. The interior of the house was dark, and the coals from a dying fire illuminated the fireplace. Cold, stiff, and sore, Phillip headed there to warm his hands. Almost hidden in the stone on the side of the fireplace, a face, dirty, with stringy braided hair suddenly came to life and shocked him. Startled, he jumped back. Behind him, McClure gasped and watched as the figure stepped from the shadows. The girl was almost as tall as Phillip, and her clothes were dirty and tattered. In a low, whispering, raspy voice, the figure finally spoke, fists curled at her side, ready to strike.

"What exactly are you doing in my father's house?"

Epilogue

Abby Weathermore would alternate between periods of drugged wakefulness and the deepest sleep she had ever known. Somewhere in the distance, she could smell fresh baked bread. Her ankle hurt terribly, but she was not able to move it. It was tightly wrapped and tied down. When she was able to raise her head, she saw her ankle encased in a series of gears, larger just below the knee, tapering down to about an inch diameter below her ankle. A gauze wrap encircled her head, but the pressure of the bandage felt good. She had a mild, dull headache behind her eyes.

Her eyes fluttered open occasionally, and she saw that the ceiling of the room was at least two stories tall. The entire room, including the ceiling, was white. The head of the bed was metal piping, and loops of tubular metal served as a backboard. A metal dresser sat in the corner, with a white wash-basin on the top and a towel draped neatly over the edge of the basin. The towel, as well as her bed linens, were the purest shade of white. There were no pictures or ornaments of any type on the walls. Clerestory windows encircled the octagon-shaped room and let in a gray-colored light. The room was warmly lit.

The only thing in the room that wasn't white was a tall metal statue which stood in the far corner of the room. It almost looked like a suit of armor. It had a head, body, and arms that were crossed in front of it. It stood on a circular base, but it did not move. The face did not appear benign however. Pointed, menacing teeth protruded from the corners of the downturned mouth.

Days ran into nights, and many nights passed while figures dressed in white came and went, caring for her needs. One particular afternoon, an older woman with curly silver-gray hair, dressed also in white, approached her bed. Abby could not be sure, but it looked like flour dotted her apron.

"Where are you from?" the woman asked. "How were you hurt? How did you ever get to be lying in the wheat fields? What's your name, Miss?"

Tears welled up in Abby's eyes, and she briefly covered her face with both hands. Opening her palm, she slapped the flat of her hand against her forehead again, and again, and again, until she felt her eyes well up with tears. *For the life of me, I can't remember!*

How it all began...

A New Year. A New Hero. The story of how
The Clockwork Adventures came to be.

What makes this book different? To understand the way in which the series developed, it's helpful to peer through our retroscope. Several years ago this book was conceived as a children's book featuring Pebby. She was portrayed as a Yorkie mix adopted by a family which was already owned by a Malamute. As the art was completed and the children's book was going to press, the editors asked for more development of the Yorkie character.

So began the character development of the feisty, loving, fiercely independent tinydog. A backstory developed, leading to the wild and imaginative idea that she came from another time and dimension. The backstory sculptured her thoughts as well as her character. If you are a dog-lover like me, and you have in-depth conversations with your dog, like me, then you know *exactly* what I mean. It was this background that gave rise to her emotions.

In Pebby's case, her work ethic was a major part of her behavior. She had worked her way up in the ranks to lead as Chief Delivery Dog of the Octagon Bakery. Why a bakery? Her speed, her memory for the layout of the town, and her friendliness are qualities that would serve her well despite her size. However, as she developed a life as Phillip's sidekick, her independent streak had the potential to cause problems as their relationship evolved.

As Chief Delivery Dog of the Octagon Bakery, Pebby delivered fresh-baked goods by pulling her beloved red wooden wagon. She was captain of a fleet of loyal, hardworking, and prideful delivery dogs.

It was not such a far stretch to envision a Victorian town that relied on dogs for this service. The world-building began in earnest, and so evolved the concept of the steampunk town. World-building gave rise to automatons, flying machines, and pollution-generating factories. This concept strayed far away from a story that was limited to a thirty-page children's book.

At this point, the children's book idea was revised, and that story became *Moushka, The Big Dog That Wanted to Be a TinyDog*, a full-color illustrated forty-four-page story. The focus of *Moushka*, copyrighted in 2018, featured the relationships in the family as well as the jealousy Moushka the Malamute experiences when a tinydog comes into the family. The tinydog is, of course, Pebby. Competitive feelings are explored as Moushka looks to find his own special place in his family's heart.

After the completion of *Moushka*, attention was directed to the story of the tinydog who arrived from an alternate universe. While world-building was in development, the first book in this series was focused deliberately on the relationships between the characters, as had been in *Moushka*.

Since the majority of the characters are teens, I wanted to be direct in laying out the thoughts and feelings of the characters. Instead of relying on just subtext, I deliberately italicized what the character was thinking at that exact moment. I chose this path to let the reader experience, not an inference from the action, but an intentional showing of what was in the mind of the particular character. I believed this to be especially critical when their thoughts deviated significantly from their actions.

This reveal allows the reader to bond with the characters in a unique way. They have an introspective view into what the character is really thinking at that particular point in time… *Silly mother, did she really think that putting my pens and pencils in stupid cups was going to make me work more? Nope, time for another round of Revolutions for the Ages!*

Finally, the book was drafted. I presented it to the illustrator, Clara Kay, to read, and she presented her terse, direct observation. *No one is going to wait for the second book in the series to find out about Norwall. You've got to give us something to make us want to flash-forward!* I understood exactly what she meant.

It just so happened that pre-Covid, my family decided to vacation in one of my favorite spots, Gatlinburg, Tennessee. It was a late decision and all the facilities that allowed pets were already booked for the week between Christmas and the New Year. I was able to find one cabin deep in the heart of the Shenandoah National Forest, miles from anything. It was appropriately called "The Storybook Cottage," and indeed, the owners informed me that many writers have stayed there while completing their novels.

There we stayed. Early each morning as the others slept, I watched the snow twinkle down outside the big picture windows. Moushka and Pebby sprawled on their beds in front of the fireplace. A second version of the book was crafted. The world-building was no longer postponed. The story of the Victorian town was woven into the tale of Naji and Pebby's trip through the Parallax Contingency, and their *incidental* meeting with Phillip.

By the end of December 2019, the revised story was nearly complete. A host of characters from Norwall added depth, foreshadowing their reappearance in future books of the series. As we celebrated the New Year in beautiful downtown Gatlinburg and watched the fireworks through the spattering of snowflakes, my wish was that the New Year would bring the release of the first book in *The Clockwork Adventures*. Then, unexpectedly, horrifically, March 2020 brought changes to our lives. The idea of the grayfog of Norwall overwhelming the populace with lung disease was already a part of the story when COVID-19 arrived. The political upheaval and division in Norwall mirrored the upheaval happening in the United States. The book sat unattended while survival became the order of the day. The characters were frozen in time as homeschooling and a new job consumed the family.

Meanwhile, artist Clara worked on her idea of having a drawing at the start of every chapter. The character's appearances came to life, adding more depth to the story. Gradually, over the next twelve months, we devoted time to complete the project.

Staying in survival mode for such a long period of time took a toll on everyone. But, I always believed in *Clockwork* as an adventure story; a story about relationships, a story about interactions between people and animals, a story about friendship and love. I always believed in the love of a tinydog, *whose sincerity has never been questioned.*

Enjoy her story, our story, about friendships, devotion, and self-sacrifice in times of pandemonium, hardship, and loss. Enjoy *The Search for Norwall,* and look forward to the next book in the series already in development, *The Circles of the Realm.*

Character Development

~ PHILLIP WEATHERMORE ~

The schema for the character development of *The Clockwork Adventures* protagonist showcases a thirteen-year-old forced to mature at warp speed. Phillip is portrayed initially as lazy, manipulative, and antagonistic toward his mother, as well as resentful of his older sister, Claire. These qualities are not especially admirable, nor likable. He is portrayed as somewhat of a loner, save for his best friend McClure. As the story unfolds, we see him sarcastically viewing the things his mother does as quite irritating. He sneaks, playing video games rather than working on school assignments.

The challenge in crafting his character was to make him initially quite *ordinary*. The extraordinary things that happen to him as the story evolves take him on a path of rapid emotional growth. The challenge was to create a likable character whose self-centered habits are not so bad as to render him unredeemable. In fact, his emotional trials lead him, in later volumes, to be the one others look up to and admire. How he gets to this point is the crux of the adventure. The story becomes more than just an escapade in time travel to another dimension. It becomes an internal adventure of his spirit and emotional growth as well.

Time after time, we will see Phillip faced with extraordinary decisions. Some he will make quickly, others, he will ponder with trepidation. Toward the end of *Part One*, we see him quickly make the decision to confront the elder McClure and actually protect the sister that he famously resented. It is this evolving relationship with Claire that drives his emotional growth in *Part One, The Search for Norwall*. He discovers, much to his surprise, that "Miss Pitter-Patter-Perfect" is not what she seems to be. It is his first realization that there may be a depth to her that he has not understood before.

We also see his friendship with Naji Najeem develop throughout the story. He finds the elder gentleman intriguing, but he is never sure he can trust him completely. Where does Naji come from? Phillip is astute enough to realize that Naji's interpretation of the English language is a bit off-kilter. Even at the end of the first book, Phillip wonders if Naji *intentionally* gave him the widget, a mysterious clockwork key.

We too, are left wondering, did Naji select Phillip? Or was it happenstance that led to the widget finding its way into Phillip's pocket? At the inevitable climax, we see him pull himself together and take charge of the situation. This urgency leads him to project onto himself the very qualities that he found annoying in his mother. We see him imitate her in the way he deals with not only his sister, and also Naji, but even the McClure family.

By the end of *Part One*, we see a different Phillip. We see him as a caretaker of the other characters. We see him crystalize his emotions into sharp focus. above all, trying to keep his family together. Will that ability help him survive in *Part Two, Circles of the Realm*? Or will the distractions overwhelm him? What will his relationship be with Pebby? And finally, what will it take for him to measure up to the extraordinary task in front of him?

~ CLAIRE WEATHERMORE ~

Claire! More than just the quintessential older sibling, she embodies everything Phillip is not. Claire. *Miss Pitter-Patter-Perfect*! The challenge in crafting her character was to make her the polar opposite of Phillip, yet keep her likable. An extraordinary student, an inventor, a math whiz, *she's everything I'm not!* opines Phillip early in the story.

Claire. Extraordinary, untouchable, remote Claire, engrossed in her private world, often ignoring Phillip or diminishing him. She finds the world on her phone and in her laboratory much more palatable. She often unintentionally makes remarks which might cause him to feel he does not measure up to her standards.

Initially quite extraordinary, we see her frustration as she is faced with ordinary tasks. Just getting out of bed at a reasonable time in the morning is too much for Claire. Helping with the laundry tests her patience, and we see her only helping begrudgingly. While we see her bask in her mother's adoration, we rarely see her interact with McClure. She calls him a "dweeb" like her brother. We only see her develop empathetic feelings for him after she becomes aware of his treacherous home situation.

So unlike Phillip, who faces extraordinary tasks, Claire comes face-to-face with her difficulty in managing ordinary tasks. An overachiever, this is not an easy adjustment for her.

Perhaps it is her other-worldliness that causes Phillip to keep secrets from her. It is not until well into the adventure that he really trusts her with the information he has discovered. In the last third of *The Search for Norwall*, we see Phillip take charge and make decisions that could change all their lives. But, the polar opposite of Phillip, Claire is forced by the situation to confront the ordinary. She assumes the household tasks, much to her chagrin. She *"does not like being Mom, it's too much work."*

Time after time, we see her faced with ordinary decisions, and we watch her struggle. We see her step well outside her comfort zone and confront the elder McClure. We see her collect the younger McClure's belongings and imitate what she thinks her mother would do. It is her evolving ordinary life as well as her relationships with Phillip and McClure that define her emotional growth in *The Search for Norwall*.

As she takes Phillip under her wing and agrees to share her lab, she transforms their relationship into one of congeniality. She shares her knowledge base in exchange for being let in on what she perceives to be the ultimate adventure. She cannot bear to be left out.

Claire does not pick up on clues suggesting that Naji's perception of the world is very different from the Weathermores. She has been engrossed in her digital world and may be short on reading personal cues. Claire is so shocked by the unfolding events that her intellect takes a vacation while her emotions rise to the surface. It is not until later in *Part Two, The Circles of the Realm*, that we see her draw on her superb reasoning power and logically analyze the sequence of events.

We cannot take her for granted. By the end of *Part One*, we see her as a reluctant caretaker of the persnickety pets and her mother's business. We see her on autopilot as she works through the daily routine. Will that ability help her survive? Or will the inevitable distractions overwhelm her? What will it take for her to take off her headphones and realize that she could be in grave danger?

~ PEBBY ~

The challenge in designing Pebby as a sidekick to Phillip was to first to determine how they would communicate. Having a talking dog was not an option. Having the voice inside her head revealed made it easy to show her irascible personality. It became a way to portray the conflict Pebby experiences.

First, although she is quite proud of her accomplishments, having attained the coveted role of Chief Delivery Dog for the busiest enterprise in Norwall, her attachment to Naji Najeem is based on mutual solitude. She has never really belonged to anyone. After meeting Phillip and spending time in the Weathermore household, Pebby felt a sense of belonging to something larger than herself. This was a brand-new feeling for her.

As we see Pebby travel her delivery route in Norwall, we meet people who love her. From Treena Trembly, her groomer, to Wassy Wymore, who hugs her too tight, to Lee Anna Loo, Director of the Hydroponics Institute, we see multiple people who want to call her their own. We experience her feelings for all these people, but we see she cannot make the commitment to stay with anyone, until the day she meets Phillip. There is an unspoken bond between them from the very first time they meet. *It was as if every clock in the universe suddenly stood still.*

Bringing her character to life in *Part One* was easy. Much more difficult is watching her character navigate the choices she must make in *Part Two*, which will test her loyalty to Phillip, and threaten her standing not only among her canine friends but also among those who love her.

~ McCLURE ~

McClure. It is no accident that in *Part One*, we never learn his first name. In a way, this story is as much about McClure as it is about Phillip. It has been said that for a child to grow up well, he or she needs one, and only one, person. The child must know that their well-being comes first with that primary person. That person, so crucial to the child's development, could be a preacher, a teacher, a parent, or a relative. But, the child must know, beyond any doubt, that they march at the head of that person's parade.

In *The Clockwork Adventures*, we meet McClure, who does not march at the head of anyone's parade. McClure is everyone; he could be anyone who grew up without the strong affections of an adult. He could be anyone who grew up with a broken emotional compass, eternally out-of-kilter.

We see McClure embarrassed by his father's actions. We see the elder McClure, unkempt, rude to his family, unable to take care of himself. We see him call his son a "loser." We see him break the heart and spirit of his child again, and again, and again.

Why was portraying this family situation necessary? This is an adventure story, but it is a story of the adventures of the spirit of all the characters, many of whom come from very different circumstances. We will see McClure deal with his issues as he is faced with difficult choices. There is much adventure and many surprises in store for McClure, and it is best not to underestimate his importance to the storyline, especially his relationship with Abby Weathermore!

~ NAJI NAJEEM ~

Enigmatic. Mysterious. An elderly tailor with an unusual accent and a persistent lung ailment. A collector of discarded items, we first see Naji as eccentric. Later, when we have the experience of visiting his secret laboratory, we discover that there is more to him than meets the eye. Still, we are never really sure if the relationship between him and Phillip is happenstance or part of a carefully executed plan by this man from another time and place.

When crafting his character, shrouding him in mystery was deliberate. Even at the end of *Part One, The Search For Norwall*, we are never sure of the reason for his involvement with the Weathermore family. We are never certain if he has deliberately involved Phillip in the intrigue, or if their meeting was perhaps nothing more than serendipity.

Of course, we see Phillip's attraction to Pebby as the draw that leads him to befriend Naji. As we see Naji actively engage Phillip and groom him to lead, we cannot help but ask, was it coincidence? Is this old tailor more crafty than we can ever imagine? Does he have an ulterior motive?

The development of the character was based on the premise that he is a well-respected and well-educated man, but a man who is not entirely forthcoming. Where he came from, as well as his role in his prior life remains a mystery known only to him. He withholds information that can help Phillip, all the while encouraging him to excel at school and be a leader. We cannot help but ask, what does he expect him to lead?

~ Deen DIGGINS ~

Deen Diggins appears in *Part One* as the Quartermaster of the Delivery Dogs. His lack of education, poor nutrition, and separation from family are typical of most teenagers in Norwall. Exceptional is his devotion to something outside of his own needs, the team of delivery dogs. We see his devotion to Pebby; his love for her is pure. We see Pebby notice he looks malnourished. We feel pain as Automatons watch their every move. We see him whisper to her *sure would like to have a dog like you Pebby, sure I would*. Such simple pleasures denied him, yet he loves her. We have not seen the last of Deen Diggins.

~ TREENA TREMBLY ~

A female character who has a larger role later in the story is Pebby's groomer, Treena Trembly. Capturing the special bond of love and trust that they share was easy, as the character is modeled after a real-life groomer. Treena has the kindest, most gentle heart of any character in the story. She is warm and loving. She is very tired of the situation in Norwall, and sneaks a secret message to Naji Najeem, begging him to help. We see the loyalty and love that she shares with Pebby as an example of self-sacrifice and loving devotion.

World-Building

Creating the Environments of *the Clockwork Adventure* Series

McClure's neighborhood was put together in a nanosecond. It was like so many neighborhoods you see as you navigate Central Florida. Massive trees shade the side streets which are covered with stained concrete pavers. Most of the sidewalks are cracked and uneven from settling of the sandy earth. The walkways are speck-led black from years of mildew, and can be quite slippery. Artist Clara and I were able to construct the front facade of McClure's house by talking through the action that hap-pens *inside* the house. We wanted the house to look quite foreboding, almost scary. Her initial sketch was spot-on and was used as the final depic-tion.

This particular house, although I had never been in it, was clear in my mind from the beginning of the story. The chipped porcelain kitchen sink, the worn wooden stairs leading up to the narrow hallway, the parent's room on the left, McClure's small room to the right, all were dreary and somber, signifying a lack of care.

My wish was for the reader to feel the dreariness and despondency that Phillip experiences as he visits for the first time. I wanted the reader to share Phillip's appreciation for his friend who endured, and never once complained.

I can, even now, imagine every detail of this house. I imagine the foyer, with the kitchen off to the left, the living room with the worn and stained furniture to the right and the sleeping man lying on his side on the blue threadbare couch. The curtains are pulled closed to keep out the annoying light of day.

Creating scenes originating in Central Florida, including the Adventura Mall, was not difficult; the world already exists. Not so with Norwall. The creation of this world was a very different undertaking; a difficult and time-consuming process. The idea of creating a mid-eighteenth-century Victorian town predestined, to an extent, the style of the architecture and the clothing. But, when I added a steampunk flare, and envisioned a world overseen by nasty automatons, all bets were off. Everything changed. The actual work of building the fantasy world began.

World-building is a skill; it takes talent, and an extraordinary amount of thought and attention to detail to bring together the elements that make up an entire universe. Parallel worlds collide in this time-travel adventure as the action toggles between modern-day Florida and a mid-eighteenth-century Victorian world with inventors, flying machines, steam factories, and automaton robots.

While most of *The Search for Norwall* takes place in Florida, as early as Chapter Two we are given a first-hand street-level view of the City Center of Norwall through the eyes of the tinydog named Pebby. She has risen in the ranks to achieve the coveted position of Chief Delivery Dog of the Octagon Bakery. It is as though, seen through her eyes, the reader is experiencing first-hand the cramped upstairs apartment of Naji Najeem, the shiny facade of the Octagon Bakery, and the dusty roads leading to the Five Feathers Falconry.

It was crucial, right from the second chapter of the story, to introduce the town and the shimmering, gleaming bakery structure, which was meant to contrast sharply with the dark, foreboding, prison-like atmosphere of the town. In order to build the world of this fantasy town, a map was constructed, representing a crude layout of the town. It had to be a quick jaunt from Naji's tailor shop to the bakery, far enough to let Pebby have room to break into a speedy run. As she travels to the bakery from Naji's tailor shop, and to the Groomerly Grooming Establishment, her route had to be mapped, as there will be incidents later when she retraces this same route back to the dog habitron.

In order for the story to make sense, Pebby's route for the day had to cover one of the outer circles of the realm. The outlying sections of the city were constructed as concentric rings around the central business district. In order to give variety to her travels that first day, and also to showcase the environment, the various biomes of the outer banks had to be constructed.

First, the lay of the land had to be determined. Most large cities are bounded by at least one river. There had to be plenty of natural water to supply the factories, most of which are steam driven. There had to be a modicum of rainfall to supply the crops for food. If there was a wheat crop to supply the bakery, then it followed that there had to be enough rain to support the crop.

Additionally, there was unusual wildlife, and rainfall that was becoming acidic. Because of the deteriorating environment, the remarkable bird species were dying. The Five Feathers Falconry became a sanctuary for the remaining avian species, as well as a laboratory to create a prototype automaton avian flyer. Even though the climate was temperate, there was a need to grow food away from the polluted atmosphere, and the idea of the Hydroponic Institute was developed. This required research into the science of hydroponics, and actually resulted in a mock lab set up on my back porch, producing lettuce, chives, onions, and a multitude of herbs.

The Hydroponics Institute sits in quite a different environment than the flat wheat fields. Likewise, the Five Feathers Falconry was constructed on the outer edge of the town in order to give the birds space, and to give Jeeson and Noora room in a field to fly the prototype.

In order to make this come together, it was

necessary to build the world right from the start. We had to set up locations that Pebby could reach pulling her beloved red wagon; we had to make the course rigorous, but able to be navigated in one day by a tinydog. She had to cover the main areas of the outer circle, yet the course had to be reasonable for her to accomplish the deliveries.

Not withstanding the location, topography and layout of the town, we had to also structure the government, the currency, the class system forced on the people, and worse, the oppression under which the population lives. How did the people become trapped in the factories? How did the government force them to live in the Habitrons? How were families torn apart? How does the government keep control? These elements so crucial to the story-line had to be determined before the storyline could continue.

In Chapter Two, the Angry Automaton appears. We see Pebby face the frightening mechanical creature as she heads to work at the Octagon Bakery. How can the metal man be threatening?

The technology had to be developed.

First, the Automaton had to be created. There were at least five prototypes for the metal man, and a prototype adapted for the "baby bot" that lives on a shelf in Phillip's room. The baby bot needed to be similar enough to raise curiosity about its origin. The

Norwellian Automaton had to be menacing, ruthless, and not a bit friendly. It had be so threatening that it would scald you in a heartbeat for an infraction. It had to inspire fear by its very appearance.

Lastly, the vessels, vehicles, and robotic creatures also had to be designed. But, there is still more to come, and the world-building of this magical place continues, just as the story continues to develop, with more surprises, more robotic creatures, and more *Clockwork Adventures* yet to unfold!

The Art Of Clockwork

Get a behind-the-scenes look at the illustrations of **The Clockwork Adventures: Part One, The Search for Norwall!**

This *Artist's Edition* features chapter illustrations and a vintage Victorian cover. Some of these designs were concepted almost half a decade prior to the release of this book. *Clockwork Adventures: Part One, The Search for Norwall* has changed a lot since it was first created. In these special behind the scenes pages, you can get a glimpse of the development of the art behind the book!

Did you know that Pebby is based off a real-life dog? Check it out! This is Pebbles, a Yorkie-Maltese mix. The way Phillip meets Pebby in the story is directly inspired by how the real Pebby was adopted! To the right are two of her first ever designs.

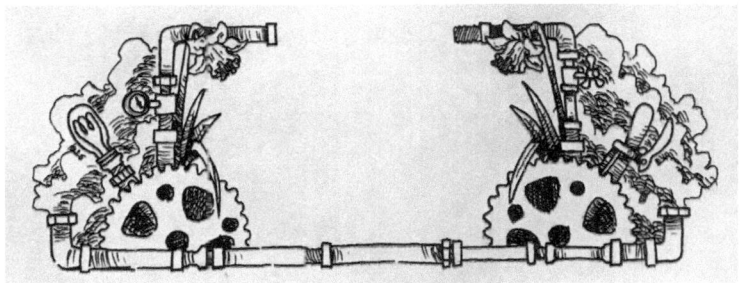

These are some of the initial designs of the border that surrounds each chapter illustration. It was important to make them look like they came straight from Norwall,

with pipes, steam, and gears incorporated into their design. The chapter illustrations reflect the inked drawings of vintage newspapers, and artist Clara Kay rendered these frames in real pen and ink for authenticity.

The first pass on the cover of the book was concepted all the way back in 2017. Back then, Pebby's name was Pebbly. The book was also going to be a picture book, and featured far fewer steampunk concepts!

Here you can see Pebby sitting between Phillip and Abby. The title then, was *Travels of Pebbly*.

Artist Clara Kay did many concept sketches during the book's development. Here are concepts of Pebby and her delivery wagon!

In the bottom right is a first draft of her portrait found on the front cover of the book.

In the upper left, beside the basic sketch of Pebby, is a rough outline of the widget that Phillip discovers in the camouflage backpack.

In the upper right is a more realistic rendition of Pebby, and a rough design of her gear vest. You can see the leather loop attached to the side, allowing her wagon to attach to it.

To the right, you can see the very first drawing ever of Phillip! This was a concept made in 2016. The second image was finalized a year later. His design sure has changed a lot!

Both illustrations of Phillip here were made when *Clockwork Adventures* was still called *Travels of Pebbly*, and was meant to be an illustrated picture book. When the book matured to a young adult novel, Phillip's design matured as well.

Naji was the first character designed for *Clockwork Adventures*, before the book even had a name. His design has not changed much over the years, nor has his relationship with Pebby.

In the image in the upper right, you can see artist Clara Kay's signature in this early concept art, dated 2016!

Meet the Author and Illustrator

Nan Kopitnik is a Board-Certified Addiction Medicine Physician. She cares for vulnerable Florida citizens in skilled nursing facilities.

She authors children's books under the pen-name Alexa Rayburn. She is the author of three children's books and *The Clockwork Adventures*, a young adult science-fiction series.

Nan has published articles in medical journals, lectured at national meetings on addiction, and counseled countless families. She loves to weave relationship issues into exciting adventure stories.

She also authors humorous stories and scripts, which can be sampled on her website. From the age of seven, she was a great fan of the novels of Patrick Dennis, which she read under her covers with a flashlight. She is currently collaborating on *Shy Sam the Wolf-Dog*, an educational book featuring the true story of one Florida family's remarkable and humorous integration of a wolfdog into their family structure.

Her latest achievement has been completing the Master of Fine Arts Creative Writing Degree Program at Full Sail University in Orlando, Florida. She is an annual vendor at MegaCon Orlando, where she sells books and merchandise from her company, TinyDog Books. She is the keeper of toy robots, and one remarkable tinydog. She is the handler of five large rescue parrots that bite with reckless abandon.

Information about her books and novels can be found at: **https://nankopitnikwrites.com** and **https://www.tinydogbooks. com**. Her books are available on Amazon Kindle, as well as Barnes & Noble Bookstores. Books and merchandise can also be purchased at **https://tinydogbooks.storenvy.com**.

Clara Kay is an illustrator, concept artist, and 3D animator located in Central Florida. She has a Bachelor of Fine Arts (B.A.) in Emerging Media: Character Animation from the University of Central Florida.

Clara is a Florida native. She enjoys horror media and challenging modern storytelling techniques. Illustration and concept art are her passion, and she loves designing worlds and characters with intricate stories. She has been writing and illustrating for her own stories since she could hold a pencil. Her passion for art and design comes from growing up playing video games. She has participated in dozens of online fan-made art anthologies called "fanzines," being an active member of the zine community. She loves tabling at conventions like MegaCon in Orlando, and enjoys presenting her work to the public.

You can visit her at **https://clarabellumsart.wixsite.com/portfolio.**

Visit our LinkTrees to see our websites and stores!

TinyDog Books

Clara Kay

Check out our other books!

Nasty Cat

In *Nasty Cat*, five-year-old Serena DeWitt gets much more cat than she bargained for!

Moushka: The Big Dog That Wanted to be a TinyDog

Life is grand for Moushka until a tinydog comes to live at the Weathermores.

The Plucky Parrot

Freddy the Plucky Parrot joins the Weathermore family and tricks them with his sassy sounds.

www.TinyDogBooks.com

Find our books, merchandise, blog, upcoming books and more!